finding

HOME

Coming Home Series

J.M. ADELE

A heart at risk
A long way from home

FINDING HOME
Copyright © 2017 by J.M. Adele
All Rights Reserved

Edited by Eeva Lancaster
Cover Design by Book Flare Publishers
Cover photo from Adobe Stock ©Yuliya Yafimik
Cover art from brusheezy.com
Formatted by Book Flare Publishers

First Edition
ISBN: 978-0-9944516-2-0

Dedicated to the wonderful group of ladies and gents I am so incredibly fortunate to call friends.

Contents

Chapter One

Hard Decisions

2006

Greyson's lungs convulsed from sucking down too much dust, diesel fumes, and cow stench, as he tossed another hay bale onto the truck. Bending forward, he spat the grit from his mouth, watching his shadow jerk as he returned a little piece of Mississippi to its rightful place.

"Fuck this shit."

The muffled protest came out of his mouth once a week, probably closer to daily in the last few weeks, as his desperation became a palpable force driving him to crazy town.

Wiping his mouth on his shoulder, he walked behind the rumbling truck, inching its way around the loose bales in the field.

"Shut up before Papà hears you."

Turning his head, Grey leveled a sneer at his brother for daring to scold him. "He won't hear, he's driving the truck. Besides, I don't give a shit if he hears. I hate this job and he knows it."

"He might know it, but he won't accept it."

Antonio threw another bale, and straightened with a groan. Removing one worn leather glove and his hat, he scrubbed a hand over his sweaty buzz cut. It was clear they were brothers in the same dark shade of their hair, their slate gray eyes, and strong chins. A legacy from their father and his Italian heritage. But their differing hair styles were the clearest indicator of their personalities. Antonio was happy to conform, while Grey's hair hadn't seen the clippers for four years. He had no interest in fitting into anyone's regulations. The ponytail he wore was a big *fuck you* to conformity.

"He'll have to accept it soon enough."

Removing his cowboy hat, Grey tugged on the ends of his hair, dislodging the piece of hay that was scratching under his collar.

"What are you talkin' about?" Anton flicked his eyes sidelong, taking a swig from his water bottle.

Plonking his hat back on his head, Greyson grabbed his own bottle. "I'm leavin'." He stared down his brother, challenge marking his face and his stance.

"What are you talkin' about? Where are you goin'?" The water bottle dangled from lax fingers, all but forgotten, as Anton gaped at his older brother.

"You repeat yourself a lot. You know that?" Grey smirked.

"Cut the shit, Grey. Where are you going? Does Mama know?"

"She's been supportive."

He bent, heaving another bale through the air to be caught and stacked on the truck by the ranch hands. His two sisters were taking turns walking beside the vehicle, guiding Papà when to stop or slow down.

"She wants me to follow my heart."

"Where to?" Shock lifted the pitch of Antonio's voice.

"The kitchen. A real kitchen where I can learn to cook from the best."

"You're not serious?" Capping his bottle and letting out a shrill whistle, Anton threw it to one of the ranch hands on the truck. "He'll never speak to you again. You know what happened to our uncle."

Yeah, success happened. If his father couldn't support that, then … Grey didn't give a fuck.

The bitter fallout from Uncle Matteo's escape still lingered in the old farmhouse. A constant pollution of ash in the air, cloying every conversation or family gathering where his absence was glaringly obvious.

Greyson clenched gloved fists, holding his body in check. He didn't want to antagonize his brother. Antonio was built for ranch life. Grey wasn't.

"I'm aware, and I'm willing to take the chance. It's worth it. I can't rot away on this ranch. It's not the life I want."

"What about the family?" Anton's arms flailed, emphasizing his point. "What about your friends? Lory?"

"Lory would want me to be happy."

His younger brother took off his hat, slapped it on his thigh, and whistled a long, low note. He eyeballed Grey under heavy brows, shaking his head. "You haven't told her. You're a chicken shit."

Grey's muscles tightened, gathering for a fight.

One side of Anton's mouth tipped up in a mocking smile. "Well ... I'll miss ya. I'd say make sure you visit, but I don't know if you'll be welcome."

The tension seeped out a little, but Grey knew it wouldn't disappear until he was in his pickup on the interstate.

"I'll visit anyway. He can't stop me from coming to town."

"Basta!" The brothers whipped their heads toward the truck where their father was leaning out of the window, motioning with his arm. "When you're done with your women's meeting, maybe you could load the truck."

"Sì, Papà." Antonio tipped his chin in acknowledgement before turning back to Grey. "Come on. Let's get this done so we can enjoy some of Nonna's pasta."

Eyeing the back of his papà's head through narrowed slits, the muscles in Grey's jaw worked out his annoyance. He'd grind his teeth to stumps if he stayed here any longer. Shifting his gaze, he watched his brother diligently working at clearing all the bales. He didn't seem all that concerned about Grey leaving. Or maybe he didn't believe that Grey would go through with it.

His determination solidified. He could no longer spend his life doing something he didn't care for. He was already half packed. It was only a matter of days. All he had to do was tell his papà.

They finally finished loading the last of about two thousand bales. Garlic wafted down the dust track and over their makeshift seats of hay, as they made their way back to the hay barn. He could see the old white farmhouse in the distance, with its dormer windows marking the second story bedrooms, and the long veranda where he'd often sit listening to the sounds of the night.

Grey's nose twitched, capturing the alluring scent. Way better than cow shit, or almost anything he could think of. He rubbed his callused palms together, thinking about going into the kitchen after they off-loaded the bales. It was a distraction from the nerves rampaging in his stomach at the thought of the conversation that had to happen soon. If he was smart, he'd let it wait until his father was full-bellied after a hearty meal.

Grey jumped down, listening to his papà's barrage of instructions, as if they all didn't know how to operate the bale elevator, or stack hay. They'd been doing this for years, for Christ's sake. Every word from that man's mouth was gasoline on the fire in Grey's belly to get the hell out. Every muscle ache, every creak in his bones, every scratch or cut on his skin, drove the flames higher.

He stretched his neck, pinched his mouth shut, and took up his position at the elevator, ready to unload his last bales of hay. If he never saw hay again, he'd be as happy as … a chef in a kitchen.

———

After showering, Greyson followed his nose to the heart of the house, listening to Nonna singing in Italian, and his sisters chatting as they set the table.

"Smells good, Nonna."

His grandmother held up a spoon full of sauce for him. "Tastes better," she replied in her native tongue.

Rarely did she speak English at home. He'd learned Italian first, despite his mother's efforts to get him speaking English. But growing up a Mississippi boy, the Italian influence had not been enough to assuage his strong, southern drawl.

"Mm. My favorite. I could smell it as we drove in." He noticed crispy curls of deep fried pastry on a plate on the bench. "Cartocci Siciliani for dessert?"

"Mm hmm, with ricotta cream." She pulled a bowl across the bench and plonked it in front of him. "You can make the cream."

He reached for the ingredients she had set out, jerking back at the stinging slap of a wooden spoon on the back of his hand.

Fuck! "What was that for?" He shook out the pain.

"Wash your hands." She frowned in disapproval.

"I just showered." He reached for the ricotta again.

Nonna wasn't backing down, wielding the spoon in front of him with puckered disdain on her wrinkled face.

"Okay." Retreating to the sink, hands up in surrender, a small smile played on Grey's lips.

He'd miss her. She was the reason he loved to cook. She was the one who'd secretly kept in contact with his uncle, and planted the seed of hope that there might be a future outside of this hellhole.

He shook off the water and dried his hands on the towel his Nonna threw at him.

"And don't forget to strain it after you add the powdered sugar."

His smile stretched out to full. "Yes, Nonna."

She might have barely reached five foot three, but she was the only person he willingly took orders from. It was probably all in the delivery. Nonna managed to frown and scowl with love.

Antonio came through the door followed by their sisters, Sofia and Marianne, still chattering away, using their hands as much as their mouths.

"Odori buono, Nonna. I can't wait to eat the lovely meal you've cooked for us."

"Your sisters helped."

"Oh ... damn. It still smells good, though."

Nonna slapped him over the back of the head.

"Ah!" He laughed rubbing the sore spot. "If I keel over from poisoning, will you do the eulogy, Grey?"

"Ask Marianne. She's good with words."

"Whose eulogy?" Their mother joined them, her brown hair in a haphazard tumble behind her neck.

"Anton's being dramatic." Marianne rolled her eyes.

As the eldest sister, she'd inherited their maternal grandmother's name, and her looks too. Mousey brown hair, pale blue eyes. She'd taken on the olive complexion from their Italian side, but that was it.

"Anton doesn't trust our cooking," Sofia explained.

She was quite a bit shorter than her elder sister and took after her namesake, Nonna, in looks and personality. Although, Nonna's dark curls were now a pale gray and tamed in a bun. If either of them held a wooden spoon, everyone knew to steer clear.

"It smells delicious, honey." She flung her arms over her daughters' shoulders. "Thank you all for your help today. We're well stocked for winter feed, and we'll be rewarded with this wonderful feast that you've prepared for us. Molte grazie, Mamma."

Lines crinkled around his mother's blue eyes as she smiled at her mother-in-law. Since he'd told her of his plans to leave, they'd gradually appeared, fanning over the deepened shadows underneath like papercuts marring her beauty.

He swallowed back his guilt, and focused his attention on pushing the ricotta and powdered sugar mixture through the strainer. She'd always been there to support him, and he was thanking her by packing his shit and leaving. But, fuck, the boxing ring between his ears had played host to Obligation versus Dreams for too long. He'd finally reached his breaking point. The ding of the bell had sounded, and selfish need had thrown up its arm as the winner.

His biggest concern was the backlash. His mama would be on the receiving end of his father's wrath. He wouldn't physically harm her, Grey knew that, but words sprayed in anger could harm just as badly. She would be the convenient target, not the deserving recipient. That was all him. He was prepared to work his ass off to get where he needed to be. It would be his way of thanking her for her faith and support. No way did he ever want to cause that woman any more pain.

Grey watched out of the corner of his eye as Nonna dished up the plates and his family took them out to the table where his father would be waiting. He finished mixing the cream, and put it aside to be piped into the fried pastries later before following his grandmother into the dining room.

Holding court at the head of the table, his papà was in the midst of outlining the plan of attack for the next week.

"… need to prepare the pastures for over-seeding, and check the fly tags. See which ones need replacing."

He looked up as Grey and Nonna entered, standing to pull out the chair for his mother. Greyson had to respect the way Papà cared for the woman. He was capable of showing love when he wanted to. It was patience and acceptance of differing views that he had trouble with.

As everyone joined hands in prayer, Grey let his head hang loose on his neck, closing his eyes to soak in the words of thanks given by his mama. She spoke of being thankful for their harvest, and for the blessing of being able to work together as a family to make their ranch successful.

Each word that curled off her tongue lay heavy on his shoulders, sinking his mood further. Was he just being a selfish dick, abandoning his family?"

He tuned back in to his mama's prayer. "… and give us the strength to be true to who we are. To follow our intended purpose, and respect that each of us has our own unique journey to take. Amen."

Lifting his gaze, he caught his mama's wink from across the table. Grey felt the squeeze of remorse around his neck. Clearing his throat, he picked up his flatware and pushed the food around the plate in search of his appetite. It had up and deserted him, just like he was doing to his family. He had to go. He was done here.

He glanced at his mother whose face was etched with concern. She cast a reassuring smile his way, but it wobbled at the edges. She had to be hurting. He knew it must pain her to carry the burden of knowing what was coming, and not be able to share her concerns with anyone. Grey wasn't being fair. He had to say something.

"Answer me, son."

Grey snapped his gaze towards his father. "Pardon?"

A gust of breath whistled out his father's nose as he watched Grey under a creased brow. "I asked if all the calving supplies had been checked. We need to be ready for the last few of the season."

"Yes. They're all ready to go."

"Good. I'll need you to be on watch. I expect calves any day now."

"I can't do that, Papà."

"Greyson," his mother's voice tried to break through the animosity arcing between father and son.

His sisters' conversation cut off like the scratch of a record, as all eyes turned on him.

Papà's mouth pinched tight. "Why is that?"

"I won't be here. I'm leaving."

He watched the muscles in his father's jaw clench, his own, mirroring the movement. Locked in a stare down, he didn't want to be the first to break. His body was so taut an ice pick couldn't have broken through his flesh. Silence blared as the stare down continued.

Placing both elbows on the table, his papà leaned forward. "No, you're not. You have responsibilities here."

Grey leaned back, shaking his head. His hands tightened into fists under the table. "Responsibilities that I don't want." He fought to keep his tone even. "You know I hate this life. I want to cook, Papà."

His father's shoulders bunched impossibly tighter. "Cook? You want to do women's work?" He shot a dark look at his wife. "Like my brother."

His mama rested a hand on his father's arm. "Lucca, please. Let him go. He's unhappy."

With a jerk, his papà flung her hand off, and slammed his palm down. Everybody jumped in their seats, but Grey didn't budge an inch.

"He has a roof over his head, food on his plate, and clothes on his back. What's to be unhappy about?"

"I don't expect you to understand, and I don't need permission." Grey pushed back from the table. Turning to leave, he saw the disbelief and hurt on the other faces around the table. "Sorry." The apology broke over his tongue, cracking into pieces. What else could he say?

"If you're going, go now. And don't come back," his father bit out.

Sophia shot to her feet. "No, Papà!"

Greyson left the room to a flurry of cries and protests. His brother attempted to calm Sophia down, and his Nonna wept. Devastated to witness such a scene for the second time.

He retreated up the stairs, anger and guilt quaking in his flesh.

You knew this would happen.

Greyson closed his bedroom door, bracing his back against it. He shut his eyes, seeing it all play out again. Maybe it was a stupid thing to blindside everyone when they were gathered in one room. Of course, it all went to shit. He should've spoken to them individually. Warned them before telling his Papà, knowing he'd react the way he did. Well, at least there'd be no drawn out goodbyes.

A soft knock at the door vibrated through the back of his skull where it rested.

"Grey? Can I come in?"

He opened the door and waved his mother in, before grabbing his suitcase out of the closet.

"Don't feel bad."

He cast a withering look over his shoulder.

"You shouldn't feel bad. I just wish you had warned me."

"Sorry. I guess … I had to let it out."

"It's okay."

Grey's laugh held no humor.

"It'll *be* okay," she corrected.

Throwing clothes haphazardly into the case, Grey's mind sought out the right words to say to her. But his brain had already vacated, and was urging his body to follow. The case was half full before he realized his mother had gone quiet. He turned around and found her sitting on the edge of the bed, silent tears rolling down her face as she watched him pack. Cursing under his breath, he went to her, wrapping his big arms around her thin frame. She shook, still containing the sound of her anguish.

"Ugh, sorry. I swore to myself that I wasn't going to do this, but it's always hard for a mother to watch her children go. We've been lucky to have you for this long." She raised her hand to his face, watery eyes fixed on his. "I knew from the time you were a little boy that you weren't made for this place, and that one day you'd leave. You were so determined to learn, and so passionate about food. And you never liked the chores Papà gave you. You should be proud that you have the courage to chase your passions. I am proud of you." She dropped her hand, wiping away her tears. "I don't want you to worry about us. Just concentrate on working hard and finding your place."

"I will." He gave her a gentle squeeze and let her go, rising to his feet. "I promise to honor you, Mama."

"You already have, Grey. Please be safe. Do you have enough money?"

"Yeah. I'm covered. Thanks."

"Stay until morning. I don't like you driving these roads at night."

His face twisted in a grimace. One more night under his father's roof? Hell, no. "I think I need to get going. I'll find a motel somewhere."

Her shoulders rose as she sighed in resignation. "Okay. I'll see you out front."

A soft tap sounded on the door just before she opened it to leave.

"Hi, Lory. Come on in." Looking back at Grey, his mama smiled a sad smile and left him with his guest.

Grey shoved his hands in his pockets, watching his friend and neighbor take in the suitcase, and the empty closet. Her big blue eyes widened and fixed on him, a puff of breath escaping her parted lips in place of words she apparently couldn't find.

Remaining upright became a challenge as his legs hollowed out, drained of the flight reflex. "Lory. I was going to tell you."

"In a text? A phone call? When were you going to tell me?"

"I wasn't supposed to leave for a couple of weeks, but my father is bootin' me out. He's pissed."

"Yeah, I can imagine." She stood in the doorway, arms hanging loose by her side as she watched him, unguarded.

He dragged his fingers through his hair, unable to pull together a good enough apology or excuse. What a fucking mess. She didn't deserve this. He'd known Lory and her brother, Clay, since they were babies. Her family owned the property on the south and west borders of his father's land. They'd been farming here for several generations already, by the time his Nonno bought the land. One of Mississippi's founding farming families, they were royalty around these parts. But the Carters were like family to him.

Lory drifted over to the bed and sat down, wedging her hands together between her knees. Her long hair fell forward to curtain her face in dark blonde, as she dropped her gaze to the floor. Moving to kneel in front of her, Grey caught the vacant look in her eyes. Leaning back on his heels, he rubbed his hands on his thighs, a little surprised that she was taking it this hard.

"You're not really surprised, are you? You know I hate it here."

"I know." She shrugged. "But you love your family. I didn't expect—" the words cut off with a choke.

She covered it with a cough that reached out and punched him square in the chest.

"I have to go. I'm sorry. Tell Clay ... tell him I'll see him around. And tell him to keep that Jake Johnson from sniffin' around you. He's trouble, Lory. Don't go gettin' mixed up with him."

"You don't have a say in the matter now, do you?" Her drenched, bloodshot eyes narrowed accusingly.

No, he didn't. But he'd sure as hell be telling Antonio to keep that fucker in check while he was gone. Keeping assholes away from Lory had been a sport he'd played with Clay since they were kids, even though he knew for a fact she had a mean left hook.

"I know you can look after yourself. You might look delicate, but you're a steel magnolia, darlin'."

To his surprise, Lory lurched forward and clamped her arms around his neck, hugging him tight before she ran out the door. He sank down to lie on his back.

It was official. He was the biggest asshole in Mississippi.

Time to skip town.

Chapter Two

A Tall Drink of Water

Chelsea stretched her arms above her head, yawning as she followed the smell of cheesy grits and biscuits wafting through the house. "Mornin', Mama."

"Mornin', darlin'. How'd you sleep?"

Her mother stood at the stove, stirring the food. Blonde hair pulled back into a ponytail and her signature pink, frilly apron tied around a slightly generous waist to protect her nightgown.

Chelsea leaned in to give her mama a kiss on the cheek, and snuck a biscuit off the cooling rack on the bench. "Ow, ow, ow!" She juggled the hot treat from one hand to the other, before dropping it back.

"Silly girl, when are you gonna learn some patience?"

Her mother pulled a plate from the cupboard and placed the offending biscuit on top, with some steaming grits, before handing it back to Chelsea. "Here. Sit down and savor it. It'll be your last southern breakfast for a while. They don't make 'em like this up at that fancy college of yours."

Chelsea removed her stinging fingers from her mouth with a pop, and plonked herself at the table. The corners of her lips took a downturn as she thought about having to leave tomorrow. It didn't feel right. Leaving here was always hard, but this time, some invisible current had her in its grip. There was a hum in her blood, luring her away. She wanted to spit out some gum and glue herself to the southern ground.

"I could always make my own, now that I'm moving out of the dorm."

Chelsea swore she heard a snort escape, as her mama's eyes narrowed. "Am I going to have to worry about your safety while you're gone? I don't want you burning anything down."

"It's a possibility. Maybe I can swap cooking duty for cleaning the bathroom or somethin'? My new roommates will probably beg me to stop once they taste my cooking. I hope my new place has a comfy mattress. I'm so done with the one in the dorm." Her shoulders shook in an exaggerated shudder. "I've been walkin' around like I've been rode hard and put away wet. I need a rest."

Mama tutted, pursing her lips. "I'll be dead before I get used to your filthy mouth. You are no southern lady. Where did I go wrong?"

"It's my protective mechanism. It keeps away the weak-hearted."

"It weakens my heart."

"It certainly weakens the hearts of men."

"Oh, good Lord. This is why I need medication."

"I'm yankin' your chain." She grinned. "I'm sure gonna miss this place."

"This place will miss you too, honey." Her mother's voice wavered and faded out as she hid her face from Chelsea.

She knew they were both referring to more than just their location.

"Only one more year, Mama," she said softly, feeling a swell of love for the woman.

Her mother turned off the stove and joined her at the breakfast table. "One more year and then you'll get a job, travel, meet people. Don't be in a rush to get back home. There's not much doin' here, sugar. Enjoy the ride while you're young."

The mouthful of cheesy goodness lost its flavor as she watched her mama's lip quiver, betraying her brave façade. Chelsea admired the woman more than anyone. It had always been just the two of them. They'd moved from Texas six years before, but that was a life she wished she could forget. Her mama had struggled, working two jobs, trying to keep the roof over their heads. Sometimes, their dinner plates had gone empty. She'd been so tired she barely had the energy to smile at Chelsea, let alone spend quality time with her.

Chelsea had spent too many brain-numbing nights next door, playing with old Mrs. Neaman's cat, and waiting for her mama to come and get her, until she couldn't take it anymore. One moment of reckless stupidity had her climbing out the window, drawn to the nearest trouble she could find. She started hanging with the older kids, spending time at the nearest take-out joint, smoking and talking shit. That's where she met Beth, another escapee.

They'd chased trouble until Chelsea found herself in a deep, dark hole. It felt like nothing could pull her out. She still couldn't recall how they'd ended up separated. Her memories of the events of that night slipped through her grasp whenever she tried to remember. It was the impressions on her senses that dug the deepest. The way her body had felt... like it was detached from her brain, too sluggish to follow the messages fired through her synapses. She recalled covering her nose with her shirt to filter the smoke from the bonfire as she struggled for breath. But the lights … the flash of red and blue lights still played the most vividly in her nightmares, tethering her to the past like the heaviest of chains.

"Where have you been, young lady?"

Silently, she'd stood on the porch, squinting blurred, tear soaked eyes under the harsh light over the front door.

"Chelsea, you're scaring me. What happened?"

The look on her mama's face as it morphed from anger to concern—

"Something bad has happened, Mama. Real bad."

—and finally, horror … *that* would remain etched in her memories forever.

Lead coated her gut as she remembered how she'd put her mother through hell. They'd moved to Alabama to start afresh. Best damn decision her mama had made. It didn't erase the past, but it softened the jagged edges of the scars left behind.

She ordered her cheeks to hitch up. "I'm enjoyin' the ride. Don't you worry. I've met plenty of nice folks. I just miss home, that's all." Chelsea made swirly patterns in the gooey mixture on her plate, trying to wipe away the memories. "Besides, six years ago you were telling me the opposite. Telling me to settle down ..."

"I know. It's hard for me to think of—" Her mama's throat bobbed, collapsing on the words as a hand flew to her chest. She gathered her composure, wriggling in her seat. "I'm just concerned you're trying to squash your free spirit. Don't ever do that, honey. Find a balance."

They ate in silence while Chelsea processed the advice. She'd done everything she could to try to undo the damage she'd caused. Getting a scholarship to college was her way of repaying her karmic debt, but she didn't think it would be this hard to be away.

"This'll always be home. You're stuck with me whether you like it or not."

Even as she said it, she wasn't sure if she believed it. Fingers of doubt slid over her collar bone, pulling her back, telling her to hold her plans. Change was coming. She jerked a shoulder to dislodge the sensation.

"Besides, what would y'all do without me making life interesting?" Taking her empty plate to the kitchen to wash, she sent her mother a smile across the kitchen counter, and got a frown in return. "Speaking of which, I'm gonna go see if Angel wants to do something, seeing as it's my last day here, and all."

Chelsea skipped over and wrapped her arms around her mother's slim shoulders, giving her another kiss on the cheek. "I'll see you later, okay?"

She received a pat on the arm and a cautious smile, sending her on her way. Chelsea was determined to make her mama proud, but she had one last day of freedom, and fun was calling her name.

―――――

Looking out of the café window at all the mom and pop businesses in town, Chelsea relished every sight, smell, and sound, packing them in her heart so she could revisit them while she was away.

There was no place like it.

She laughed at herself, tempted to check her feet for sparkly red pumps.

Taking another sip of her sweet tea, she surveyed her friend, Angel, as she ate her bagel. With raven hair and pale skin gifted by her father, and green eyes and features as her mother's legacy—God rest her soul—Angel presented a delicate beauty befitting her name.

Angel knew about deep, dark places. That's where they met as teenagers. At the bottom of that hole. By the time Chelsea got to town, Angel had lost her mama, and the love of her life. The first, tragically taken too young by a drunk driver out of control, and the second, forced to leave by an egotistical snake in the grass.

Together, they'd latched onto and dragged each other out. Chelsea guessed that's why Angel's dad let her hang around his family. He'd seen his daughter come back from the abyss with Chelsea's help. He saw beyond the trailer trash label she'd worn since birth, to find something good.

Unlike her own father. Bless his cold heart.

Her hand tightened around the glass as her teeth ground together, annoyed she'd broken her promise to ban that asshole from her thoughts.

Scrubbing him from her mind, she remembered saying goodbye to Hank, Angel's dad, instead.

"Be a good lass, but not too good," he'd said with a wink.

If she was looking for a man, she'd be looking for a younger version of him. But that wasn't happening. She was just fine all on her lonesome.

"How come your daddy is still single?"

Angel's face blanched as she blinked huge eyes at the question.

"Aw, shit. Sugar, I didn't mean that anyone should replace your mama, I just wonder how a good lookin' man like your daddy manages to fend off the ladies? Tall, dark hair, pale blue eyes ... He's a looker, sweetie."

Angel scrunched her nose and reached for the sweetener, pouring it into her mug. "Whatever you say, honey. I don't know, you'll have to ask him. Can we just talk about somethin' else?"

"I'll bet Miss Penny from the bakery wouldn't mind buttering his buns, if ya know what I mean."

Angel clapped her hands over her ears, squeezing her eyes shut. "For the love of God, would you please stop?"

Laughter bubbled out of Chelsea's throat. She shouldn't tease, but Angel was an easy target.

"What about you? Any man candy around here worth takin' for a ride?"

"Oh, my—" The smack of Angel's palms on the table echoed through the tiny shop, causing a few heads to turn their way.

Chelsea raised an amused brow.

"I have more important things to worry about than the opposite sex. It didn't turn out so well for me before, so why would I subject myself to that torture again? And what about you, huh?"

Chelsea leaned back in her seat and crossed her arms. "Plenty of man candy where I'm goin', sugar. They're pretty to look at and fun to play with, but that's as far as I'll go. Men are more trouble than they're worth. You know how I feel about that."

Angel merely nodded.

They stared each other down, assessing who was going to break first.

Chelsea uncrossed her arms, feeling bad that she'd ruined their last day together with such a sore subject. She leaned forward, whispering conspiratorially, "Wanna go play switch the mail?"

Angel snorted, a smirk breaking the scowl on her face. "We haven't done that since sophomore year."

"I know. It's well past time for us to do it again." Chelsea grinned at her friend. "How 'bout we go shopping instead?"

"We can look, but that's it."

They made their way out into the street, matching strides, always in tune with each other.

"Are you sure your daddy is okay with you taking the day off?"

"Yeah. All I did was mention your name, and his face went all soft. I didn't even have to convince him. He's unofficially adopted you. In fact, I think you might be his favorite." Angel mock scowled at Chelsea as she shoved her on the arm.

"Naw. You're his little Angel." Chelsea looped their arms as they meandered past the window displays.

"Are you ready to go back to the big smoke?"

"Yes and no. Fall is so beautiful there, but I miss y'all so much when I'm not here. I have some great friends. You'd adore Jenna. I'd love to bring her back with me one day. She'd probably fit in my suitcase. I love all the history. Every turn around every corner is a step back in time. And there are heaps of people our age sharing the college experience. The traffic sucks, though. All those crazy Massholes behind the wheel. It's some scary shit, let me tell you."

"I wish I could come visit you sometime, but you know I can't leave my obligations here."

Her best friend amazed her. She had two young children to look after, while holding down a job in the office of her daddy's auto shop. She appeared happy, for the most part. But Chelsea could tell there was something missing. Some fire that had died to an ember and needed something … or someone, to stoke it back to life. They both knew who that someone was. What they didn't know was if they'd ever get to see him again.

Chelsea swallowed down the anger and guilt that always accompanied thoughts of Aiden and the reason he left town. She prayed every day that the good Lord might bless Angel with all the happiness she deserved. Faith was something that Chelsea had struggled with every now and then. But when it came to her friend's happiness, she had all the faith in the world.

"I know, honey. I know." She hugged her friend's arm tighter, and pulled her to a stop as she spotted a little boutique children's clothing store. "Ooh, look at the adorable little jeans. I have to get something for the kids."

"No, Chelsea. It's probably expensive in there. I've deliberately avoided going in there since it opened."

Angel tugged on Chelsea's arm, urging her on, but she stood her ground.

"I have some tip money saved up. Let me do this for them, please?"

Angel chewed on her lip, her eyes darting between the mannequins on display and Chelsea. Her shoulders slumped and Chelsea knew she'd won the battle.

"Okay. But only one item each. Don't go crazy. We have to go get them soon, anyways."

"Sure thing, sweetie." She was already halfway through the door, dragging Angel behind her.

————

The gas pump buzzed and clicked loudly, filling the air with fumes as Angel filled the tank. Chelsea leaned casually against the car, watching people out of the corner of her eye. She noticed Vince Walker filling his Ford, amazed that he'd gotten so tall. He was three years younger than her, and had been a cocky freshman when he'd asked her out. Moving away for college seemed to roll time forward, like a runaway train, rather than the tedious ticking of hands on a clock.

She jiggled her leg, trying to shake off the gnawing feeling that she wouldn't be coming back here to live. It sank in further, the closer she got to catching her plane.

Fucking crazy talk.

She might've been running away when she arrived, dragging heavy shit with her, but somehow, arriving here had lightened the load and made it all seem bearable. If she lost her connection with these people and this town, she'd be lost. The nervous energy ramped up until she was tapping her heel a hundred miles an hour, ready to take off.

Her attention shifted to a man she'd never seen before, and her heart instantly picked up its rhythm.

"Who is that tall drink of water?" Chelsea locked her sights on the stranger entering the gas station.

"Where?"

"He just walked in to pay for his gas. Long, dark hair. Brooding good looks. Tight ass cheeks in Wranglers."

Angel's eyes popped wide. "Keep your voice down!"

"Ass cheeks!" From the back seat, Addy tested the words on her child-sized tongue. Judging by the huge smile on her cherubic face, she liked the way they sounded.

Angel groaned. "Don't say that word, sweetie. That's an adult word." Unamused, Angel sent Chelsea a glare as she finished at the pump. "Thanks, Chels. Daddy is going to pitch a fit. Thank you very much."

Chelsea winced, keeping her gaze on the man as he spoke with the attendant. "Sorry, sweetie. You should be proud, though. She's a smart little sponge, aren't ya, honey?" Chelsea waved through the window at the little girl, before addressing Angel again. "I'll make it up to you. The gas is on me."

As she sauntered off, she put an extra sway in her hips to make use of her boots and swishy skirt. What was the harm in letting her free spirit soar just a little? She had her mama's blessing, after all. And something about the dark stranger reeled her in like a magnet. Her effort was rewarded when the man turned, stopping in his tracks on spotting her.

She made it to the door as he reached forward to open it for her. "Why, thank you, stranger," she drawled as she brushed past him into the shop. "Haven't seen the likes of you 'round these parts before. Are you just passin' through?"

"That was the plan. I'm just on the lookout for somewhere to eat supper." His voice caressed over every nerve ending, making things tingle.

Chelsea hummed in delight, never one to hold back her thoughts. "You should come to the diner. Fill up that body before you leave. There's not much to look at in the next town, anyways. The view and the company are much nicer here."

"No doubt." His pale gray eyes devoured her from under heavy lids.

"If you'd like some company, the diner is half a mile down the road. I'll see you there in a bit." It wasn't a question. She knew he was keeping up with her perfectly by the way their bodies vibrated and swayed towards each other. Her mouth watered at the thought of watching him eat, and talk, and look at her the way he was doing now.

His voice followed behind as she moved towards the register. "What's your name, sugar?"

Looking over her shoulder, she smiled. When a man wants to know your name, he's intrigued, if not half sunk. "Chelsea. What's yours, sugar?"

"Greyson." His barely-there smile was the sexiest damn thing she'd ever seen.

Her eyes dropped to the straining material covering his chest and biceps, before rising to meet his stare again. Nope, not just the smile. The whole delicious package. Stupidly, she wanted to go deeper. Wanted to know what made him tick. Whether he had the soul to match the body. She doubted guys like that actually existed, and trying to find one was a pointless exercise for dumbass romantics.

"Likewise, Greyson. I'll be seeing you real soon."

She watched as he blew out a long breath, threw him a wink, and went to pay.

Damn, her stomach was full of dancing lightning bugs. Or maybe it was a glut of waving red flags. She'd never been this excited to spend time with a man. Lucky for her, both of them were leaving. She could still have a little fun before she left. She wasn't going to go too far. She didn't do that anymore.

Much.

———

Like the rest of town, Lucy's Diner was stuck in a time warp. They had the jukebox to prove it, complete with vinyl records. It had a nice homey feel to it, though—another thing she'd miss while she was gone.

The bell on the door jingled as it slapped shut behind her. An aromatic cocktail of grease and coffee hung on the air, assailing her senses, and triggering her hunger. Chelsea turned and waved to Angel as she drove off shaking her head. Her friend thought she was crazy, meeting a strange man who wasn't hanging around for long. She'd learned to be more selective and trust her instincts when it came to men, despite her impulsive tendencies. Unwilling to repeat the fatal mistake from her past.

Maybe she was crazy, but there was something about him … She wasn't completely irresponsible. The diner was her turf and it was safe. There'd be people here that would look out for her.

She had this under control.

Chelsea's blue gaze roamed the cracked red vinyl booths, until they landed on the deliciousness that was Greyson Stranger. She didn't know his last name, so Stranger it was, and that's how she wanted it to stay. This was just a short detour to let off some steam before she had to get back to the serious business of paying for her sins.

Her smile stretched wide as she watched him take her in, the heat in his eyes blazing. His long, dark hair hung over one eye, brushing the tops of his wide shoulders. He leaned back in the chair and rested his arms across the table in front of him, with a hint of a smile in greeting.

Slowly walking towards him, she kept eye contact, half because she wanted to make an entrance, and half because she couldn't look away.

"Is this seat taken?"

Greyson waved his hand across the booth as if to say, "Be my guest."

Chelsea slid into the seat and rested her chin in her hands, still staring at him.

"Hi."

"Hi." He smirked.

"You hungry?"

"Yeah. I've ordered a piece of pie and sweet tea. I didn't know if you were gonna show up, so I figured I'd … fill up my body …" He wiggled his fingers to put air quotes around his use of her phrase. "… before gettin' back on the road."

At the mention of his body, Chelsea's eyes dropped to his straining T-shirt again. It was hard not to look. The man was gorgeous. "Well, sugar, if I invite a man somewhere you can always guarantee I'll show up. A piece of pie and some sweet tea sounds mighty fine right about now."

The waitress appeared in time with Chelsea's declaration. "Ili sweetie, good to see you again. You having what he's having?" The older lady stood with pencil and pad poised, and a ready smile.

"Thanks, Doreen."

"Okay, hun." She bustled back behind the counter.

Chelsea turned back to her companion. "So, tell me about your first kiss?"

Greyson's mouth dropped open and he huffed out a laugh. "Excuse me?"

"First kiss. Come on. Spill."

"Mindy Lawson, second grade, on the swings. How about you?"

"Decker Turner, two years old, in the playpen." She grinned. "What did you think you'd grow up to be when you were a kid?"

"Superman … How 'bout you?"

"Lois Lane." She smirked, batting her lashes playfully.

A deep laugh rumbled out of him, sending tingles down her neck.

"Do I get to ask a question?" He raised a dark brow.

"Only if it's not personal."

"Your first kiss isn't personal?"

"No." She shrugged.

"So, I can't ask what your last name is?"

"Nope."

"Or your number?"

"Nooo." She shook her head, dramatically.

He sat up straight and scratched the stubble on his chin, one side of his mouth quirked. "Arrabbiata or Carbonara?"

"Ooh, good one. It depends on my mood. Arrabbiata, most of the time."

"Spicy … Nice." He leaned towards her, his eyes dipping to her lips for a second, before seeking her gaze again.

She put her hands on the table, mirroring him as she leaned forward. "Red or white wine?"

"Whatever goes with the dish."

"I like an adventurous man." The smile broke out on her face again.

"I'm on the biggest adventure of my life."

"Where ya headed?"

"Isn't that a personal question?" He raised a brow and moved his hand closer so their fingers touched.

"Touché. Yes, it is."

The clink of plates on the table broke the intensity between them.

Chelsea took in a desperate breath as they both leaned back. "Thanks, Doreen, you're a darlin'."

"You're welcome, sweetie. Enjoy!"

They each took a forkful of pie, and chewed as their eyes roamed over each other. The taste on her tongue was amazing. The country song playing on the jukebox barely registered over the sound of Grey's lips smacking together as he enjoyed his food. He made a low hum in his throat, and she let out a whimper. It was the most intense foreplay she'd ever experienced.

She couldn't help feeling sad at the thought that this couldn't go anywhere. It should have been a warning signal, when fleeting hook-ups were the only relationships she dared to entertain. The type she could control. Maybe it hadn't been wise, starting something with this man. It echoed of her past. Of a stupid decision that cost a life. She feared she was setting herself up for a painful experience, rather than the fun she'd hoped for.

Picking up her glass, she gulped down some cool, sweet tea, looking away from him for a beat.

"Feelin' a bit heated, sugar?" The amusement was obvious in his voice.

The glass thunked on the table as she put it down too forcefully. "I am. You wanna get out of here?"

"What's the hurry? Are you tired of me already?"

"Nope. It's just the opposite. I'm afraid I've bitten off more than I can chew, but like the greedy girl I am, I'd like to gorge myself some more."

She had lost her everlovin' mind.

His jaw tightened and he paused, his eyes flashing to her mouth. She watched that jaw loosen as he continued to chew and swallow slowly. His gaze drifted back to hers, and he picked up his drink, draining it in one long chug before pushing the glass away.

"You're a wild one ... Tempting."

He sat so still with his eyes boring into hers, his face an intense mask. His eyebrows had dropped. He looked almost angry ... or maybe frustrated. It did nothing to dispel the heat that gathered in her core. If anything, the hint of fire in his eyes set her desire for him at furnace level. She'd never experienced an attraction like this before, putting her at a distinct disadvantage. She needed to be the one in control, and she felt anything but.

"I need to get back on the road. If I don't get out of here now, I'm never going to leave," he muttered, before he stood. Reaching into his back pocket, he pulled out his wallet, and threw some green onto the table. His warm palm caressed her cheek, as his thumb drifted across her bottom lip. The touch set off all sorts of tingles, further awakening parts that had no business being excited in a 1950s diner.

Chelsea's heart thundered in her chest as he leaned down to place a soft kiss on her lips. The barely-there touch seared more than the hottest chili.

"The first kiss is always personal," he whispered in her ear, before walking out of her life.

For good.

She sat for the longest time, staring at where he'd been sitting, trying to calm the hell down. Wondering what the fuck had just happened, and why she suddenly felt so bereft. Like her carefully planned future now had a gaping hole she had no idea how to fill.

Chapter Three

New Friends

Chelsea finished placing photos of her mom, and Angel and the kids, on the bookshelf above her desk. Worn out after a long day of moving and unpacking, she slumped on her desk chair, admiring her decorating efforts. A royal purple, satin comforter lent a luxurious quality to the standard-sized bedroom. She'd draped a colorful scarf over her bedside lamp, added some finger paintings—courtesy of the Murphy kids—to the walls, and stocked her bookshelf with books, trinkets, and photographs.

Her classmate, Dakota, had offered Chelsea the spare room at her place, and Chelsea had jumped at the chance to get out of the dorms. Not that the dorm rooms were bad, but there was something about a having a vinyl covered floor and sharing a building with a few hundred people, she just couldn't stomach. It would be nice to have a room to herself.

She made her way out to the living room where Dakota was lounging beside Ryan—the only male in the house—peppering his ears with her chatter. He didn't seem to mind, letting it bounce off him while his hand rested on her thigh and his eyes glazed over. Guaranteed, he only heard one percent of what she was saying.

Hannah, the final tenant, sat on a ratty recliner playing Xbox. The computer-generated sounds of revving engines battled with the conversation on the sofa. It all looked suspiciously like the recreation room in the dorm, but that was where the similarities ended. There weren't students lined up to use the bathroom, or hundreds of people milling about the building. This was a home. Her new home. She figured it was like a new pair of leather shoes that had to be worn in until they molded to her feet. And if it didn't, she would be leaving in the summer, anyways.

Ryan turned his head, acknowledging Chelsea's entrance with a slow perusal of her body, cutting off Dakota mid-speech.

"Hey, gorgeous. All settled in?"

Aw, shit. And he seemed so sweet when she'd met him. He had that twinkle in his eye. Like he knew he was cute and every woman should watch out. *Not happening, sunshine.*

Chelsea noted the annoyance on Dakota's face, before flicking her eyes towards Ryan, and pasting on a smile.

"Yep. All set." She nodded before shifting her attention back to Dakota. "Thanks for letting me stay here." Offering her friend a genuine smile, she tried to ignore the feeling that she was intruding on something.

"Not a problem. You saved us from having to interview a whole heap of weirdos."

"How do I know you're not weirdos?" She cocked a blonde eyebrow and crossed her arms.

Hannah snorted, but didn't take her eyes off the screen as her fingers flew over the controller.

Ryan's face stretched into a huge grin, his dark eyes full of mischief. "You don't." He appraised her with an interest she had better sense to return.

Tightening her arms, she managed to stop a growl from escaping.

"I think we should all go out to celebrate the new addition to our little family. You ladies up for it?" He wiggled his eyebrows.

She was amazed that the sparkle in his eye grew even more pronounced as he voiced the double entendre. It may as well have been a flashing neon sign that screamed 'player'. The entire time he'd been checking her out, his hand remained on Dakota's thigh, and a frown had marred Dakota's pretty face as his blatant flirting continued.

Chelsea had dealt with guys like him before. Sometimes they were good for a bit of fun, but not when another woman's heart was on the line. She felt a rush of sympathy for her friend.

"Sure. Sounds like fun. Why don't you invite some other guys to make things even?"

It was Ryan's turn to frown as Chelsea circled the sofa and grabbed Dakota's wrist, pulling her up. "Hey Dee, why don't you come help me choose something to wear?"

Like Dakota had a choice. They were already halfway up the stairs before Chelsea had finished the sentence.

Guiding them through her bedroom door, she shut it quietly before dropping Dee's arm.

"Girl, is he just overly friendly or is there something goin' on between you two?"

Dakota shrugged, seeming nonchalant, but something in her dark eyes told Chelsea she was irked by the question. "He's a nice guy. He just likes to flirt."

"And you like it when he flirts with you?"

Her shoulders bounced again, as she scratched at her eyebrow. "Yeah. It's a bit of harmless fun. Why wouldn't I like the attention of a gorgeous guy?"

Chelsea rested her hands on her hips and pursed her lips. Every woman liked the attention of a gorgeous guy. It's when their attention wandered that problems began.

"You didn't seem to like his eyes wandering over to me, and I can assure you, I didn't like them on me either. Whatever he's got goin' through his head, I'm not interested. Are we clear?" She reached over to squeeze Dakota's shoulder.

"Yeah, we're clear." Dakota laughed. "Why are you making such a big deal out of this?"

"I don't want there to be any misunderstanding between us. I really appreciate you inviting me to live here. I've seen stuff like this break up friendships before. I'd hate for things to be awkward. Promise me you'll talk to me first if you have any issues with our arrangement?"

"Yeah, okay. I promise."

Dakota snorted, her bemused expression stopping just short of an eye roll. She wasn't taking this seriously. Chelsea only hoped that Ryan would get the message and back off.

"Hey, if you guys are talking about Ryan behind his back, I'd like to join in." Hannah's tall, lithe body glided into the room, and landed on the edge of Chelsea's bed. She flicked her light brown plait over her shoulder and leaned back on both hands. "Welcome to the family. Ryan's roving eyes clearly found you interesting." One cheek caved in with a dimple, as dark blue eyes assessed her from behind cat-eye framed glasses. "I can see the appeal. Love the accent. Nice rack."

Chelsea's brow shot up and she dropped her chin to inspect her T-shirt. It wasn't like she'd dressed up to move house. She was in her sloppiest gear; yoga pants and an old Boston University tee. What was wrong with these people?

"Hannah." Dee flopped onto the mattress beside her friend and crossed her legs. "Chelsea's going to think we're a bunch of deviants."

"That description would be accurate of Ryan and myself, but I'm sure she knows you're normal, Dakota." Hannah tilted her head to the side, smiling at Chelsea's confusion. "I'm bi. But don't fret. You're not my type. I go for quiet, bookish types. They're usually wild cats in the sack."

Oh. Go, Hannah.

"What's Ryan's excuse?"

"He's just a horny college student intent on spreading his seed far and wide."

Dee smacked Hannah on the arm, but giggled at her remark.

"Nice visual. Excuse me while I vomit." If Chelsea hadn't already been turned off, she certainly was now.

"I'm afraid our Dee has developed a little crush on him."

"No, I haven't. We're just being friendly."

"Mm hmm. Real friendly." Hannah lowered her glasses to stare at Dee over the rim. "You were friendly about three times last Saturday night. Is that about right, Dee?"

"We were drunk." Dee's eyes went all dreamy, and a ghost of a smile tugged at her lips. "Three times? Really?"

"Yeah. I checked with the neighbor. He agreed."

Dakota threw her hands over her face and giggled. "Shit. Sorry, Hannah."

"It's fine. You were just getting back at me for last year."

Dakota groaned. "Don't remind me. Dave. Then Mindy. Then Dave *and* Mindy."

Chelsea's hands stuck to her hips as her eyebrows rose higher and higher. "So, it's true. All y'all *are* weirdos. Will ear plugs and an eye mask be enough to drown you out, or should I just start packin' now?"

"Ear plugs and an eye mask? Interesting. We could do something with those," Hannah piped in.

Chelsea's hands slipped, dropping her arms to hang loosely by her sides. What the hell had she signed up for?

Her two housemates burst out laughing.

"We're just messing with you!"

Chelsea wasn't sure if they were just joking about her choice of personal protective equipment or the entire conversation.

"So, you haven't slept with him, and Hannah hasn't had a threesome?" Yeah, it was none of her business, but she wanted to know.

Dakota shook her head, a demure smile playing on her lips, giving Chelsea no clue to the truth.

"We weren't joking about the threesome. Threesomes are the best." Hannah stared off into space, a wicked smile playing on her lips.

It wasn't often she met someone more outlandish and forward than she was, but Hannah had her beat. They'd all seemed normal when she checked the place out before summer break. Now, she was a little suspicious of just how close these three actually were.

One thing, she was sure of—living with these people was going to keep her on her toes.

They rifled through her closet, choosing what they were going to borrow for the night ahead. Chelsea joined in the impromptu fashion show, feeling a tiny bit of home click into place. She'd done this with Angel countless times. They were similar in size, Chelsea just an inch taller than her best friend. She didn't know how Hannah and Dakota were going to fare, with Hannah being a foot taller, and Dakota, shorter by the same amount. But clothes flew everywhere as they threw themselves into the task. Hannah opted to show off her impressive shoulder tattoo with a halter top, while Dakota's choice of a yellow dress set off her darker skin tone—the extra length sorted by the use of a belt.

Chelsea trailed the fashion queens into the bathroom, preparing to put on her mask for the night. Maybe prettying up her outside would get her insides in on the partying plan. She sponged on some foundation, smiling at the two ladies beside her as they bantered back and forth, hoping that the make-up would cover whatever funk she had going on.

Now, she was the newbie. It was natural to feel out of sync …

Hell, no, it wasn't. Not for her.

Where the fuck had she gone?

She was still in Alabama, watching Greyson walk away. Half an hour in his presence and her world had flipped on its head. Maybe it was time to hang up her party skirt and get serious about being an adult. She'd never felt like she could let loose here, anyways. Not like at home. This was temporary, and she had something to prove.

"Hey. You okay?"

She snapped out of her troubled thoughts, taking in their reflections as Dee rested her head on Chelsea's arm.

"Oh, yeah. I'll be fine, sugar. Don't worry about me. Just a bit tired, is all."

"Are you sure you want to come? It's okay if you want to sit this one out."

"Naw. You're sweet. It'll be fun. Allston, here we come."

Yay.

Ugh.

Ryan puffed out his chest when they all made their way out to the kitchen to find him. Beer in hand, he was already in party mode, spreading his arms wide in appreciation and welcome.

She had to admit that he was a good-looking guy, in a boy-next-door kinda way. Light brown hair that curled into loose waves, dark brown eyes, and olive skin. He had a certain appeal. Yeah, he was a terrible flirt. But then, so was she. She just needed to discourage him so he'd get the message. This was going to be fine, she thought, as she crossed her fingers behind her back.

———

They turned up at the Silhouette, possibly the best dive bar ever. In Allston, anyways. She'd been here once, the year before, but they'd painted a mural on the exterior over the summer. A tribute to some famous Joes, in black and white on a red background.

Cheesy Christmas lights and a rowdy college crowd greeted them with a warm, exuberant embrace. Chelsea was surprised to find that Ryan had followed her suggestion and invited a couple of friends—also college boys—she guessed, as they slapped each other on the back.

Tall, thin, and blonde, Cameron was an engineering major. He seemed a bit shy—perfect for Hannah. Watching the way his face turned pink every time Hannah leaned in to speak in his ear, was entertainment enough for the evening.

The other guy, Jackson, had plenty of meat on his bones. He was probably fond of a barbecue rib or five, but he was tall too. His size became a little less imposing as they warmed a couple of bar stools. Jackson was studying business, like Chelsea. In theory, they had plenty to talk about, but the conversation was stunted by the lure of sports on the screen, and Jackson's roving eye for the other ladies around the bar. She should have been offended. She wasn't. Truth was, she was relieved. She kept imagining long, dark hair, a wicked smile, and tight Wranglers.

Chelsea sighed as she sipped her beer, and turned her attention to the game on the screen. After a minute of staring through it, she scrubbed the heel of her palm across her forehead, trying in vain to erase the memory of that kiss, and the stupid, meaningless conversation that had her body humming. As fleeting as their interlude had been, she couldn't shake the weight of it. Not just the strength of the attraction between her and Greyson, but the way he'd simply walked away, taking a chip out of her confidence.

It was completely idiotic, letting a stranger she'd just met do that to her. She wanted to kick herself repeatedly with a steel-toe boot.

Chelsea had sworn never to put herself in a position where a man had any power over her. But with the emotional tumble of her last day at home, she'd been a careless dumbass. What was she thinking, running off to meet a strange man at the diner? She thought she was being smart by picking a safe place, and then what did she do …?

She'd asked if he wanted to leave.

With her.

Alone.

She groaned and shook her head as a shiver coursed down her back. Thank God he left. She could be dead right now.

"Hey," Dakota yelled in her ear. "Where're ya at in your head? 'Cause it's not a good place, I can tell." The words were barely decipherable. She was slurring so badly.

"Wow, Dee. Your breath could sterilize a hospital. How many shots have you had?"

Dee and Ryan had been heating up the dart boards for the last half hour, while Hannah and Cameron played pool. It was a testament to her mood that she'd chosen to sit out the fun and games.

Dakota waved a hand in the air, swinging her head around. "Oonly fweee." Her fingers wiggled before she settled on holding up four.

Dakota's dark hair and eyes morphed to blonde and crystal blue as Chelsea's mind warped into her dark past for a second.

"Beth, honey, you are hammered. How many beers have you had?"

"Mm. Maaybeee fwee?" Beth held up a hand wriggling all five fingers as she giggled.

Chelsea snapped her eyes shut and prayed for amnesia before she did something stupid.

Ryan's arm slid over Chelsea's shoulder, his face coming close as he leaned down to talk in her ear. "Hey there, gorgeous. Are ya having a nice time?"

Ryan's articulation was more pickled than Dee's. He dragged out the 's' sounds. Heated breath laden with tequila wafted across her chin. She coughed as he leaned back, showing her a drunken grin. She turned her face away, cringing for Hannah and Cameron's benefit as they rejoined the group.

"Yup, how 'bout you? Did Dee whip your butt?"

"No, but I'd like to whip yerzz."

She tossed his arm off, throwing him off balance so he stumbled backwards into Cameron, and shot to her feet.

"You ready to go?" she barked at Dakota, spearing Ryan with a look that could slice him in half.

Yeah, men were bad news. She'd needed a reminder. And now she'd had two in the course of two days. Lesson learned.

"Easy. I was just kidding around," Ryan slurred.

"I don't appreciate jokes about debasing me, or any other woman for that matter. And how could you let Dakota get so drunk? Are you a douche, Ryan? Because I'd really like to believe that my friend has better sense than to get mixed up with a douche. And that she'd never invite me to share the same roof with one. Do I have to worry about my safety? And Dee and Hannah's?"

"Whoa." He held up his hands, still leaning on Cameron for support, eyes as wide as his droopy eyelids would allow.

Chelsea uncurled her fists and dropped her chin as she took in the looks of shock on the surrounding faces.

Shit.

Okay, maybe she'd overreacted.

"Sorry. I'm sorry ... I'm gonna head home. Ladies, I'd feel a lot better if you were ready to leave too." She crossed her arms and shrugged her shoulders, trying to defuse the situation with a smile.

"Yeah, I'd say we're done here." Hannah leaned up to give Cameron a kiss on the cheek, and left him pink-faced with one last message whispered in his ear.

They made their way through the crowd to the exit. Dee using Chelsea as support and Hannah helping Ryan. Chelsea checked her phone. They still had half an hour before The T finished for the night. She'd just saved them a taxi fare. *Woohoo.* Way to find the bright side. The small blessing didn't ease the guilt and embarrassment she had churning in her gut. Let's hope she wasn't going to have to look for a new place to live tomorrow.

Dang, she missed home.

Chapter Four

Back to Business

Chelsea's fingernails clacked on the keys of her laptop, taking down notes while the professor droned on. Paying attention was proving to be a challenge, especially with the weight of Dakota's questioning stare heavy on the back of her neck.

She'd managed to avoid Dee and Ryan that morning, both sleeping off their alcoholic binge session. But Hannah had given her sideways looks, pleading ignorance when Chelsea asked whether there was something on her face.

Sitting in class, she felt like a bug under a magnifying glass with a beam of sunlight aimed at her. Finally, the class finished, and the sound of students talking and gathering their stuff roared to life. *Thank you, Jesus.* She sat unmoving, hoping that Dee would need to be somewhere else in a hurry.

"What was with you last night?"

Chelsea's shoulders tensed at the question. "I was really hopin' you were so drunk you'd forgotten about that," she whispered over her shoulder, not wanting everyone to know about her pitchin' a hissy fit.

"Not a chance. So, what gives?"

Dakota wasn't concerned that everyone would hear, drawing the attention of those around them with her loud mouth, as she wrestled her laptop into her bag.

Chelsea prayed for patience, closing her eyes for a beat. "You were late this morning. I'm surprised you made it at all. I thought you'd still be passed out in bed." She focused her attention on packing up, pleased that she'd volleyed the surrounding questioning eyes back to her friend.

"Hannah's hangover cure. Works like a charm," Dakota announced to their audience before leaning down to speak in Chelsea's ear. "Don't think you're getting out of explaining yourself."

"Later," Chelsea hissed, descending the stairs to the exit.

Dakota stuck to her tail like a blood hound. "Seriously, Chelsea? I vouched for you, and now you're behaving like a crazy person. Ryan was just joking around."

Chelsea ducked into an empty alcove, lowering her voice to a harsh whisper. "What he said was inappropriate.

It made me uncomfortable. Yeah, I shouldn't have snapped, but he doesn't know me well enough to make jokes like that. We have to live together, Dee."

"Exactly." Dakota sliced a finger through Chelsea's personal space, eyes blazing.

Chelsea groaned, dropping her chin to her chest. "Look. I'll apologize for my outburst. Hell, I'll even clean the kitchen for a month ..." She raised her eyes and fixed them on Dakota's. "... but I won't put up with any crap from him. Or any man."

The tense lines of Dakota's face and shoulders unraveled instantly. "Oh. I get it ... What happened to you?"

"Nothin' happened to me." *Not exactly.*

Turning her back, she moved into the corridor, hoping to leave this conversation behind. "I appreciate your concern. Maybe if we spent some time getting to know each other better, I'd feel more comfortable with all y'all, and you'll get to know my ... quirks."

"Sounds like a plan. But you're still on dish duty for a month."

Leaning forward to open the door, Dee nodded for Chelsea to go first. It was a kind of truce even though Dakota's mouth was still pinched in annoyance.

"Thanks."

With a sigh of relief Chelsea made her way outside, taking in the warm breeze and the hint of chromatic change on the horizon. Greens giving way to an array of yellows. It was beautiful. In another month, it would be spectacular. She didn't want to spend her last year with animosity marring her time.

She savored the scene, feeling a mix of home sickness and nostalgia for this place. Guilt and worry tugged at her.

Maybe she'd made the wrong decision, moving in with a friend. The good Lord knew she wasn't an easy person to live with. She had enough baggage to fill a sink hole, and apparently, it was spilling over into her final farewell.

Turning to Dakota, she put on her best apologetic smile. "Have you got another class now, or can I buy you coffee?"

"It just so happens that I'm meeting Hannah for coffee in Washington Square. Why don't you join us, and then you can say sorry for ruining her chances at getting some last night."

"Hannah and Cameron? I couldn't tell if he was really keen on her, or just trapped in her clutches. I bet he's pissed at me too."

They strode side by side through the throng of students and headed for the T stop. The ground seemed to firm up with each step, as they settled back into a familiar, easy camaraderie. The whole living together thing ... that was going to take some getting used to.

"I think he was a little scared of Hannah. He had 'virgin' written all over him." Dee spread her fingers and wiped her hand through the air like she was cleaning a mirror.

"Poor Cameron. My guess is he's not used to the attentions of such a vibrant woman."

"Vibrant? Yeah, that's the perfect word. I'll add eccentric to that."

"Intimidating," Chelsea offered.

"Sexually aggressive."

They both dissolved into giggles, bumping shoulders.

"Hey, ladies. Wait up."

Ryan's voice found them through the crowd, and they both spun around to search for him. Dee spotted him first, as he jogged through the cluster of bodies in his gym gear. She scooted off to give him a hug. Chelsea stood back, hesitant to approach, even though he seemed overjoyed to see them.

To see Dee, she corrected herself.

"Hi there. Where ya headed?"

Straight white teeth flashed a huge smile. His gaze washed over Chelsea, the tightness around his eyes hinting at the tension between them.

She needed to sort this out. Now.

"Hey, Ryan. I apologize for jumping down your throat last night. I overreacted. You were drunk, I get it. But don't go sayin' shit like that to me. Ever. Ya hear?"

"I just wanted to have a game of darts with you, Chelsea. That's all I meant."

Her eyebrows shot up, and she searched his face for signs of a lie, finding none in the wide set of his ingenuous eyes. Either he was a talented actor or he *was* being honest. She hadn't even considered that his comment was completely innocent. *Oh, God.* Now she really felt like a bitch. She'd judged him on first impression, and twisted his words to mean something she'd expect a player to say rather than a friendly challenge.

Who was the douche now?

"Oh, shit. Ryan, I'm so sorry. Me and my big mouth." She clasped the strap of her messenger bag, cringing. "I have a real short temper. I tend to shoot my mouth off before I ask questions. I apologize, again."

She glanced at Dakota, silently questioning if it was okay to invite him along. Dee's smile stretched in approval. "Would you like to come for a coffee? We're meeting with Hannah. My treat."

Chelsea offered the olive branch, feeling a little sick in the stomach that she was making such a mess of things already. She thought she was a better judge of character than that.

Ryan tapped a finger on his chin, playfully looking to the heavens for the answer. "Hmm. Coffee with Ryan's Angels. Sounds like heaven." His arms swung around their shoulders, playfully nudging them in the direction of the train station.

"Ryan's Angels? Your ego is bigger than the Super Bowl." Chelsea scoffed.

"A man can dream."

"Keep on dreaming; that's all it will ever be." She ducked out from his hold, striding out in front.

Things were still shaky between them. He was too familiar with her, even though she'd made it clear she didn't feel comfortable with him yet.

She gnashed her teeth, contemplating her situation, until an unpleasant thought jolted through her. Her steps faltered as the blood drained from her face. *Is that how she'd treated Greyson? Had her brash behavior turned him away?*

She was the worst kind of hypocrite. She didn't want to be treated like any man's play thing, and yet, that's how she'd been treating men for years. A whimper escaped her lips as she put a hand over her stomach. Her two companions, deep in conversation, obliviously followed behind.

Ryan had thrown a mirror in her face, and she didn't like what she'd seen.

Lord. What happened to turning over a new leaf? Atoning for her sins? Setting herself up for the future wasn't enough. She needed to grow the hell up before she ended this chapter of her life. How could she face her mother, or justify her mother's sacrifices, if she was running all over town behaving like the man who'd ruined her mama's life?

Her gut dropped to her feet. All of a sudden Alabama seemed like it was at the other end of the Earth from where she was standing.

Only one more year.

————

Chelsea breathed in the rich scents of simmering sauces and food prep wafting from Abbiocco's kitchen, an appreciative hum vibrating her throat. She'd worked here as a server for over three years. Outside these walls, she couldn't help but feel like a stripper in church. Not that she was losing her clothing on the regular, although it would sure help pay the bills. She felt exposed here, like they all knew her sordid past, and that she was only pretending to fit in, and were laughing behind her back. But at Abbiocco, she was one of an eclectic mix of misfits—everyone so different—and yet, all the pieces fit perfectly. This place was her home away from home.

Stopping at one of the tables, she looked around the deserted room, feeling emotions swell and clog her throat. Basking in the familiar inviting atmosphere, she was suddenly in danger of tipping over the edge she'd teetered on since she left home—since the diner, and everything that had happened with Ryan.

Pulling out a chair, she sat her ass down. Swiping her moist eyes with the back of her hand, she felt stupid for having a weak moment. But she bowed her head and let the tears drip, anyways. She deserved a break, damn it.

Rifling through her pocketbook, she yanked out a Kleenex, and tried to clean herself up before anyone saw her.

Girl, pull your shit together, pronto.

On the far side of the room, Chelsea could see the cooks working through the kitchen window. Could see their mouths moving, but couldn't quite make out what they were saying above the clash of metal utensils and equipment. She ran a hand over the crisp white linen covering the wooden table, mentally listing all the things she had to do before dinner service.

Chelsea stood, slinging her pocketbook over her shoulder, as she weaved through the room. The spread of tables, broken up by an occasional potted tree, their branches bare but for a string of lights. Pendant lights hung low, casting muted light throughout the room. Exposed brick walls lined the space in a darkened earthy tone, while a pyramid of glass in the center of the ceiling invited a view of the heavens. The effect was a cozy, magical atmosphere, despite the large space.

She'd been told Abbiocco was an Italian term used to describe the drowsiness you experienced after a large meal. That was kinda how she felt after each shift. Content and fulfilled. Definitely tired.

The kitchen door busted open as Dane, the restaurant's host, made his way over. "Babe! I thought that was you." He enveloped her in a warm hug before grabbing her arms and pulling back to inspect her face, his manicured brow drawn low. "What's going on. Why have you been crying?"

"Dane." His name squeezed through a tight throat.

"You're not gonna quit, are you?"

"Dane," she said more firmly.

"Aren't you happy to see me?"

She rolled her eyes. *Such a drama queen.* "Dane! Take a breath, and lay off the grip. You're hurtin' my arms."

"Oops! Sorry, babe." He let her go. "I'm just so happy to have you back. You know there's nobody that works the front of house like you ... And that awful bitch, Sonja ..." He snarled and held up a finger. "Do you know what she did? She served dishes to the wrong party, and one of the guys there was allergic to egg. Luckily, they realized it wasn't what they had ordered. We had to comp their desserts and his meal. She didn't bother to water her tables, and then she skated at the end of the night."

Jamming his hands on his hips, he glared at Chelsea. The diamond studs in his ears caught the light, mocking the fierce expression on his face. Dane may be man-scaped and moisturized to within an inch of his life, but he was scary when he wanted to be. She almost felt sorry for Sonja. Almost. If there was one thing Chelsea couldn't tolerate, it was lazy, selfish, careless people. Dane was none of those things.

"Did you tell her the shakers weren't going to fill themselves?"

"No, I told her not to come back. She smirked and said I had no authority to make that decision."

Chelsea's mouth flattened, unimpressed that they were still saddled with the peach.

"Beau sorted her out for me." Dane's eyes scanned the bar wistfully.

It was no secret that he had a crush on the bartender. She didn't blame him. Beau was hot. With brown hair and eyes to match, and a chiseled jaw covered in scruff. He was comforting and formidable at the same time.

"That man is my hero. Pity he's married. I'd be his bar-back any day."

"Married and super straight. Never mind, honey, there's a man out there for you."

"Hmm. He's probably still hiding in the closet." Dane turned back to Chelsea. "What about you? Did you snag yourself some hot Alabama tail while you were there?"

"Nope. I've decided to retire from the dating scene for a while."

Dane laughed for a solid minute before he realized she wasn't laughing with him.

"Wait. You're serious?" Those plucked eyebrows danced up his forehead.

"Yeah. I am."

"What? Why? One of us has to get some. How can we talk about sex if we're both in a man drought?"

"There's plenty more to life than men, Dane."

"Yeah, but none of it is as much fun."

"Shoes are fun. Ice cream is fun. Shopping and dancing are fun."

"None of those things will keep you warm at night, or make your toes curl in pleasure. Oh, babe. No, no, no. You've gone and lost your mojo."

His pitying expression pissed her off. "My mojo is right where I left it." *In a diner in Alabama.* "I appreciate your concern, but I don't need your pity. And I don't need a man." Chelsea raised a brow, and started to make her way to the kitchen.

"Three months." He called out after her.

She spun around, trying to taper back her annoyance. "Three months, for what?"

"I'll give you three months before you give in to temptation. If you can't make it that long, then you owe me a day at the spa."

"And if I prove you wrong?"

"I'll buy you those Manolo Blahniks you've been drooling over."

She sucked in a breath. "The boots?"

"*The* boots."

She pursed her lips and narrowed her eyes at him. "I'm offended that you think me so weak and so easily bought."

"I'm preying on your weaknesses for my own sick pleasure. It's true. You *should* be offended."

"You're going to be broke by Christmas, so you're the one who'll suffer, ultimately. It's a win for me and a loss for you. Why not? You're on."

She breezed past him into the kitchen to say hello to everyone and pack away her things, already imagining the suede beauties on her feet.

Piece of cake.

Chapter Five

What The?

"Jenna, honey! How've you been?" Chelsea flung her arms around her petite friend, feeling the scratch of Jenna's raven bun, rock hard with hairspray, just under her chin.

Catching up with the dinner service team at the Host's Station after hugging her way through the population of the building, she swore the smile was tattooed to her face. She soaked in the love, feeling like she'd been gone for a year, rather than just over a month.

"I'm doing fine. It's so good to have you back." Jenna slapped a no-nonsense hand on Chelsea's back, and stepped out of the embrace.

Jenna was a ball of muscle, reminding Chelsea of a gymnast, although it wasn't the gym that sculpted her body. It was yoga, and loads of discipline. She'd never seen Jenna's hair down in the three years they'd been working together. Not even when they caught up outside of work.

"Got your tip jar ready?" Chelsea gave the bun a playful tap, half expecting to hear a wooden sound.

The tiny dynamo's hand snapped up, quick to straighten things out where they belonged. A total waste of time. There was no way anything was getting through the solid crust of hairspray fortifying that up-do. Still, Chelsea couldn't help wondering if anything was hidden under there, and she loved teasing Jenna about it.

"Okay, ladies and gentlemen, stop wasting time. What're we in for, Dane?" Jenna barked, getting down to business, her tilted eyes zoning in on the restaurant's host.

"We're fully booked tonight. We've got an eight-top in your section." Dane cocked a brow in Chelsea's direction. "Business meeting. It's Mr. Clermont, and his party. He asked to be served by you."

The hair rose on the back of Chelsea's neck, as unease and excitement warred for the top emotional spot. Mr. Clermont was a frequent customer, and she'd worked hard to build a rapport with him, knowing that it would secure her a regular source of good tips. But the man had grabby hands. So far, he'd only brushed her arm, or her knee, 'accidentally.' But when the alcohol started flowing, he got this look in his eye, like he was mentally stripping her naked and throwing her on the table.

Chelsea propped her hands on her hips, ready for battle. "Okay, anything else I need to know before I study the menu?"

"The chicken manicotti is to die for. We've had to eighty-six the fettucine with truffle because of some hold up with the supplier. Oh, and there's a new apprentice chef starting sometime soon. Not sure when."

"Apprentice? Seriously?"

"Yeah. Surprise!"

"Okay. Thanks, Dane. We'd better get our asses moving."

Chelsea darted around, setting up for service, slowly getting her rhythm back with a few more pieces of home clicking into place. As a sophomore, she'd worked with her mama in the little bakery and café in town. Maybe that was why this place had a special place in her heart. It evoked memories of home. A slice of pie, and a cold, sweet tea enjoyed for a fleeting moment.

Damn it.

She shoved a table into place, wondering why the moments she was so desperate to forget are what often replayed in her idle mind. Why did her brain fixate on the men she didn't want, or that didn't want her? Not all men were bad. Dane was a good guy. *Gay.* So was Beau. *Married.* Hank was a phenomenal human being. *Old and, ew, Angel's father.*

She bolted up straight as the realization struck.

Well, shit. I'm lonely.

Years of meaningless liaisons, proving to herself that she didn't need anything more. That she was the one with the power. And now, her heart decided to slap her upside the head and tell her it's all bullshit.

Greyson Stranger, you are a sonofabitch.

Jenna grabbed another table, sliding it beside Chelsea's. "Hey, are you okay?"

Her shoulders sagged. "Yeah, I'm just …" Chelsea searched the glass ceiling for an answer. "Going through some sort of quarter-life crisis, or somethin'." She shrugged and went back to her task. "I've been here for three years. I'm home sick. It's hitting me hard, I guess. Plus, I've moved in with a bunch of horny crazies."

"Sounds like the perfect place for you."

"Hey, watch it." Jenna merely raised a brow, staring Chelsea down. "Yeah, okay. You're right. But I'm changing my ways. I've sworn off men."

Jenna's jaw dropped in exaggerated disbelief before a thoughtful look changed her expression. "Are you swapping sides?"

They grabbed a tray of flatware, setting the tables as they spoke.

"What?" Chelsea's brow creased in confusion, before it hitched up again as Jenna's meaning sank in. "Oh, no. I'm off the dating scene altogether."

Jenna shot an accusing finger in Chelsea's direction. "Right. Who are you? Is the real Chelsea stuck in the trunk of a car somewhere?"

"The real Chelsea is under construction. We're sorry for the inconvenience. Please wear protective clothing while in the vicinity. Thank you for your patience."

"Oh my God. You're serious." Jenna stood with a centerpiece poised in midair, her jaw slack, even if her bun wasn't.

Dane sidled up beside Jenna, slinging his arm around her shoulders. "She's deadly serious. We have a little wager riding on her willpower. She thinks she's getting *the* boots, but I'll be enjoying a day at the spa by the end of this month. Care to join?"

"Nuh uh. I'm staying out of this one. I'm too worried about her mental state to take advantage like that." Jenna stepped forward, dislodging Dane's arm from its perch.

Dane didn't seem offended. He was used to Jenna's aversion to physical contact. "Oh, Jenna. So serious. What's wrong with making the most of an opportunity when you see one?"

"Said the wolf to the lamb. You have no shame."

"Shame is for fools."

"You should have plenty to go around, then."

Chelsea threw up her hands. "Children! No fighting before dinner service. I'll prove you both wrong. End of discussion. Let's get to work."

How could she be lonely when she had friends like these?

She made her way to the server's station, bracing herself for the onslaught. Mr. Grabby Hands would be coming in soon. If things went her way she'd have a nice bit of cash tucked away by the end of the night. She just hoped she could keep Mr. Clermont in check.

Lord, spare me from assholes.

———

Chelsea worked around the room like a pro. Her feet throbbed as she refilled drink orders and changed carafes of water. Being back here was like slipping on her favorite pair of shoes. Molded to perfection, comfortable, familiar, and loved. She liked to think they would be sparkly and red.

The energy in the room buzzed along her skin more than it ever had. She couldn't explain what was different.

Jenna was in sync with her, as usual. Dane was his entertaining self. Maybe it was the fact that her section seemed to have attracted the rabble tonight. She'd done more trips to the bar than she could count, having to cut off two tables from the alcohol supply already, and she had yet to serve dessert. Abbiocco wasn't normally that kind of place, but maybe their customers were on a sports high or something. This *was* Boston. Sports ruled around here.

Clermont's table pumped out the decibels, mostly due to his own flapping gums. Drunk off his ass, the tentacled touch from Clermont's hands paired with his nasal laugh had Chelsea's patience fraying rapidly. She barely managed to keep a firm hold on her server's smile with each slimy caress.

This had better be a massive tip.

"Chelsea. Baaabe. Get me another Patrón? Aaand we'll have a fresh bottle of vino for my colleagues."

Didn't your mama ever teach you some manners? She concentrated on keeping her expression open and friendly, but damn, her eyes wanted to roll as she turned towards the bar.

Pain shot through her butt cheek as his wayward hand grabbed it in a rough hold. The shriek ripped out of her throat before she could stop it. Spinning around, she constructed her best beauty-pageant smile.

"Sugar, I appreciate the compliment, but see this here table?"

He nodded as she waved her hand, his lascivious smirk firmly in place.

"This table is like a vehicle. It's best if you keep your limbs inside the vehicle at all times, to avoid them being ripped clean off by passing traffic. And you'll be needing your limbs to be able to pay me a *huge* tip at the end of the night. Not to mention they'll be your only source of lovin' for the evening. Are you understandin' the road rules, hun?"

His flat expression told her he understood all right, but he wasn't liking what she was putting down. Damn, she was really hoping for that tip. Why were men such obnoxious bastards?

Not all men, she reminded herself.

"He bothering you, Chelsea?" Beau loomed large behind her, staring down at Clermont like he was the sludge that collected in drain pipes.

Chelsea slid her eyes back to Grabby Hands, feeling slightly braver with the reinforcement at her back. "Are we all good, Mr. Clermont?" She waited for his loose-necked nod. "Bless your heart," she aimed the nasty remark at Clermont before patting Beau on the arm. "He's fine, sugar. Thanks for backin' me up. I'll follow you to the bar, I have another order to fill."

————

Another hour later, with only one table left occupied in her section, and a few campers scattered throughout the rest of the room, Chelsea was ready to get some shut eye. The sounds of the clean-up could be heard coming from the kitchen, and their worst elevator music played from the overhead speakers. She'd helped bus tables so they could all get out on time, and now busied herself at the server's station preparing for the next day.

Clermont only tipped fifteen percent, leaving without so much as a thank you. *Egg suckin' dawg.* She'd already divided her tips with the rest of the staff, and was left with enough to feed her coffee addiction for the rest of the week. Just.

Dane drifted into her space, bumping her shoulder with his to get her attention. She didn't bother raising her head.

"What's up, Dane?" She may as well have said, 'leave me alone, for the love of God.' Her patience was thinner than a piece of gauze full of holes. Exhaustion sank to her bones. Too much Alabama sunshine and relaxing at home, and she'd gone soft. Plus, that damn buzz was still in the air, and it was starting to get her goose.

Her shoulder jerked forward as Dane bumped it again, more insistent that she paid attention this time. She threw down the napkin she was working on and turned to glare at him.

He held up his hands in surrender and jerked his chin towards the back corner of the restaurant, flicking his eyes in the same direction. "The new recruit," he whispered, for some damn reason.

Like the newbie sitting in the ba—she turned her head, nearly falling into Dane when she noticed who occupied the table in the corner. She felt his steely gaze across the expanse of the room. Blood pumped to her limbs, prepping her for flight. She wasn't sure in which direction she intended to go.

What were the odds?

How was this happening?

Her thoughts fell from her brain like chalk dust falling from a chalkboard.

"He's been staring at you for the last twenty minutes."

She snapped her eyes back to Dane. "What?"

"Damn shame you've sworn off men. He is one tall package of delicious. He gives Beau a run for his money. I may have to reevaluate my crush ..."

Dane rambled on, but the buzz swarmed her ear drums and rattled the center of her chest. She stood stiff, her inability to move at odds with her body's need to flee. Or, maybe it was that she needed to run over and jump Greyson Stranger's bones.

Emptying her lungs, heat singed her flesh as she began to twitch, her leg jiggling on the spot. *Shit.* She was going to have to work with him. Life had to be joking. *Why did she have to go and make that promise ...? Ugh,* no. That was the old Chelsea talking. She was supposed to be growing up. Her head fell forward and she stared at the sensible black pumps she was wearing. She tried to imagine those Manolo's adorning her feet, but the image glitched like her vision was on the fritz. *Damn buzz.*

"... And then an hour in the steam room before soaking in the hot tub." Dane was already planning his day at the spa.

Cocky sonofabitch.

"Oh, you're hilarious. You can forget about the spa because those boots will be mine."

"I'm pretty sure he'd be yours if you asked him. I can feel the lust from here."

She groaned, and turned back to the server's station. "Shut up. Just, shut up."

Chelsea directed the words at her friend, but it was a plea for the buzzing to stop. It must be her body reacting to the realization that she was in trouble—again.

Shit. Fuck. Shit.

Chapter Six

I Have Arrived

After the final twelve hours behind the wheel, way too much gas station food, and numb ass cheeks messing with his swagger, he'd arrived.

Boston.
The big city.
Looong way from the ranch. Yeehaw.
Grey's chest expanded as he sucked in a dose of freedom, checking out the brownstone he'd be calling home for the next few months, until he could get his own place. Man, his uncle must be rolling in it.

He found the hidden key and jogged up the steps, feeling the prickle of blood returning to his rear end. Opening the door, the smell of wood polish hit him as he took in the kind of opulence fit for a magazine cover. *Holy shit*. He stood blinking for a minute, not wanting to set his dirty, cowboy boots on the shiny floor. Grey half expected the butler to make an appearance.

His instincts led him straight to the kitchen, head rearing back as his hand dropped his bag at the sight. State-of-the-art European appliances. Extra wide, double ovens. Heat lamps. It was an entertainer's dream. He wondered how many kickass parties his uncle had thrown here.

The temptation to put the room to use had his hands itching. This was a long way from the country kitchen he'd grown up in. All his favorite memories involved learning how to cook from his Nonna and his mama in that basic kitchen. Some of his worst memories too. As a young boy, his father had berated him for wanting to spend his time with the women. Being dragged out by the ear to 'go on and do some real work.' His parents fighting over keeping him in his rightful place versus developing his passion and talent.

Reaching into his back pocket he took out his phone and dialed his mother, knowing she'd be waiting for his call.

"Grey?"

"Yeah, Mom, it's me." He smiled at the sound of her voice.

"You made it safely. Thank the Lord."

"Stop. You worry too much."

"You're my son, it's my job to worry about you. How is your uncle?"

"Living the life by the looks of his pad." He smoothed a hand over the stone benchtop. "I haven't seen him yet. He said he'd be working late."

"When do you start?"

"Not for a couple of days. I thought I'd check the place out tomorrow. Get my bearings."

"Well, make sure you get some rest tonight."

"I will." He drummed his fingers on the bench, looking at his reflection in the oven door. The image shadowed, enhancing the unmistakable guilt marring his features. "How's Papà?"

"He's in bed. Early start tomorrow. You know how it is."

"Yeah." He knew how it was.

"Are you okay, Mama? Has he been hassling you about me leaving?"

"I'm fine …"

The pause and the crack in her voice almost undid him. He put his hand on the keys in his back pocket, for a second considering turning around and heading home. But that would make a mockery of all the times his mother had come to his defense.

Anger brewed as he thought about the stubborn old bastard that'd raised him. What pissed him off the most was how much he loved his father despite his overbearing behavior. But trying to appease him was not the answer.

"He's not talking to anyone. Don't worry. He'll get over it soon enough."

"Hm." He hoped that was true, rubbing his fingers over his forehead to erase the tension pounding behind his skull.

"Get some sleep. Call me after your first day at the restaurant."

"Okay, Mama. Love you."

"Love you too, honey."

Leaning both hands on the bench, he faced his reflection head on. Jaw clenched and eyes piercing, his determination flashed like a Times Square billboard. He couldn't wait any longer. Taking the stairs two at a time, he found his bedroom, dumped his bag on the floor, and grabbed the towel that had been left on the bed. *Thank you, Uncle.* After the fastest shower of his life, he jumped back in his pick-up, and set off to check out his new workplace.

Greyson's truck crawled past the front of Abbiocco, stunned at the sight through the windows. The place was beautiful in a rustic, old-world kind of way, without looking dated. He slowed almost to a stop until the car behind him honked.

Sorry, man.

If he had any doubts about chasing his dream, they disintegrated with the spike in his pulse at finally being here.

After parking at the back entrance and banging the side of his fist on the door, he pulled the collar of his jacket up and slipped his hands in his pockets, eager to get inside and out of the cold. Light spilled at his feet as the entrance opened in invitation.

"*Buonasera, Zio,*" Grey greeted his uncle, a little shocked at how his midnight black hair was now the color of steel.

"Greyson. Good to see you made it." Matteo waved him inside, giving each cheek a kiss and enveloping him in a hearty hug.

The heated air from the kitchen seemed to reach out, pulling him into its warm embrace. He gratefully accepted, feeling an instant sense of belonging to this place.

Grey's feet anchored to the floor as he surveyed the scene before him. Gleaming stainless-steel benches, stacks of bowls and pans, and the ranges and ovens, all called to him. He couldn't wait to sink his teeth into the challenge of creating *the perfect balance of textures and flavors to make the mouth sing.* An expression he learned from his Nonna.

The kitchen was in the middle of the dessert service. He watched the Chef de Partie and her patissiers scoop rochets of sorbet, arrange macaroons, and trickle what looked like berry coulis onto an array of plates. Tiramisu, sfogliatelle, and a coffee semifreddo also featured on the line.

The smells shot a message to his stomach, reminding him that he hadn't eaten since lunch. He swallowed the saliva pooling in his mouth, and rubbed a hand on his belly to quiet the growling.

Matteo laughed. "You hungry? We can fix that."

"Thank God. I didn't want to have to face another dose of take-out. Road trips are great and all, but the food sucks."

"Fretta," Matteo barked into the room, pointing to the clock on the wall. He waved his hand at the controlled chaos, turning to Grey. "You've arrived on a particularly crazy night. But, it's good for you to see how busy we can be. You'll learn to cope, or you won't survive. It's the life of a chef. Always pressure against the clock. Always trying to exceed expectations, and innovating to make your mark and keep things fresh. You will see."

He followed Matteo further into the room.

"I'll show you around, and then we will do your paperwork."

It was obvious how Matteo's powerful presence commanded respect in the dip of each employee's head, and the way they did his bidding without question. They trusted his expertise and guidance.

Grey had barely spent any time with the man, but he respected the hell out of Matteo. Over twenty-two years ago, he'd rejected his birthright and Nonno's expectation that his first born would inherit the cattle ranch and continue the family legacy. Matteo ended up in Boston, where he apprenticed under one of the leading chefs of the time. After building up his own reputation, and saving enough to invest in his own restaurant, Abbiocco was born.

Declared an outcast after his unsanctioned exit, Matteo hadn't met Grey until he was ten; after Nonno died, lifting the ban. Sporadic visits from his uncle eventually dried up all together when Matteo and Lucca had a falling out. That was one skeleton that remained locked tight in Grey's father's cupboard. Not even Nonna knew what drove the brothers to blows.

Secret communications between Nonna and her eldest son kept Greyson updated on Matteo's successes, stoking the flame of his own ambitions. And now, here he was. He knew the repercussions of his actions, because it appeared that history was set on repeat. The two black sheep had found each other again.

They entered the surprisingly small office where bare brick walls made it feel more like a cave than a work space. A desk lamp provided the only light source, adding to the cozy feel. Other than the desk that took up the center of the room, the only other furniture was a filing cabinet, bookcases in each corner behind the desk, and a bench seat to the side of the doorway.

Greyson sat, wedging his knees under the lip of the desktop. He eyed the bookcase, recognizing some family photos of him with his brother and sisters as children, and a couple of Mama and Nonna in the kitchen, balanced precariously in front of the stacked cook books. None of his father or grandfather. The Agrioli men were masters at holding a grudge.

Matteo's chair squeaked as he wheeled around to reach for the policy and procedure manuals, dumping them in front of Greyson.

"Some light reading before you start." Matteo raised a single brow. "Now, once you sign, I'll have you for two years. I don't tolerate quitters. If you're not prepared to bleed, burn, sweat, and blister for this, then don't sign. The program includes over four hundred hours of related instruction. I expect two hundred percent effort and top marks. When you're here, I'm not your uncle. I am Chef. Do you understand?"

"Yes, Chef."

"*Bene.*"

Matteo pushed a stack of papers across the desk and held out a pen with a burning severity in his gray eyes that said, '*don't fuck this up.*'

I don't intend to.

He passed the papers and pen back, rubbing his sweaty palms on his jeans.

"Is Lucca still against you being here?" Matteo's gruff voice sounded suddenly tired.

"Yeah."

"*Hmph.*"

They sat watching each other with a hundred unanswered questions, refusing to make a sound. He could see it on Matteo's face, and his head was clogged with them.

What happened between you and my father all those years ago?

Why are you giving me this chance?

He didn't give voice to either, choosing to continue sizing up the man he'd idolized for years.

"Grab a plate, go on out the front, and take a seat. Watch how things work front of house. I'll meet you out there."

Grey took his food, dodged his way around the busy staff in the kitchen, and scanned the restaurant for an empty table. There were plenty this time of night. He picked one in the back corner. *Perfect.* He'd get a full view of the room, and not have to watch his back. Not that there were any rogue animals to worry about here. Just rogue humans with too much alcohol in their veins.

The place looked even more amazing up close. It had a vibe going on that had everything to do with satisfied customers and staff, and little to do with the decor. Greyson wolfed down the delicious cuisine before he leaned his arms on the table and surveyed the room again. His whole body tensed when he caught a flash of platinum blonde.

No. It couldn't be.

Shaking his head, he sat back and relaxed. *Of course, it wasn't her.*

The view of the blonde's rear was a sight to behold in that black pencil skirt, and the fitted white shirt showed off a trim waistline that would fit in his hands nicely. He willed her to turn around so he could see if the front was just as enticing.

She whirled around to attend to a table, and his heart stuttered to a stop. Rebelling against his body as it roared to life with a thousand possibilities.

Holy shit! It is her.

Chelsea.

Boston, you're full of surprises.

He didn't know if she was a welcome complication or a disaster waiting to happen, but he tightened all his muscles to stop himself from springing out of the seat. He didn't want to scare her off. He'd sensed she'd be a hard one to pin down when they met. And he'd be damned if he didn't enjoy the chase.

This time there'd be no walking away. For either of them.

Fate was a genius.

Chapter Seven

I'm Taking You Home

Chelsea tried to resist peeking over her shoulder, only failing a few times as she worked with Jenna, tidying up. Anything to ignore the ten-ton weight of Greyson's gaze on her back. He hadn't bothered to approach her, and she refused to go there again after the way he had rejected her last time. Whatever scared him away back in Alabama probably still bothered him now. Every second that passed without him coming to speak to her was a hatchet chopping away at her confidence. The ground under her feet had wavered between shaky and solid since meeting him. But, it was her own damn fault. She was way too fond of playing with fire.

Her head turned again, involuntarily tracking her boss as he walked over to Greyson's table and took a seat. They spoke for a little while, though she couldn't hear them, before turning their eyes on her. She stiffened, but nodded with a smile, like his attention didn't bring out goose pimples on her skin and send her heart thumping behind her breast.

"What's with you and the new guy?" Jenna broke through the spell Chelsea was under.

"Hm? What? Nothing," she squeaked, before clearing her throat.

"Oh, yeah. There's something. You guys keep doing those longing looks across the room. It's sickening. You do realize attraction is largely a response to a cocktail of hormones and brain chemicals, and the body sizing up an appropriate person to mate with. It's all about biology. Genes! Not sexy at all. If you want to be a slave to your body, that's your business, but I'm staying the hell away from the whole sad scenario. The planet simply cannot sustain the current rate of population growth—"

"Jenna, Chelsea …" Thankfully, Matteo broke into Jenna's rant before Chelsea worked up a migraine. "I'd like you to meet Greyson. He's my new apprentice. I hope you'll make him feel welcome, you'll be seeing a lot of him."

Not nearly as much as she'd liked to.

Before her vow, that was.

Grey stretched out a hand towards Jenna. "Pleasure to meet you."

Jenna took the offering, releasing a shy giggle while squirming uncomfortably. Chelsea levelled a disbelieving stare at the pocket rocket as she shrugged and scurried away, unable to comprehend how easily this stranger had crumbled Jenna's ironclad pragmatism. And thinking there wasn't a chance in hell of resisting him, if Jenna fell for his charm so easily.

Chelsea's eyes snapped back to Greyson when she felt the touch of his hand on hers, his fingers grazing the pulse at her wrist as he raised her arm. She twisted in his grip, and pulled their arms down so they were now engaged in a friendly handshake, instead of having his lips anywhere near her skin. Not again.

Feeling dang proud of herself, she lifted her chin, and gave him a genuine smile.

"Welcome to the team. I'll do my job, you do yours. Try not to suck. And, good luck."

She pumped their hands a few times, escaping when she saw her campers finally leaving. There, on the table, were a couple of Benjamin Franklins. She clutched them to her chest, a huge smile breaking free, until she spun around and saw that Greyson wasn't far behind, watching in amusement.

"Whoa, back away, buddy." She warned, stuffing the money into her pocket.

"That's not what you said in Alabama."

"Well, that was a mistake, and a different Chelsea altogether. In Boston, I'm all business."

"Is that right?"

"Sure is, sugar."

"Hm ..." His eyes scanned her face, thoughtfully, before dropping to watch her hands tugging nervously on her apron's ties. "Ya know, I couldn't believe my eyes when I walked in here tonight."

"Oh? Never seen a Michelin-starred restaurant before?" She crossed her arms and took a step backwards.

"As a matter of fact, no. But that's not what surprised me."

He took a step closer, and she could see the pulse jumping in his neck, and smell his scent; freshly showered, if she had to guess, but she'd rather not think about it at all.

"Seeing the intriguing woman I left behind, and thought I'd never see again. That's what surprised me." Pinning her under his gray stare, his expression was unreadable, but for the intent sparkle in his eyes.

Her body instantly responded to his call, but her mind screamed, *kiss my go to hell.*

"The woman you left behind? You make it sound like I was yours to leave. If there's one thing I'll never be, it's yours, or any man's. Excuse me."

Pushing past him, she headed to the office in the rear of the kitchen to retrieve her pocketbook. She knocked on the open door before entering, and nodded at Matteo who was sitting at his desk, bifocals perched on the end of his nose. Matteo looked up from his computer screen to offer a smile. He rocked a severe case of hat-hair from wearing his toque blanche all night. His chef's jacket barely showed a stain. The man was so meticulous.

Taking a hundred out of her pocket, she tossed it on his desk. "Would you mind splitting that between everyone? It's my last tip for the night."

He nodded, tucking the note in a cash box.

"You okay if I scoot home now?" Looping the strap of her pocketbook over her shoulder, she searched for her phone while waiting for his answer.

"It's too late to catch the T. Do you want a ride home?"

She looked at the screen on her phone. Quarter past midnight. *Damn.* She thought about the hundred still warming her pocket, but squirmed at the thought of wasting it on a taxi fare. She had a trip home for Christmas to pay for, and she wanted to fatten the small nest egg earmarked for big things after graduation.

"How much longer do you plan on stayin'?" she asked, already imagining him with his keys in hand.

He grimaced, and Chelsea's shoulders dropped before he even spoke. "I have another hour's worth of work to sort out. Sorry."

"I'll take you."

Her body stiffened, hands clenching on the strap of her bag, and eyelids falling shut in denial of the deep voice coming from the doorway.

Matteo spoke up when she didn't respond. "Thank you, Greyson. That's very nice of you. Are you okay with that, Chelsea?"

Er, no. I'm not okay with being stuck in a confined space with Mr. Sex On a Stick.

"Well, actually—"

Dane popped his head in to say goodnight. "I'm taking the girls home. Pete already left. Are you good for a ride, Chels?"

"Yeah, I'm taking her," Grey confirmed as Chelsea huffed and propped her hands on her hips. He took the opportunity to grasp her elbow and steer her towards the door.

"Like hell—" she protested, but Dane cut her off.

"Making new friends. That's our Chelsea. You two are adorable together."

"Traitor," she hissed over her shoulder, her feet stumbling to keep up with Greyson's lengthy stride. Dane's cackle was the last thing she heard before the door shut behind them.

Grey didn't slow down until they reached his truck. He unlocked the door, and had her in the passenger seat before she could get her wits together enough to plan an escape. The door slammed loudly in her face and she watched, slack-jawed, as he rounded the hood and made himself comfortable behind the wheel.

"What do ya think you're doin'?"

"Taking you home. Where are we headed?" Revving the engine, he tapped his thumbs on the steering wheel and watched her, waiting for directions.

"I don't even know you." She wondered if Jenna's comment about being stuck in a trunk somewhere would come to fruition, her eyes were wide with fear... and maybe a little excitement. "You could be a serial killer."

The corners of Grey's mouth tipped up. "Now you're worried about me being a serial killer. I've been working towards this opportunity for years. I'm not going to stuff up my chances by becoming a suspect in the murder of a co-worker. Plus, I've known Matteo for a long time. Do you think he would've let me drive you home if he didn't trust me?"

She slumped back in her seat. "*Hmph*. Do you even know your way around Boston?"

"Nope. I've been here for approximately two and a half hours," he said, pointing to the time on the truck's stereo.

She twisted in her seat, reaching for the door handle, but Grey leaned his big body across her lap, pulling it shut.

"Uh, uh, uh. Seat belt on."

She sucked in a breath as he pulled on the belt and buckled it, brushing her hip in the process.

He grinned, putting the truck in gear and reversed out of the lot, looking both ways in contemplation of which direction to choose. "Hm. Eenie, meanie ... left."

"Wrong." The word came out in a rush with the air that had been trapped in her lungs.

He pulled the wheel to the right and flicked on the radio. Bon Jovi blasted into the space, fraying her already stretched nerves. Grey turned it down and went back to tapping his thumbs. Chelsea tucked her hands under her thighs. It was safer that way. She faced the windshield, but kept giving him the side eye, watching his hands and forearms flex as he drove. His presence was impossible to ignore as it filled the cab, engulfing all her senses. His smell, the sound of his thumbs keeping the beat, his quiet humming, and the heat radiating from his body—all of it was amplified, bringing her body to life. She was barely aware of where they were, enough to give directions, remaining focused on him until they reached the house.

"This is it?"

"This is it," she confirmed, sizing up the house, wondering what he thought of it.

The porch light illuminated the blue front door, and she noticed a glow around the edges of the blind in the living room window. Flaky paint on the siding of the New England style home was a little embarrassing, but hey, it was a student share house—a roof over her head—and she was absolutely thankful for that.

"So, now I know where you work *and* where you live. I'd say we're getting pretty personal, don't ya think?"

Chelsea turned on him, spearing him with the full force of her disapproval. She wanted to slap that shit-eating grin right off his pretty face. Pretty wasn't the right word. He was ruggedly handsome. Those gray eyes were killer under heavy brows, and against the backdrop of tanned skin and long dark hair. He wore a leather jacket over a snug tee. She turned her face away before she let her eyes drift down to his jean clad thighs.

Reaching for the handle, she managed to exit the car unhindered this time, but the slam of his car door echoed hers. Snapping her gaze across the hood, she shook her head in disbelief.

"Oh, no. No, no, no. I appreciate the ride home, but you are not walking me to the door. Get back in the truck, mister."

Grey's grin grew wider. *Smart ass.*

She took a few steps, Grey copying her movement from the other side of the truck.

Her jaw clenched, eyes narrowing. "You can't be serious. What? Are we in middle school now?"

"You're used to getting your way, aren't ya? I'm just doing my gentlemanly duty and making sure you get inside all safe and sound. No offense, but this doesn't look like the best part of town." He waved a hand at the street before continuing up the steps to wait by the door.

Chelsea waited for a minute with hands clenched and thighs pressed together, feeling more pissed off and turned on than she had in … ever. *Goddamn smart ass.*

Just as she started to follow, the front door flew open. Dakota stood in her sleep shorts and tank, looking between them in confusion.

"I was wondering if you'd lost your key, but now I see you've found someone instead." Turning to Greyson, she held out her hand. "Hi, there. I'm Dakota."

"Greyson. Pleased to meet you." He shook her hand, nodding briefly before fixing his gaze back on Chelsea.

Under the weight of a frown, she watched Dakota flash her eyes and mouth a 'wow' while fanning her face. Chelsea had to bite her lips to keep from growling.

"Who's at the door?" Hannah crowded in behind Dakota, introducing herself to Grey. Within seconds, they'd all disappeared inside, leaving Chelsea gob smacked.

Oh, great. Now it's a party.

After a minute, she trudged in after them, just wanting to fall face first into bed, and not at all liking the fact that Greyson Stranger had invaded her personal life so easily, after her vow to go cold turkey on men. What was his game, anyways?

Entering from the hallway afforded her a view of Greyson's back as he stood in the kitchen. With his hands slung in his back pockets, his shoulders looked even wider. The pose seemed relaxed, but there was something in his stance; an underlying tension that said he was uneasy. Chelsea stretched up onto her toes to see who he was talking to. Her brow shot up at the look on Ryan's face as he stood, arms crossed, and pissed off in front of the fridge.

What the fuck?

The fatigue wiped from behind her eyes as annoyance took its place. "What's goin' on here?" She stormed past Grey and got all up in Ryan's face, not asking why she'd targeted Ryan rather than the intruder.

"Nothing, sweetheart, just questioning your new friend's intentions. It's a little inappropriate to be having visitors so late at night, isn't it?"

In a haze of red, Ryan's face started to morph into a punching bag. This guy knew all the ways to get her riled up and ready to pitch a fit. Chelsea's mouth flattened as her eyes narrowed on him. The frown dropped from his face, taking a bit of color with it, and his throat bobbed in a gulp. Somewhere in the background she heard a faint, "oh, oh," and a snicker in feminine tones.

Giving him a pointed stare, she prepared to serve him a dose of whupass. "Last time I checked, I was a grown ass woman who contributes an equal share of the rent here. So, if I want to have a visitor at one o'clock in the goddamn morning, I'll have a visitor. And as long as I don't disturb anybody's beauty sleep, there's not a goddamn thing you, or anyone else can say about it." Spearing her finger at Ryan and then Grey, she continued, "I've had a double dose of assholes tonight, and I am done. I'm goin' to bed." In a role reversal, she grabbed Grey by the elbow and dragged him to the door. "Thank you for the ride home. That was real nice of ya, but you need to leave."

"Nice to meet you!" the girls called at their backs.

"You too. I'll be seein' y'all," Greyson returned with a grin.

Grrr. "You have some nerve," she barked.

"Sweetheart, you have no idea."

He spun as they reached the door, and grabbed the frame before she could push him further. Reaching out, he grasped her upper arms, holding her in place with his gray eyes as much as his grip.

"What're you doin'?"

"Picking up where we left off."

She sucked in a breath at the promise she saw in his stare, utterly transfixed and speechless for once in her life.

His hands loosened and coursed their way up to her shoulders, neck, and face. She felt their slow caress, fireworks sparking under her skin and into her blood stream. Chelsea's heart thundered, a mixture of fear and thrill, in anticipation of what he might do next.

She didn't want him to kiss her.

She wanted it so badly she feared she might pass out if he didn't put his lips on hers right this second.

Her lids fell as his face moved closer to hers. She felt the brush of his warm breath before the softness of his lips touched her cheek, close to the corner of her mouth.

Too close to be friendly.

Close enough to be tantalizing.

Too far to be satisfying.

A growl rumbled from her throat, and then his hands fell away, taking their warmth with them. Her eyelids fluttered open in time to see him get in his truck. It was too dark to see inside, but she knew he watched her as the engine revved to life. With her hand raised to her cheek, she watched him drive away, nerves collecting in a lump at her throat.

It was the strangest thing.

The loneliness …

That gaping hole in her future …

He'd plugged it for the brief time they'd spent together. Like it was shaped to fit him.

She wanted to deny it, but there it was.

Totally fucking insane.

She'd never been more scared.

Chapter Eight

Helpful Advice

Flinging an arm over her eyes, Chelsea whimpered. She'd just checked the time on her phone. Four in the frickin' morning. Number of hours of sleep? Nil. Zilch. Zip. Nada.

Fuck!

She had kicked her covers to the floor over an hour ago, but the sweat on her skin refused to evaporate. That damn buzzing continued to zip beneath her skin. It was as if Greyson was still with her, watching her in that intense way of his. He was certainly in her thoughts, stoking her lust even as she denied it momentum.

Her fingers itched to walk their way down her body to satisfy the cravings he'd ignited. Hands locked in the sheets, she held back the urge. The new Chelsea didn't give in to her impulses. She had control. Barely, but she had control. The old Chelsea would've invited him in without protest, and promptly kicked him out when she was finished with him.

There was nothing wrong with a woman who had a healthy libido. If it was good for the goose, why the hell couldn't the gander play too? Society's double standards sucked. But, she must admit that there was no excuse for treating another person like a disposable product. She'd never considered that a guy might want something other than a no strings relationship. Now, she wondered if she'd hurt some hearts along the way. Shame delivered a lashing, as frustration doubled the blow. She'd take the punishment for as long as it took to make things right.

The sweat began to cool, leaving goosebumps in its wake. She kicked her legs off the side of the bed, grabbing a hoody before she headed to the bathroom. A splash of cold water did nothing to clear her head or fix the frightful reflection in the mirror. She snapped up a tissue to clean the leftover black smudges of mascara under her eyes, but only managed to smear them into wide gray bruises. Gorgeous. Why the hell did she care? Who was she going to see at four in the morning?

Figuring some early morning TV might bore her enough to send her back to sleep, or at the least distract her, she flopped on the sofa and started flicking through the channels. She wasn't sure how long she'd been there when Ryan decided to join her.

"Hey. Whatcha watching?"

She shrugged. "Infomercials."

"My favorite."

"Whatever turns you on." She gave him the clicker and folded her legs up, wrapping her arms around them.

"Hey, sorry about last night. I'm just looking out for you."

"I can look out for myself, Ryan." She almost bared her teeth.

"Yeah, okay." He didn't sound convinced.

Lord, save her from men.

"So, that guy."

Here we go. "Greyson," she said slowly.

"Yeah. That guy. How do you know him?"

"He's the new apprentice at work." She turned towards him, dropping one foot to the floor and tucking the other under her knee. "Why do you even care?"

"I told you. I'm looking out for you. I'm the man of the house. It's my duty."

Seriously? "Is that right?" she drawled, arching a blonde brow. "Sugar, I grew up without a male in the house, and I've done just fine. My mama taught me how to handle myself, and what she couldn't teach me, I learned from dealing with assholes along the way. So, please spare me your misplaced macho bullshit."

He crossed his arms over his chest. eyebrows sinking down low. "Why are you so goddamn defensive?"

"Why are you being so high handed and possessive?"

"I'm not being possessive, I'm being protective."

She barked a humorless laugh.

He dropped his arms and expelled a weighted breath. "Jesus … Look, can we just start over? Again?"

"Only if you can back off."

"I'll do my best."

His mouth tipped up in a smile that made him seem innocent. She knew the truth.

"Most women like to be cared for."

"I think you'll find that I'm not like most women. Never heap all women in one basket, sugar. That's your first mistake."

"Don't you agree there are certain patterns of behavior that each gender conforms to?"

"Have you been reading self-help books or somethin'?" She clasped her hands together in her lap. "Sometimes a woman wants to fix what's wrong, or go into her cave and switch off. We don't always have to talk about our problems for the sole purpose of gaining empathy or clarity. So, don't go assuming you know women."

"Okay. Point taken." He twisted to face her, maneuvering his body to mirror Chelsea. "What about Greyson? He seemed pretty possessive."

She shivered at the thought of Grey feeling possessive over her, not sure if she liked the thought of it. "I barely know him, so he has no right to feel that way. And neither do you."

"He may not have the right, but he feels it. Believe me."

She believed him all right. The way Grey had dragged her out of Abbiocco. The kiss he'd laid on her that promised all sorts of things she wasn't ready for. Again, she wrapped her legs in a hug in an effort to rid her skin of goosebumps.

"Hey, I didn't mean to upset you. If you want him gone, just give me the word."

She wanted to laugh at his bravado, but she wasn't that mean. There was no way Ryan could take Grey. There had to be a thirty-pound disadvantage in Ryan's corner.

"What word would that be?"

"Hero," he deadpanned.

She collapsed back on the arm of the sofa clutching her belly in a fit of giggles. "Oh. Ryan. That was priceless. I'll be sure to holler that at the top of my lungs if I ever need a knight wearing a shiny metal suit."

He put his hands on his chest. "I could get a suit of armor if that's what you want."

"I just want to live in a peaceful, harmonious house."

He shook his head, pointing a finger at her. "No, you don't. You love a good verbal slinging match."

"Well now, see? We're startin' to understand each other." She smiled.

"Yes, we are." He jerked to a stand. "Do you want some pancakes?"

"Can you cook? I thought that was women's work. You know, with you being the man of the house and all."

"I know how to cook eggs, pancakes and ramen noodles." He counted each item off the list on his fingers. "The three basic food groups a student needs for survival. My mom made sure I could do those, at least."

"What about mac and cheese?"

"Correction. Four. Four major food groups." He held up another finger.

"And no fruit or vegetables?"

"I can throw on some sliced banana if you want."

"Sold." She grinned, smacking a fist into her other palm.

"That would imply that you're paying me. What currency are you offering?" He made a gimme gesture with his hand.

"Oh, Jesus, Ryan. You need to cut that shit out. I'm not interested in becoming a member of your harem." She rolled her eyes behind his back as she followed him into the kitchen. "Speaking of, what's the deal with you and Dakota?"

"What do you mean?" he called from inside the pantry.

"Oh, come on. Your hand on her leg ... sitting close on the sofa .... Have you slept with her?"

He backed out, holding the flour, and faced her wearing a sly grin. "Are you jealous?"

Oh, my God. Her mouth pulled tight in annoyance. "Not in this lifetime, but I'll give you points for persistence."

"Relax, I'm just kidding around."

Going over to the sink, she squirted some soap on her hands and scrubbed them clean. "Just cook the damn pancakes. I'll cut the bananas."

"Yes, ma'am." He clicked his heels together and cracked an egg into the bowl.

"Please tell me you have maple syrup, and it's free of charge and innuendo."

"All free, so long as you get it yourself."

"Now, that I can do."

———

It didn't take long before the wafting smell of breakfast woke the other sleeping beauties and called them downstairs. At five in the morning. She almost laughed when they came stumbling in.

Chelsea watched from across the table as Dee sat beside Ryan, bumping her elbow into his, with a smile that fell short of flirty and ventured into dopey territory. Ryan seemed to buy it. They looked cozy. She wasn't as concerned for Dakota after talking with him. He wasn't a heartless bastard. Maybe he and Dee were after the same thing. Just a short fling to scratch an itch. There was nothing wrong with that if both parties were up front about it.

Chelsea speared another piece of banana, cutting off the pancake beneath and smearing the lot in a puddle of syrup, savoring the taste on her tongue with a hum.

"Chelsea's making porn noises." Hannah cocked a brow as she popped another bite of her own.

"I am not. I said hmm. That's not moaning."

"Sounded like a moan to me," Dakota sucked some syrup off her fingers and bared her teeth in a cheeky grin.

"At least I'm not sucking my fingers, Dakota Does Dallas."

"Never been to Dallas."

"I have," Hannah supplied, smiling a secret smile.

"Are we talking the actual Dallas, or is there a suggestion behind that comment?" Chelsea leaned back, holding up a hand. "You know what? Never mind."

Ryan wisely changed the subject. "So, Head of the Charles is on this weekend. I'm going to need a cheer squad."

"You row?"

"Yep, I'm an oarsman. How else do you think I maintain this oar-some bod?" He rubbed his hands down his chest and abs, striking some sort of pose that looked more like it belonged in a doctor's office than on the cover of a fitness mag.

"Oh, no. Don't bring out the Dad jokes. Save them for another decade down the track."

"Are you coming?"

"Yeah, but I'll have to bail early because I've got the supper shift."

"Okay." He dropped his fork on the plate and pushed it away. "It's Hannah's birthday next Wednesday. What are we doing to celebrate?"

Chelsea's head swiveled back to Hannah as she finished up her pancakes. "It's your birthday? Damn, I have to work." Clearing her and Ryan's plates, she washed the sticky syrup off her fingers.

"Aw. That's too bad. I was thinking we could take Hannah out for a bite and maybe go to a bar afterwards. What do you think, Ryan?"

"Babe, I'm always up for the bar." He laid a wink on Dee, coloring up her cheeks.

"You could come into Abbiocco before you go out drinkin'. I'll make sure you get a table in my section."

"Even better." Ryan turned to Hannah. "What do you say?"

"I say that'd be great." Hannah pushed her chair back, picking up her plate. "And now I'm going back to bed. It's too goddamn early."

"I agree." Dee rose, pulling on Ryan's arm. "You coming?"

"Are you offering?"

Chelsea grimaced. The man could not help himself. The problem was, his attention wasn't selective. She hadn't been that bad. Flirting with more than one guy at a time was just plain mean.

"Get outta here. I'll clean up."

"Thanks, babe," Ryan said, following Dee out.

"Not your babe!" Chelsea shook her head, wondering if he'd ever stop.

————

Rugged up in jeans, a sweater, and a jacket, Chelsea huddled in a camping chair on the grassy Riverbend Park near the Weeks Footbridge. The cuppolas perched atop the different houses in Harvard stood out across the skyline with their striking white structures, and shiny, colored domes. Chilly winds whipped along the Charles River where boats sliced through the water as they raced to the finish.

"Would you like to borrow my scarf?"

"Yes, please." She couldn't get the words out fast enough as Dee handed over the knitted garment.

"Southern girl. Not built for this climate, are you?" Dee turned to get some sun.

"Nope. I should've known it'd be colder by the water. How are the rowers just wearing tank tops? I don't care if they're exercising, it is fucking freezing."

"Do some jumping jacks or something. Ryan's race should be up next."

"Is he the cock?"

"It's called the Coxswain, and no he's not." Dee's face tightened, unamused.

"Jeez, Dee, I know. Relax, I'm joking. Can we go and get a warm drink, after?"

"Yeah, I guess so." She uncrossed her legs and re-crossed them with the opposite leg on top, leaning forward. "What is your problem with Ryan?"

Chelsea covered her nose with the scarf and blew out a heated breath, trying to defrost her face as she queued the confession on her tongue. "He's me."

"Huh?"

"He's the worst parts of me put on display. He shoves my bad behavior in my face, showing me how immature I've been, and it's … uncomfortable." She dropped the scarf back in place under her chin. "And I don't like how he flirts with both of us at the same time. For the record, I've never done that."

"He might flirt with other women, but he's in my bed at the end of the day."

"So, you are sleeping together."

"Yeah. He told me he loves me, so be nice. Please?"

Oh, honey. This wasn't going to end well. "I'll do my best."

Cheers roared from the spectators on the river banks and bridge as another group of boats sped past. The Head of the Charles was *the* annual event for rowing. Teams from across the globe came here to test their stuff against the best of the best. Electric excitement crackled along the course, lifting Boston to the world stage for the weekend.

The team from Boston University glided past in their maroon and white, and Chelsea and Dee jumped out of their seats, yelling and clapping. She could only just make out Ryan's determined face, second from the back as he heaved his blade through the water. So, he could commit to something and work hard. He deserved a little more credit than she'd been giving him. Watching his boat disappear around the bend, she vowed to cut him some slack.

She wouldn't get to see this next year. Her stomach dipped as she tugged on the scarf, securing it against the icy breeze. She also wouldn't be freezing her ass off. That was a plus.

Cranking her head towards Dee, she almost heard ice crack as she moved her frozen muscles. "What did Hannah say she was doing, again?"

"Early birthday lunch with her family."

In a warm house. "Lucky bitch."

"Have you found out anything about the new guy?" Dee's eyes fixed on the river as she tapped her fingers on the arm of her chair.

"Greyson?" Chelsea said his name like he hadn't been in her thoughts constantly since his surprise appearance at Abbiocco.

Shifting her gaze to Chelsea, Dee scoffed. "Yes. Greyson. Are you being coy or obtuse?"

Yeah, Dakota wasn't buying the innocent act.

Was it that obvious?

"His folks run a cattle ranch in Mississippi. He was a cowboy."

"A cowboy? Lucky bitch." Dee quirked an eyebrow and grinned. "What's he doing up here in the city?"

"His grandma taught him to cook. He'd rather be in a kitchen than a barn. End of story."

"Oh, come on. There's more to him than that."

"I'm sure there is, but it's not a good idea for me to get to know him. I've sworn off men, and he is a temptation I don't need."

"You? You have sworn off men?"

"I made a deal with myself to change my ways. And Dane bet me a pair of Blahniks that I wouldn't last until the end of the year."

"Who's Dane?"

"We work together at the restaurant. He's the host."

"Right. I don't see you wearing those shoes any time soon. Not with Greyson under your nose. He is too irresistible."

"Aren't you lusting after Ryan?"

"Of course."

Her gaze shifted to the water again as those fingers continued making silent music.

Chelsea snapped her head around and bunched her shoulders on hearing a loud crunch accompanied by shouting and gasps from the crowd. They watched, jaws slack in disbelief, as two boats collided, splashing and rocking while they righted themselves and got back in the race.

Her hand flew to her chest where her heart slammed against her ribcage. "Holy shit. Did MIT just get taken out by … who's the yellow team?"

"Peking University. And I think they're the ones who are worse off." Dee folded up her chair, ready to go.

She walked to the water's edge to watch the boat struggle its way towards Eliot Bridge. "Yeah, they're taking in water. Damn. Sucks for them." They weren't giving up. Her lips tilted up. That was impressive.

Chelsea pulled her attention back to packing up, before looking up at the bridge, distracted by a flash of white. "Is that …" Squinting her eyes, she raised a hand to block the sun. "… a bride and groom on the bridge? They must be hard core rowing fanatics."

Hm. Weddings. Her brain fired with all sorts of possibilities. A grand scheme in the making. She had to think of all the benefits and the potential liabilities. Her plan would have to be solid before she shared it. This was something they had to take advantage of before the opportunity was lost. She bounced on her toes, eager to get hold of a pen and paper. Even a napkin would do.

"Let's go get that drink."

———

Sitting on the bench in Matteo's office, Chelsea watched, amused by his attempts to ignore her. He was a stubborn man. She was worse. She'd sit there all damn day if she had to.

"Did you know the space next door is up for lease?"

Air whistled out of his nose in a drawn-out breath. "I had noticed that, yes."

"Are you looking into it?"

"Why would I need to do that?" Cursing, he hammered his finger on the backspace key.

"Can't you see it?"

He tossed her an impatient look. "What am I supposed to be seeing, Chelsea?"

"It has an identical glass ceiling, doesn't it?"

"*Sì.*"

"You could knock out part of the dividing wall to give staff access to your brand-new function center. Think about it. Weddings, bar and bat mitzvahs, engagement parties, all under the stars with catering by the famous Matteo Agrioli from Abbiocco. Do you know how much the wedding industry is worth? We could team up with hotels to do a package deal, and attract people from all around, with your reputation as the juicy carrot."

Matteo's hands stilled on the keyboard, his attention now firmly on Chelsea.

"You're not saying anything. Why are you not saying anything?" She bit her lip and clasped her hands.

"I'm thinking of the possibilities, good and bad."

"Okay. That's encouraging."

"I'll need market research. Cost projections. A business plan."

"Uh huh." She nodded, her blonde waves bouncing eagerly. "I've already started putting it all together."

"Have you, now?" He tapped his fingers on the desk and pushed his glasses up his nose. "The construction noise is going to mess with my lunch service."

"Yes, but the dinner service will be mostly unaffected. We can schedule the noisy, messy stuff during Mondays, when we're closed. We'll talk to the contractors about minimizing the impact. You might lose some days, but I can't imagine it being more than that with most of the work happening next door. It will be a few private rooms, separate from the restaurant except for the staff access between. What do you think?"

Taking his glasses off, he fixed his unfathomable metallic gaze on her. She couldn't fight the urge to squirm as he made her wait for his answer.

After a minute, he spoke. "We're going to need a bigger kitchen."

She laughed and slapped her hands together. "Yes, we are." Throwing the real estate agent's card on his desk, she sprang up from the seat. "Give them a call and make an appointment for a look see."

Propping his glasses back on, he affixed his eyes back on his monitor. "Get me those projections, asap."

"Done."

Only just beginning.

As soon as she had the thought, she realized she wouldn't be sticking around to see it through. But the current continued to swirl in her blood, leading her to this place. She understood that now. Boston was enticing her to stay. Her two homes were putting up their dukes in a confusing battle she didn't want to think about. Alabama would win in the end.

Wouldn't it?

Chapter Nine

Celebrations

Chelsea walked through the bustling bodies in the kitchen, the symphony of sizzling, bubbling, and mixing, joined the chatter of the staff. Several cooks and chefs manned the lines, prepping for the night ahead. Things were relatively calm and organized. The first orders of the night wouldn't start coming through for another hour or so. As always, the mouth-watering smell of food stirred her stomach and her taste buds. Stealthily, she nabbed a sliver of prosciutto to calm the cravings.

On her way through, she spotted Greyson and Albert, the Sous Chef, with their heads together. The sight of her sexy stranger sent hunger pangs of a different variety coursing through her body. She placed a hand over her heart, telling it to settle down, and her feet slowed to a halt, deliberately disobeying her order to keep going.

"Tuck your fingertips under, so the side of the knife rubs against your knuckles."

Albert pointed his finger dangerously close to the chop zone making Grey pause what he was doing. She watched his throat as he swallowed, and his face screw up in adorable frustration. The difference between cooking at home and cooking in a professional kitchen was a gaping canyon that he seemed determined to conquer. She didn't know how they did it. Cooking was like some foreign language to her. A skill necessary for survival, but it eluded her nonetheless.

That was another thing she had in common with Ryan. Her mouth flattened. She was beginning to realize she was more like him than she'd like to admit. It wasn't just their penchant for the chase.

"Yes, like that. See how much faster you can move and with less amputations? Win win." Albert flicked a dish towel over his shoulder, nodding in approval.

The sous chef had earned his spare tire after twenty years in the business. He looked damn proud of it too, rubbing it like a pregnant woman as he tottered off toward the cold storage, leaving Grey to it.

She should keep walking.

Remember the Blahniks. Remember the Blahniks.

"Hi. How are ya doin'?" She reckoned it didn't hurt to be polite.

Grey didn't flinch. His hands kept their rhythm, with his concentration firmly cemented to his task. Probably a good thing or there would be an amputation after all. But she was a little miffed that he didn't even look at her.

He was all kinds of hot and cold. One minute she was drowning in his intensity, and the next, she was watching him walk away. She could still hear the bell from the diner door every time she thought of that moment. It pricked at her ego, deflating it to a pathetic shadow of its former self. It was best if she stayed far away.

She shuffled backwards, unsure whether to swallow her pride and disappear, or to stand her ground. It was a dilemma she'd never experienced before. All kinds of firsts were coming at her, and she didn't know what to do with herself.

"All good. How about you?"

He speaks! Her heart started a gallop. "Fine. I'm fine."

A fleeting look from the corner of his eye told her he agreed with her. There was enough heat loaded in that look to rival the wood-fired pizza ovens. She raised a hand to her throat, adjusting her collar for some extra air flow to cool the burn.

Dane sauntered behind them on his way to the front of house. "Mud wrap." He smirked and winked, picking up his pace when she sneered at him.

"Boot up the ass," she threw at his back.

"Wouldn't be the first time I've had something up there," he cackled as he pushed through the door.

Turning back to Grey, she straightened the front of her shirt and cleared her throat. He was back to ignoring her, his hands moving furiously to get through the mountain of slicing he had to do.

J.M. ADELE

"My friends are coming to celebrate Hannah's birthday tonight, so put some extra love into their meals, okay?"

"I'm just the prep guy tonight, but I'll make sure to chop the garnishes extra pretty."

He cleared the sliced peppers into a container and took his knife to the sink to wash, before grabbing the next lot of vegetables. Chelsea admired his focus. He executed everything with precision. It showed in the set of his shoulders, the draw of his brow ... the strength in his arms. She had to wonder if he did everything like he was competing to be the best.

And she was standing there like an idiot.

Chelsea gnawed on her lips and tugged at her shirt. "Okay. Good talk," she chirped, before taking off.

Throwing her shoulders back and expelling the sexual tension through tightened lungs, she reminded herself that she didn't need a distraction. It was her final year. She had so much going on between organizing the function rooms next door, and the huge project that she'd be working on at college. She had to start thinking of what she'd be doing after graduation.

Her mama wanted to open a little café where people could come and drink coffee and eat cakes, with the added bonus of a second-hand book exchange. The space would have cozy little book nooks with coffee tables and wing back chairs. She could see it now. But she wanted to be able to buy into the business as a partner, and for that she needed to find a job. And leave this place far behind. And that meant Greyson too.

As she reached the door, she turned back, answering the unspoken call of his narrowed gaze watching her retreat. The current stirred again. *Well, shit.* There it was.

The truth laid bare. He was the source of the pull. Only, it was strengthening from the ebb of a tide to the tug of a rope, lassoing her dreams and spinning them in a different direction from the way they'd been heading.

He was undoing all her good intentions.

And she was damned if she didn't want to let him.

———

"Hey, how're y'all doin'? Would you like another round of drinks?"

Chelsea gathered up the collection of glasses from her friends' table, shooing Ryan's hand away when he tried to help. She'd done her best to put smiles on their faces tonight. Hell, she had a giant smile on her face for some reason. It had to be contagious. Maybe it was the new addition in the kitchen, or maybe she was just super happy to have a chance to make things right with her roommates. She didn't care. She was just enjoying the high.

Decorated as if she were her own present, Hannah wore a balloon strapped to her wrist, and a tiara topped with sparkly plastic letters that read *birthday girl*. She'd brought along three more friends from college, making it a party of six. The group were behaving themselves. Just. They were probably saving the real partying for the bar later on.

"No, let's order dessert. I'll have a taste of your friend over there." Hannah leaned her chin on her palm, a dreamy look in her eye as she set her sights across the room.

Chelsea followed her line of sight. "Jenna?" Whipping her head back to Hannah, Chelsea made sure her eyes held a stern warning. "No. You leave Jenna alone. She is too pure and good to be sullied by the likes of you."

"Ooh, burn," Ryan snickered.

Chelsea bit her tongue with a grimace, but it was too late to suck the words back in where they belonged. "I didn't mean that you were dirty—"

Hannah sliced a hand through the air, cutting Chelsea off. "Well, I am that. Don't worry, I'm not offended. But you should know that the more you defend your friend's honor, the more appealing she appears."

"I'm pretty sure she doesn't swing that way."

"Really? Because my *gadar* is pinging."

Chelsea watched Jenna as she flitted between tables, a polite smile on her face, and that bun that didn't move an inch. As if she felt the scrutiny, Jenna shifted her eyes to their table, tossing a deer-in-the-headlights look in Hannah's direction.

"You're scaring the crap out of her. Stop it."

Hannah crossed her arms over her chest, making the balloon on her wrist tangle with the pendant light above. "Phooey. You're no fun. Bring out the sweets!"

Chelsea reached over to set the decoration free. "As you wish, Queen Hannah."

Hannah's hand flew up to check that her tiara was still in place, sending the balloon careening into Chelsea's face. She smacked it away and took off for the kitchen.

What Hannah didn't realize was that Chelsea had organized a cake. It'd cost her a mint, but she wanted to do something nice to make up for the rough start they'd had since she moved in. She hustled over to the reach-in, finding the elaborate creation already on a stand and decorated beautifully by Elise, one of their patissiers. Three different layers of cream and sponge brushed with rum syrup, all coated in frosting and toasted sliced almonds. She would almost kill for this cake. It was traditionally for weddings, but what the heck, they deserved to live a little.

All Chelsea had to do was prop it on a bus cart, and add the candles and sparklers.

Only, the damn things wouldn't light.

Burning flame nipped at her fingers. "Aargh, shit!" She dropped the lighter, shaking her hand, and cursing some more. Before she knew it, her wrist was clasped in a firm grip, and her fingers were shoved under the nearest faucet.

"What the heck are you doing?" Grey growled in her ear.

"I was trying to light the sparklers. What the heck are you doing?"

"First aid."

"I can hold my own hand under the water." She tugged on her arm, making him tighten his grip.

"Then, why didn't you?"

"I was … I would've done that next."

"Uh huh."

"I know how to treat a burn. I'm not an idiot, for Lord's sake."

"Why weren't you using the gas lighter instead of that useless thing?" He pointed an accusing finger at the cigarette lighter she'd been using.

"Excuse me for thinkin' that a cigarette lighter would be able to *light* something *flammable*. I didn't think it'd be this hard."

"Haven't you ever lit a sparkler before?"

"I always go for the rockets on the fourth of July. I like to go big."

"Yeah, I got that impression about you." He turned off the faucet and cradled her hand in his, reaching for a towel.

His eyes lifted to hers and she marveled at the thick black lashes shading his silver stare. With her hand still locked in his, he watched her unabashedly, drawing out that hum of energy she always experienced when he was near, and ramping it up a notch with the addition of his touch.

She returned his scrutiny. Why the hell not? If he was going to blatantly stare, she'd take the opportunity to do the same. It was no hardship taking in the rugged planes of Greyson's face. She wanted to drift closer and fold herself into him, but she still had enough of her wits to realize where they were.

Greyson let her hand slip from his grip and went to retrieve a butane lighter. With a click, he touched the flame to the sparkler, setting off miniature fireworks. He'd hijacked the bus cart and was out the door before she'd moved a muscle. Chelsea forced out a breath as her hands landed on her hips. She had to respect the way he'd taken charge even as she scrambled to catch up.

The party broke out in song when they saw the cake coming, and a few other patrons joined in. Chelsea sang out loud and proud, happy to be a part of her friend's celebration. Grey watched on in silence, with a hint of a smile on his lips and his eyes on her. Her toes curled in her shoes like she was trying to keep her feet planted, because the Lord knew they wanted to turn in his direction and drift into new possibilities with him. Ones she shouldn't be considering.

"Make a wish," Grey reminded Hannah before she blew out the candles.

"I fully intend to. Thank you, Greyson."

"My pleasure. Happy birthday and have a good night."

He spun around to leave, but Dakota wrapped her hand around his arm. "Wait up, what are you doing later?"

"Tucking myself in tight."

Chelsea caught a groan before it escaped. She could visualize tucking him in all too well.

"Aw, don't be like that. Come out with us."

Chelsea watched Dee's hand flex on his arm, and fought to keep her eyes from narrowing. She had no right to feel jealous. He wasn't hers.

"Not tonight. I won't finish up here until late. Sorry."

He folded his arms over his broad chest, leaving no room for argument, and not appearing sorry at all.

Dee wasn't exactly apologetic about leaving her hand right where it was either. Her lips popped out in a pout. "How about Halloween?"

"I don't have anything special planned. It's my night off." A casual shrug of one shoulder had his arms loosening slightly.

Dakota's pout stretched out in a smile and her hand finally dropped. "Excellent. A bunch of us are going to Salem for the celebrations. We'd love for you to come."

What the fuck, Dee? Chelsea's jaw ached from clenching too tightly. She was going to kill her friend.

"Yeah, okay. I'll get the details from Chelsea. Thanks." He cut a glance at her before going back to the kitchen, a coded message in the cool depths that she had no hope of deciphering.

She straightened her shirt with a frown, and got to work on slicing up the cake and serving it out, adding a dollop of cream for the few that wanted it.

"Where's your piece?" Hannah asked around a mouthful.

"I'll save a piece for me. You can take the cake home, I'll just box it up for you."

"Can't you sit and eat with us?"

"No, that would be unprofessional. I have other tables to serve too, Hannah."

Dee snickered. "Oh, come on. Sit down. It's not like they're clamoring for your attention."

This time she did let her eyes narrow and her mouth tightened in annoyance. She got the impression Dakota was spoiling for a fight, but she didn't have a clue why.

"Why'd you have to go and invite him to Halloween?"

"Shame on you, Chelsea. Where is your Christian hospitality? He's new to Boston. I thought it'd be nice to show him some sights."

"Exactly what *sights* did you have in mind? Because I don't think Salem is at the top of your list."

"Whoa, kitties. You're spitting and hissing all over my birthday party." Hannah tried to prevent things from getting all kinds of feline nasty.

"I was trying to do Chelsea a favor and extend a welcome to a newcomer. I haven't done anything wrong."

Dee's indignant chuff pissed her off even more, but she needed to quit with the trigger finger.

"Sorry, Hannah."

"It's okay, I'm getting used to your temper. If I ever need anyone on my side, I know who to call. Thanks for the surprise." Hannah raised a fork full of cake in salute and shoved it into her mouth.

"You're so welcome. I'm glad I could look after you tonight. I'll be back with the cake."

Chelsea cast a glance at Dee as she packed up. The high she'd been riding all but fizzled out. Dee returned her perusal with a saccharine smile, making Chelsea's back teeth grind together.

Sometimes, friends were enemies in disguise. She just had to figure out if Dakota was one of them.

Chapter Ten

A Little Encouragement Goes a Long Way

Greyson knew this would be hard. He'd been prepared for it. But experiencing the reality of something was always more taxing than anything a person's mind could conjure. He'd been running all night, restocking ingredients as the chefs barked out their needs. His body was up to the test. All those years of hard labor on the ranch had done him good. He didn't begrudge the hard work he'd endured at all. But the finesse required to feed a farm animal was vastly different to feeding hordes of hungry restaurant patrons. Every now and then, he took the time to admire the speed and agility of the chefs on their respective lines, knowing that would be him someday soon.

Chelsea's frequent visits to the server window drew his eye unfailingly, despite his efforts to stay focused and not fuck anything up. He didn't want to give his father the satisfaction of watching him crawl back home a failure. But every time he felt the stroke of her attention, it pulled at him like he was already on her leash. He should have been nervous, but instead, he felt like he'd been plugged into a power socket. Her being there made him want to work harder, to succeed, *and* to get her alone. Who said he couldn't have both?

She'd come on strong in Alabama, sparking his interest. And then he'd seen past the playful tease to a vulnerable center, igniting all sorts of feelings he hadn't known were possible, and had him damning it all to hell when he had to get back on the road without taking a bite of that apple. He knew one bite wouldn't be enough. Then, miracle of all miracles, she turns up under his nose. It had to be a sign from the big guy upstairs. There was no way shit like that happened for real. And if he didn't take notice of a sign like that ... he was a dumbass. He'd bought a ticket in the lottery that morning, hoping to stretch his lucky streak.

Only thing was, the Chelsea from Alabama was nowhere to be seen, replaced by a woman who was all work and no fooling around. She'd looked after her friends tonight without joining in the fun, choosing to remain professional. The irritation and disbelief plastered on her face when Dakota invited him to Halloween had him questioning whether this was the same woman at all.

But then, he thought back to how her hand had trembled in his grasp, and not because she'd singed her fingers, but because of the energy arcing between them. And the way her pulse bounded in her neck the other night when he'd kissed her. His gut told him she was as much in danger of getting pulled into this thing between them as he was, every time her eyes met his and latched on to something deeper inside.

She was scared, that's all.

The woman was used to getting her way, and he hadn't given it to her. She didn't *want* to be happy to see him. Her body was definitely excited to see him. He'd have to tug those defenses down to get the rest of her interested.

"Hey, lover boy."

Grey just about jumped out of his skin as Dane suddenly materialized beside him, and he damn near snarled.

"Whoa. Note to self. Never sneak up on the newbie. Please don't kill me."

Greyson relaxed his hand slowly from its white knuckled grip on his knife.

"That's it. Put the knife down." Dane coaxed, motioning with his hands.

Grey's eyebrows dropped even lower. "What can I do for you?" His tone was less than friendly, but the clatter of the knife on the board spoke of resignation. He knew Dane enough by now to know he didn't let go once he had a mind to do something.

"It's not what you can do for me, it's what I can do for you. And probably what I can do for my country, because she's likely to become a threat if she doesn't get some. But let's not go that far just yet."

"What in the hell are you on about, Dane?"

"You're a man of few words, I get it. But you've got to make them count when it comes to Chelsea."

"Is that so?"

"She doesn't trust men. I don't count because I'm not trying to get into her panties, and I don't want anything from her other than her fabulous company. But the slime balls that hit on her every night, they reaffirm her ideas about what a man is good for. In her mind, it's a limited list."

Grey measured Dane from the corner of his eye while storing away the valuable insight. His hands balled into fists, tightening at the thought of Chelsea getting hit on by a never-ending line of assholes. He didn't like that. Didn't like it at all.

"What is it with you two? You looked like you'd seen each other before, on that first night."

"We met in Alabama."

"Oh, you're a hometown boy?"

"No. I was just passin' through."

"Must have been some meeting. Did anything happen?"

"None of your goddamn business," he growled, eyebrows slamming down.

Dane clapped his hands together in front of his mouth, blinking back tears, before throwing his arms around Grey.

He squirmed out of Dane's embrace. "What the fuck are you doing?"

"You already care about her." Dane smiled, patting away tears with his ring fingers. "Let her know that she comes first. Build up her trust. Provide her with security and stability. She's never had that with a man. Ever. If you can do that while setting her panties on fire, then she's yours. I'm pretty certain that you've got that last bit covered already." Dane's grin showed off his perfectly bleached teeth.

Grey loosened his fists. "Why are you telling me this? What's in it for you?"

"Possibly a day at the spa." Dane shrugged.

Grey's mouth sank at the corners.

"But I just want to see her happy. For real."

He turned to face Dane front on, crossing his arms. "What has the fucking spa got to do with me and Chelsea?"

"You know you're really intimidating? I sense that you're a teddy bear, deep down. I'd like to speak with the teddy bear."

"Dane." Grey gritted his teeth to hold back his temper.

"No teddy bear?"

Grey merely cocked a brow.

"Okay, first, you should know that we made the bet before you arrived."

What the fuck? Steamy air sucked in Grey's nostrils so fast he nearly choked.

"Chelsea's got it in her head that she'd be better off without men in her life, so she's sworn off dating for a while. I said she wouldn't last three months and I stand to benefit from a day at the spa if she fails. But, if she keeps her chastity belt firmly locked, then she gets the pair of designer boots she's been drooling over for months."

"Are you telling me I'm in competition with footwear?"

"Footwear is not a joking matter. But, I digress. The real issue is your ability to redeem the male of the species."

Grey blinked and looked away. "I've been sucked into the twilight zone, haven't I?"

"Come on, man, keep up. I'm concerned about her. She's not herself. You need to restore her faith in mankind before she leaves after graduation. We don't want her to leave, do we, Greyson?"

"She's fucking leaving?"

"No, Greyson, she's not leaving because you're going to entice her to stay. Sweetie, you'll need to think quicker if you're going to keep up with Chelsea."

Matteo's voice boomed across the kitchen. "Dane, get back to your station, people are leaving. Greyson, we need help on the dessert line."

"Yes, chef."

He went to fulfill his uncle's request. Keeping his head in the game was all he should be worried about, but the space between his ears was crowded with the blonde bombshell in the tight skirt. He'd buy her the fucking shoes himself if he had to, *and* send Dane to the spa. If he worked his ass off, in a few years, he'd be able to buy her a whole closet of shoes.

He knew he had to figure out a way to balance his desires, because he wasn't prepared to let either of them go.

———

"Shit! Sh, sh, shhhhh."

Chelsea smeared lotion into her freshly showered skin as she darted back to her room to answer the persistent ringing of her phone. The shrill sound cut off a second before she flipped the stupid thing open.

"Damn it!" Her greasy fingers smudged the screen as she punched the call back button.

"Hey, baby girl. How are you?"

"Hi Mama. What're you doing still up? It must be one in the mornin'." She wedged the cellphone between her shoulder and her cheek as she wiped her hands dry.

"Oh, I went to bed early, but some hot rod tearing down the street woke me up and my brain started to race. You know how it is. So, how was the restaurant tonight? Did you make some good tips?"

Chelsea heard the clink of porcelain, and pictured her mama having a cup of hot chocolate, sitting at the breakfast bar. Probably in her favorite cup with the chicken dressed in an apron, and a chip missing from the bottom edge. Fat tears sprang from Chelsea's eyes because she missed that dumb chicken. Too much. Smudging them away, she pulled in a breath and regrouped.

"Yeah, I did okay."

She thought she sounded convincing, but the pause on the other end said otherwise.

"Honey? Tell me what's weighin' on your mind. And don't tell me *nothing* because I'm your mama, and I know applesauce when I hear it."

Her lips tilted up at the corners, rising with the tide of homesickness lodged behind her ribcage. She could do with one of her mama's hugs, but if she was back home, she wouldn't be in this mess to start with.

"I miss home. I miss you. But opportunities are opening up for me. I feel like I'm being pulled away from everything I know and love that I might rip clear down the middle."

"Aw, honey. This place will always be here. Your life is just beginning to shine. If things are happening there, then that's where you need to be for now. I'm not going anywhere, and neither are the Murphys."

"But we had plans."

"Yeah, we did. There's no rush. Maybe God is telling you that you have some lesson to learn before you can move on, or move back."

Yeah, like stay away from men. Chelsea barked a laugh.

"Oh, oh. There's more. What's this really about?" Her mama sipped her drink, the sound, so familiar, travelling down the phone line.

"I didn't tell you, but before I left 'Bama this time, I met someone. Nothing happened, Mama. I swear. We just shared a meal at the diner and then he left." She filled her lungs for the next part "Well, it turns out he's the new apprentice chef at Abbiocco."

"Okay?"

Her mama paused, waiting for her to say more, but what the hell could she say?

"Well, what's he like?"

Tempting as hell. "A little broody, and pushy. Serious. Too gorgeous to be harmless."

"Is that what has you worried? You think he's going to hurt you?"

"I think he's the first man I've met who's capable of getting under my skin."

"Well, honey ..." A deep sigh cut off the sentence.

"Well, what?"

"Dang, it's hard being so far away. I feel useless. I want to meet him. I can't give you advice without knowing who we're dealing with here. You know I'm not the best person to give you advice on men, anyways. I guess, listen to your heart, but let your head have a say too. Sometimes, what we think we want isn't what we need at all."

"Yeah. You're right. I need to keep my head on straight. Thanks, Mama."

"So, tell me about all these opportunities."

Lying on her bed, she chatted with her mama about her projects, relishing the connection to home. Each minute wiped away the confusion of Alabama versus Boston. Home was her foundation, and where she'd placed her heart. The things she was doing in Boston—they had an end date. She would graduate college. The extension of Abbiocco would be completed within twelve months. Eighteen months, tops. Matteo would have to look for a project manager to see that through. Her dream of opening Books, Nooks, and Nibbles with her mama would always be her long-term plan. And Greyson, he was only a fleeting distraction too. She wasn't looking for forever. What a total waste of time. No man was built for that. It was simply against the laws of nature. Women were delusional if they believed the fantasy in romance novels. She sighed and tucked herself under the covers, relieved that the ceiling was right where it was supposed to be and not raised to some impossible height.

Placing her cellphone beside the bed, she switched off her lamp, but the phone lit up and dinged with a message.

It's Grey. Dane gave me your number. How's the burn?

She sat up, turning the lamp back on with fumbling fingers.

Damn it, Dane.

There was no way she'd be getting any sleep now, not with the amount of adrenaline coursing around her body.

He was thinking about her, and that put him front and center in her thoughts again. After several attempts and much abuse of the backspace button, she sent a reply.

The burn is painful. Thnx for asking.

She'd barely hit send when the phone lit up in her hand with his response.

You're welcome. Goodnight.

Goodnight? That was all he was going to say? Expelling a gust of air in disgust, she mulled over the message.

Slowly, her mouth curved up. He'd been worried about her, going to the trouble of getting her number and sending her a message after he finished work. Not the next morning. No, he couldn't wait that long.

Falling back against the mattress, she pushed a palm over her mouth to stop herself from grinning like a fool. She shouldn't have been pleased at all. She thought Alabama had won the fight, but now Greyson Stranger had put Boston back in the game with only a few words.

The tear down her middle ripped a little more.

What the fuck was she going to do?

Chapter Eleven

Witchcraft

Salem was turning it on for All Hallows' Eve. She was here two years ago, and seeing it for the second time was no less exciting. People, transformed into all things gore, ghoul, and magic, clogged the Salem streets. Bodies bumped, and sounds clashed as the underworld rose to the surface for the night.

Hannah, Dakota, and Chelsea, opted to dress as a coven of witches, while Ryan decided to zombie up. Greyson tagged along, wearing his jeans, a long-sleeved Henley under a leather jacket, and a freakin' cowboy hat. She had to wipe her mouth when he showed up at her place with that thing on. Cowboy hats were rare up here. It made her miss home even more, while making him that much more irresistible. Her resolve was weakening by the second.

How bad could it be to treat Dane to a day at the spa?
Let him have his moment of glory.
Who needs shoes, anyways?

And then Grey would look at her. Not just a glance. Not even an ogle. No. He'd look deep, like he wanted to see under the layers of protection to her vulnerable center. Every time he did that, her heart would start to pound and sweat broke out on her skin. She'd squirm and fidget, detaching her gaze from the pull of his, but almost immediately sliding her eyes back to his because she couldn't look away for long. Her lips were going to be a mangled mess, unfit for kissing, if she continued chewing on them.

Aaand, now I'm thinking about kissing him. Ugh.

Chelsea tucked her broomstick between her legs, and tugged on the course strands of green hair tickling her face. She'd end up ditching the goddamn wig before the end of the night if it kept getting in the way. Adjusting her pointy hat so that it pinned back her bangs, she grabbed her broom again and jogged to catch up with her friends.

Ryan eased his stride to fall back beside her. "Why don't you just lose the wig?"

"Because my hair is pinned flat to my head underneath, and I refuse to walk around looking like I've escaped from the theatre."

"Everybody here looks like they've escaped from the theatre." Ryan's nose screwed up as he threw a glance at the back of Greyson's head. "Almost everyone. Why don't you take the pins out?"

"Why are you so worried about my hair?"

"I don't care about your hair. I'm worried that you're not having fun because of a dumb wig."

"I'm having fun." She bared her teeth in a mock smile. "See? Fun."

"Very convincing."

"What would you know? You're undead. You only care about eating flesh and brains."

"Yours would be particularly juicy, I was hoping you'd flash more of it tonight." He stuck his tongue out in a lewd gesture, sending her skin crawling.

"There ya go again."

"You know I'm only joking. I'm not a cannibal."

Her eyes narrowed. "You weren't referring to that kind of eating."

"See, if you're going to leave yourself open with comments like that, my reply is going to come from the gutter."

She turned on him, pointing her broom handle. "Or, you could control yourself because you know it makes me uncomfortable."

"God, you're so uptight."

Her body locked in place, refusing to go any further as she zeroed a death stare on her roommate, steam puffing out of her fake nose.

"Okay. Sorry. I take that back." He reared back.

Chelsea's mouth pinched and she squeezed her shoulder blades together, surveying the scene around them while she cooled off. Every time she cut him some slack, he went and ruined it with his immature innuendo.

Grey slowed down and waited for her to catch up, his eyes boring holes in Ryan's head.

"Hey. It's the Ecto-1."

The Ghostbusters' trademark Cadillac Hearse drove past them, lights flashing.

"How do you even know the car's name?" Dakota scrunched her nose.

"She's a closet pop fiction geek." Ryan voiced his revelation, a mocking expression taking over his face.

She held her chin up despite the heat that rose to her cheeks as Grey settled his eyes on hers.

"I loved those movies." She cleared her throat. "Ya know, I think I remember there's a Dunkin' somewhere around here. And maybe a bar."

Chelsea licked her lips in anticipation of a drink and a treat, to wash down the nasty taste in her mouth. Why did Ryan have to be such a jerk?

Hannah rested an arm behind Chelsea's neck, and pointed at the crowd gathering in the Salem Common. "Let's go check out the Witches' Magic Circle."

"Can we get a drink first? Like, with alcohol? They have beer near Witch Village. Let's go there."

"After." Hannah turned to the group. "Are you guys game?"

"I'm game." Ryan tipped his chin in a lead-on gesture.

Chelsea reluctantly followed, knowing what the circle was all about after seeing it two years before.

Witches and warlocks in elaborate robes and pointy hats held court in the center of a large circle of onlookers. They played tambourines and shakers, joined by a couple of guys banging on drums. Smoke rose from a small table where they'd lit some candles beside a plastic skull. Posted around the center space, large speakers on stands added technology to the mix, reminding everyone of the present age. A collection of food trucks and carnival rides provided a colorful and aromatic backdrop to the ceremony, the smell of fried, fast food wafting through the park.

Hannah propped her chin on Chelsea's shoulder. "The giant jumping castle in the background kinda takes away from it."

"Yeah, but we can still honor the dead and enjoy some rides afterwards," Ryan pointed out.

"Boring. Let's go to the costume parade." Dee turned away. "Where's Grey?"

"Don't know, don't care," Ryan mumbled under his breath.

Chelsea ignored him, craning her neck to see where Greyson had gone. She spotted him easily with his cowboy hat acting as a beacon. Holding a paper bag, he was headed straight for her.

"I thought you ladies might like something sweet."

"Ooh, fried dough. Yum." Hannah shoved one in her mouth immediately.

"Thanks, Greyson." Dee licked hers before taking a seductive nibble.

Oh, please.

He seemed to enjoy the females fawning over him in thanks, a pleased grin gracing his features.

Not her. She didn't fawn. She took hers with a polite, "Thank you."

"Sorry Ryan, I didn't get any for you."

"I can pay for my own," he snapped.

Her head spun on her neck. "Ryan! Jesus. You can have mine."

Chelsea shoved her treat at his chest, and he fumbled to stop it from ending up in the dirt.

She noted Grey's hands were empty. "You didn't get anything for yourself."

"Nope. I was gonna get a beer."

"Sounds great. Let's go. Y'all want to come?"

"I want to watch the witches." Hannah's attention was focused on the coven dancing inside the ring of onlookers.

"Okay, then. We'll just head down Hawthorne and Derby. You can come find us in Witch Village when you're done."

"I could go for a beer," Ryan piped up.

"Me too." Dee curled a hand around Grey's elbow, before wiggling her fingers at Hannah. "See you later."

Chelsea hesitated, a queasy feeling in her gut. She wasn't going to leave Hannah alone.

"I thought you were game, Ryan?"

The jerk was already leaving.

Dee pulled on Grey's arm, urging him away. "Grey? Are you coming?"

He ignored her question, standing his ground and staring Hannah down. "Are you goin' to be okay on your own?"

"Yeah. I'll be fine. I'm a big girl."

"In a strange place. At night. Surrounded by kooks." Grey's expression was as sober as it gets.

"Sounds like home to me." Hannah winked.

"Then you need to move."

"I'll stay with her," Chelsea offered, her heart doing all sorts of flips at his concern for Hannah's welfare.

"You don't have to do that." Hannah walked backwards, edging closer to the action.

"I don't mind."

"I'll stay too. The beer can wait." Greyson levered Dee's fingers off his arm. "Go catch up with Ryan. We'll see you later." He smiled politely and moved closer to the circle's fringe where Hannah stood enthralled.

"Hmph. Suit yourself." Dee stalked off, broomstick in tow.

Chelsea watched until Dakota caught up to Ryan, making sure she was safe, before joining Hannah.

"She's not happy with you."

Cutting a look at Grey, Chelsea kept a safe distance, ignoring the way her body wanted to burrow under the protective net he was throwing out. He looked after people. Cared for them. Even those he hardly knew.

"She'll live."

Dee, on the other hand … not so much.

Sliding her hands under her cloak, Chelsea cocooned herself inside as the evening chill set in. She could barely hear the warlock's words, as a man preaching into a microphone looped behind the group, pleading for them to be saved. Her brow bunched, watching his righteous march. They weren't worshipping the devil. They were speaking of love and remembrance. She caught Grey with the same dip in his brow as he watched the guy retreat.

"It's nice of you. To stay with Hannah."

Grey crossed his arms, tucking his hands under his arm pits. "It's nothing. Like I said, the beer can wait."

She managed to divert her eyes back to the warlock on the microphone. The beat of the drums and the enchanting ritual fed energy around the circle, joining the crowd as one. It pulsed through her fingertips and down to her feet, with overtones of joy and celebration lifting the somber ceremony. She swayed as it swept her along, slowly building to a crescendo.

The hard part was coming, and she braced her feet apart to steel herself.

When he asked everyone to call out the name of a person they'd like to remember, Chelsea croaked out, "Beth." Hugging herself, she squeezed her eyes shut to ward off tears, and breathed through her nose until the threat passed.

Warmth infused her side and she relaxed her arms, opening her eyes to find that Grey had moved close, watching her with his metallic gaze. Forcing an exhale through pursed lips, her tear ducts burned for release. Damn him for being so sweet. She hadn't heard him call anyone's name, but there was something in those eyes that said he understood. He hid it well, but not deep enough to be out of her reach.

She pried her gaze away to check on Hannah. Chelsea barely knew her two companions, but she'd grown dangerously close to caring deeply for them. Too fast.

Hannah winked, a ghost of a smile playing on her face, before she turned it up to the sky. Just the tiniest movement. The flutter of an eyelid. But it held enough power and reassurance to release the well of emotion stinging Chelsea's eyes. Her lips quirked up as she tucked her chin to her chest, tears dripping at her feet. She hadn't wanted to be a part of the circle, denying the bad memories from rising to the surface, but she was glad she was there. Blocking thoughts of Beth had been a dishonor. She deserved better than that. She deserved to be remembered even though dragging up the past exposed Chelsea's raw wounds. Flanked by these two, under their protective wings, she'd found a safe haven to purge the grief and guilt she'd carried for years. Physically, at least. If she had to verbalize the agony, she didn't think she'd survive the festivities.

Grey's hands slid into his pockets, and he backed away under a tree as the music started. The witches encouraged the crowd to join in the singing and dancing. She and Hannah linked arms and skipped around, singing loudly. Her eyes caught his every time she passed his way, the pull growing stronger with each turn. His inscrutable mask gave away nothing of how he felt, but the way his eyes followed told her so much. He wanted her, but he wouldn't come and take her. She had to go to him.

Fuck, it was so tempting. To let all her walls down and set herself free from her self-imposed prison. It wasn't just her body that screamed at her to do it, her soul wept at the possibility. She'd been holding her shit together for so goddamn long. But if she gave in, she feared she'd never come back. This force, this energy arcing between them, pulling them together … it was fucking terrifying. She couldn't deal with it right now.

She stopped skipping, while everyone clapped and cheered as the circle was closed. "Hey, let's go get that beer."

Her friend nodded. "Ready when you are, babe."

———

Belly full of beer and nachos, Chelsea found herself sitting in a dim candlelit room with about fifteen others, listening to a psychic pull random information from thin air. She didn't think there was any threat of actual communication with the dead, but some vibe in the room made her twitchy. Perhaps it was because she was sandwiched between Ryan and Grey, who both sat with arms crossed and one ankle on the opposing knee. It seemed Hannah was in charge of the itinerary for the night, and nobody liked her choice of activities.

Strangely, Dakota chose a seat beside Grey, quietly absorbing the show. Or maybe it wasn't strange, and Chelsea was letting her green side take over. Not the Oz kind of green, either. It was more the mammoth proportions of the big guy who split his pants every time he got mad.

Hannah appeared oblivious, hanging on every word coming out of the psychic's mouth. Lord bless that free-spirited woman. She embraced everything she did, wholeheartedly. Chelsea could learn a thing or two from her. She unfolded her arms, placing her hands between her knees, and sat up.

"May I approach you?" The psychic had Chelsea in her sights.

"Me?"

"Don't be scared. I have a message from your loved one."

"*Pfft*. Oh, I'm not scared, honey." She rubbed her palms together, shuffling her butt back in her chair.

You're such a liar.

"Your loved one with a B sound. A female. You were close, but not related."

Chelsea's muscles tensed, the twitchy feeling intensifying under her skin.

"She said to let go of the blame. It was her choice. You were not responsible."

Her vocabulary vanished as her body locked tight. What could she say? That information couldn't be randomly plucked from the air. Unless this psychic somehow knew her from Texas, there was no way she could've known Chelsea had been carrying the burden of blame for her wild ways ... and the irreversible consequences. She squeezed her palms between her knees as her mind reeled. Was that really Beth?

"She said to tell you she's okay."

Well, I'm not.

"I have a message for you too."

Chelsea's focus turned to Greyson as the psychic addressed him.

"This spirit is very clearly your grandfather. A forceful personality. He refused to wait his turn. He said he's sorry for being so stubborn, and that you must follow your heart, wherever it may lead you."

Grey tipped his chin up in affirmation, choosing not to speak. Angling himself towards her, he pulled one of her hands onto his thigh and clasped their palms together, unspoken questions suspended in his eyes.

Are you okay?

Who is Beth?

"I got you." The words rumbled out in a deep, calming whisper.

Oh, honey. You have me more than you know.

She fixed on their joined hands, her eyelids tapping out a frantic rhythm. He'd brushed aside his own revelation to take care of her, the security net still blanketing her. She half expected to see a cascade of rubble as another of her walls came crashing down. He'd offered her a safe place to forgive herself for all her failings. A chance at normal. She'd vehemently denied the small voice in her mind that said, 'what if?' What if she allowed herself to trust enough to find love? What if she found someone who would cherish her? Didn't she deserve that? That's all Beth had wanted.

As the psychic moved through the room, Chelsea struggled with herself to stay seated. She focused on the connection with Grey. The way he held her hand steady, as if he knew she needed an anchor because she was suddenly lighter than before. He gave their joined hands a shake to get her attention, and tilted his chin towards the door. She didn't need to be told twice. She stood and followed him. Breaking free, she took a gulp of night air, letting his hand slip from hers.

He flexed his fingers. "You've got a good grip."

"So I've been told." She winced. She'd let her tongue loose again. Damn, it was hard holding back around him. "Sorry about that. Knee jerk reaction. I'm trying to be a better person and that means less inappropriate flirting."

"It's only inappropriate if it's unwelcome."

"Well, I just crushed your hand. I'm sure you weren't thinking about my grip around anything else."

"I haven't stopped thinking about parts of you wrapped around parts of me ever since we met."

Her lids dropped low as she took in the firm set of his jaw. His molten gaze warmed her up, making her body pliant and ready for his touch. Maybe she could let him in? For the time she had left, anyways. And finally give herself a taste of something she could hold deep inside for the rest of her days.

"That can be arranged."

"Oh really? Forfeiting your bet so early in the game? Shame on you, Chelsea. I thought you were made of tougher stuff."

"How do you—" Her eyes popped before narrowing. "Dane ... Oh, he is going to get a whupping next time I see him."

"He's a good friend. You have a good group of people who love you." He pushed some hair out of his face and glanced at the door they'd just exited. "And some questionable tag-alongs."

"You don't like Ryan, huh?"

"I wasn't referring to Ryan. But, no. I don't like him. He wants what I want." Those eyes mapped her features.

"He can't have me. And, for the record, I don't give a rat's ass about the bet."

"Good. I'm glad to hear it, because you and I are gonna happen."

"Now?" She bounced on the balls of her feet.

He barked out a laugh, flashing his teeth. "No. I don't sleep with witches."

"Oh. That's a shame, because I'm pretty sure witches sleep naked."

His brow shot up. "Is that right?"

"It's just a rumor I heard from someone in the know."

"I'll dream about that until the time comes."

"When will it be time to come? Because I'm lookin' forward to the coming part."

The smile spread across his face in a slow seductive tide, as his lids grew heavy. "It's going to be explosive."

"When? When is it going to explode? I hope we have some towels on hand."

Laughter burst from deep in his belly, the sound rivalling the revelry in the street. "Oh, you are a peach." He reached out and pulled her into his frame.

Enveloped in his arms as he shook in amusement, she couldn't contain her smile. He was all kinds of warm and hard, and big ... and hard. Yeah, she might've burrowed in close enough to feel something against her stomach. A girl had to check these things. He had all the right gear to get the job done.

He also had so much more that she wasn't prepared for. He had heart, and compassion. He'd known that she needed to get out of that room, and he'd made it happen without pressing her for a reason why. And then he'd made her laugh while getting her panties wet. He was a goddamn rock. A big, gorgeous, steady rock. Her arms crept around him as she turned her face into his chest and breathed him in. She listened to the beat in his chest, absorbed the rise and fall of air from his lungs, and felt her own match it.

She'd been so torn between belonging in two different places that she hadn't imagined she could feel so content in a place like his arms.

Maybe home had nothing to do with geography.

But if you want to call someone home, you must both be in the same city.

And there was the problem.

Chapter Twelve

Giving Thanks

Chelsea gathered her bag and smoothed her hair as the train pulled to a stop in Beacon Hill. She had a fair way to walk to get to Matteo's place, so she had her runners on with her heels tucked in her bag. Looking around at all the beautiful multi-million-dollar homes, her nerves started to congregate. She'd never seen his house, but she figured it would look something like its neighbors. Maybe her dress wasn't good enough. She'd nearly fallen backwards off her chair when Matteo invited her for Thanksgiving dinner, but she reckoned he probably wanted to discuss the details of the function center. He didn't have any family that she knew of. What else was he going to do for Thanksgiving?

She dug her heels in and contemplated calling him to cancel, before shaking herself for being stupid. He'd invited her because they had work to discuss. She'd grown up spending time in Angel's big old plantation home. She wasn't out of place there. It had its own library, for Lord's sake. She ordered her feet to start marching, doing up the buttons of her coat to ward off the chilly air.

On her tail, the rumble of horsepower tracked her path before a pickup truck pulled up beside her. She did a double take when she recognized its worn black paint. Slowing her steps, she watched Greyson reveal himself as he wound down the passenger window.

"What are you doing here?"

"Get in." He smirked.

"No."

"Get in. I'm taking you to supper."

She tugged the strap of her bag higher on her shoulder. "I have a previous engagement."

He snorted. "Honey, I know all about your plans. I'm your ride for the evening."

She bit her tongue, holding back the filthy thought that immediately came to mind.

"I know what you're thinking, dirty girl. Get in the truck. Did you think Matteo would make you walk by yourself at night? I know it's a good neighborhood and all, but you can't trust anyone these days. Not when you look like you do."

A gush of heat burst its way from her heart to her core and she shuffled her feet, clearing her throat.

"Why should I trust you?" She joked.

"I think you know me better than that by now. If I wanted to hurt you, I could've done so already."

Maybe physically she was safe, but her heart and sanity were definitely in danger from this man. The door popped open and she jumped in the warm cab. His scent arrested her senses, joining the smell of ...

"Why does it smell like pizza in here?"

"I had lunch on the run today."

"You had takeaway?"

"No, I whipped one up before driving around to find an open convenience store."

"Oh."

He pulled down a street lined with brownstones, and trees in cages growing through the pavement. Tiny gardens fenced by intricate wrought iron bracketed the front steps to each house. It was a beautiful step back in time, in modern color. She watched a garage door to one of the houses slide up before they drove in. Paving stones formed a driveway, lit by iron chandeliers running its length. Marble tiles covered the adjacent area where chairs that belonged in a palace sat near the staircase leading into the living space.

"Is this Matteo's?"

"Yep."

"His house has its own drive through?"

"Minus the fast food." He pushed a button on a remote and the garage door rolled down behind them.

Her eyes darted everywhere, taking it all in. "The garage has a sitting room."

"I know."

"Why are you here, taking me to Matteo's?"

"Because I live here too. For now."

"Okaaay." Her brow bunched. "Why is Matteo housing the new apprentice? Sorry, no offense."

"Because he's my uncle."

She paused. "Oh, I see."

Now she understood why a chef who never took on an apprentice had made an exception to the rule. Lucky Greyson. How wonderful to have been born into a family where the future allowed you choices. And thanks to her mama, she was alive and working on opening up her own choices.

He turned off the engine and angled to face her. "What do you see?"

"You said he'd known you for a long time. Since birth, I'm guessing. You wanted off the ranch, so you thought you'd try the city. It was nice of him to give you a job and a place to stay."

The gray in his eyes grew stormy as his eyebrows slammed down. "I applied in the usual way. I had to do a trial in one of his friend's restaurants to see if I could make the cut. I did, so here I am. The housing situation is just temporary, until I can get out on my own. He's my uncle. If I can't ask him to help me out, who can I ask?"

"You're right. I'm sorry. I know you work hard and you deserve this opportunity."

"Damn straight, I do."

She wanted to sink into the seat as he stared her down with molten eyes. "Hey, I didn't mean to offend you. I just don't know if you realize what a huge thing it is to be accepted into Abbiocco for an apprenticeship. Matteo doesn't take apprentices. Ever."

"He knows I can cook. We were taught by the same woman. We have the same passion."

"I'm sure you do. And the same eyes. I see it now. Are you related through your mother or father?"

"On my father's side."

"So, you're Greyson Agrioli." She held out her hand. "Pleased to meet you."

He took a hold, but didn't shake, anger still brewing in his gaze.

"Now I know your name and where you live. This is next level kind of personal, Greyson." She offered a conciliatory smile.

"It's about time you caught up, Chelsea."

Releasing her hand, he leaned across to open her door, crowding her against the seat. With his face dangerously close to hers, he rested a hand on her thigh and dropped his gaze to her mouth. She held still, resisting the urge to lean forward and take what he teased her with, though her pulse thundered through her veins and her panties were ruined. His anger hummed through his touch on her thigh and the way he watched her like he wanted to pounce. In a display of delicious restraint, he denied them both.

She swallowed.

He was right. They were going to explode when they finally came together.

"Let's go. I have food to prepare."

Chelsea cleared her tight throat. "Yes, let's."

————

"Oh my God, what is in this stuffing?" Chelsea licked her lips and scooped some more food onto her fork.

Sipping his wine, Matteo's eyelids sank in pleasure before he answered from the head of the table. "Spicy sausage, bacon, some herbs, toasted homemade bread, garlic … Nothing too special."

"Oh, it's special." She pointed her knife at her plate. "Is this on the menu at Abbiocco tonight?"

"No, this is Greyson's recipe. Cotto a puntino."

She swung her eyes across the table. "Okay, I don't know that phrase. You did the turkey?"

"I did everything." He waved a hand at the spread of food. "And it means *cooked to perfection*."

"The squash?"

"Mm hmm." His lips quirked as he chewed.

"You didn't make the wine."

"No, but I know how to."

"Do you have to be good at everything you do?"

"I *am* good at everything I do."

One blonde brow winged up as she took a sip of her wine, watching him over the rim. Damn, he was sexy as fuck. Squeezing her thighs together, she had to remember they weren't alone.

"So, what's the plan after you finish your apprenticeship?"

"I'd like to work my way up to sous chef. Maybe try working for the competition, and see how they do things. But Albert's gotta retire some time."

"*Troiata*." Matteo scoffed, swirling his wine glass. "The competition can't have you. But there are people before you in line for Albert's job."

"It's my decision, where I take my career."

"Yes, it is. But I'm not investing all this time and money into developing your talent to have you gift it to my competitors. We will find something new for you when you're ready."

Grey snapped his mouth shut, drawing it into a flat line. His gaze flicked to hers before dropping to his plate.

She watched the muscles in his jaw flex and tense, and she wanted to reach out to soothe them.

Maybe having choices handed to you came with a price. She knew nothing about Grey's life and the sacrifices he'd made to be here. It couldn't have been easy, moving clear across the country to start a career, knowing he wouldn't be seeing his family on the regular. She'd survived college because she got to go home a couple of times a year. But to make a permanent move ... that was something else entirely. Maybe if she wanted something badly enough ...

Matteo broke through her reverie. "I might be thinking of expanding into New York City in the next few years. I'll need someone to head up the restaurant there. I'm not moving, but I will be heavily involved in getting things started. This is my name at stake."

Her skin tightened, and she rested her silverware on the plate before she dropped it. "New York?"

Grey uttered the same question, but with cautious hope in his voice rather than the despair she heard in hers. She swiped her wine and took a gulp.

"Yes. I have some real estate there, and connections in the business."

Grey's attention fell on her. She watched the pulse in his throat tick, unable to look him in the eye.

"We'll see."

"What about you, Chelsea?" Matteo turned to her. "What are your plans after graduation?"

"Oh, I'm heading back to Alabama. Mama and I are going into business together."

"Doing what?"

"Mama loves baking. She does cakes for weddings and parties. She's real good at it. We want to open a little book shop and patisserie where people can sit in big comfy chairs and read while they eat a sweet treat."

"Sounds quaint. What else are you going to do?"

Grey's shot a dark look at his uncle. "Zio."

"What? That's not going to be enough for her."

"It's up to her what she wants to do with her life."

"I'm just pointing out that she has too much motivation and vision to be content with running a little cake shop."

"Maybe they won't stop there. Maybe they'll franchise it and end up spread across the U.S."

"Boys, when you're done arguing over my future, I'd like to add that y'all need to butt out of my business." Spearing a finger at Matteo, she spoke through her teeth. "You asked, I answered. If you're not happy with the answer that's not my problem." Pushing her chair back, she stood gripping her napkin. "Thank you for dinner, it was delicious. I'm going to head home now. Y'all have a pleasant evening."

"No. We have dessert. *Ti devo delle scuse.* Sit." Matteo collected the plates and headed for the kitchen.

"He apologized."

She tossed the napkin on the table. "I know what that meant. I've heard it enough over the last three years. I need to leave or I'm going to miss the T."

"You're not getting the train home. I'll drive you."

Slamming her fists on her hips, she aimed a scowl at his smirking face. "Are all the men in your family pushy and pig-headed?"

"No. My brother, Antonio, is more like our mother. Gentle and sweet." Rounding the table while holding the wine bottle, he put her glass in her hand and took the other, leading her out of the room.

She trailed along behind him. "Well, where is he when I need him?"

"If you're looking for gentle and sweet, you'll be sorely disappointed."

"I'm not looking for gentle."

They stopped in the living room where a grand piano filled one corner, and elaborate silk curtains hung from the windows.

He offered her a seat, joining her on one of the sofas. "What are you looking for?"

"I'm not."

Studying her, he pulled his long hair off his face and tied it behind his neck. "Liar."

"I'm not interested in saddling myself with a relationship that'll end in tears."

Thinking that she could have a fling with him and walk away unscathed was the definition of insane. And if she didn't walk away, eventually he would. They'd barely started, and already he meant more and had burrowed in further than any man before. She should stop this now, before her life spiraled into something unrecognizable.

"Wow. Your parents must've shown you a happy example of love."

"My mama has shown me nothing but unconditional love, even when I didn't deserve it, but then that's the nature of *unconditional*. As far as my sperm donor is concerned. He is the devil's asshole. He took advantage of mama and then tried to pay his way out of the permanent repercussions. Mama loved me too much to go through with it."

"And for that I will forever be thankful." Sliding his arm along the back of the sofa behind her, he inched closer. "Your mama never married?"

"Nope. She never bothered with men after that. Most men are only after one thing, and they're not willing to deal with the consequences if a tadpole gets to the target."

"Are you tarring us all with the same brush?"

"Every man who has ever pursued me."

"I don't want to sleep with you. I think we established that already."

"Yet. You don't want to sleep with me *yet*. But when you do, you'll be done and on your way." *To New York.* She drained her glass and propped it on the end table, feeling his eyes boring through her temple.

"I don't think I'll be done. I think I'll be just beginning."

"Maybe I'll be done." She cocked a brow and stared him down, presenting a steel exterior while inside, she wept for the impossible.

His eyes turned to flint. "I call bullshit. You think that by being the one in control, that by not getting attached ... you remain in power. But the real reason behind your behavior is that you don't believe you're deserving of love from a man. You're scared of rejection, so you never allow yourself to get too close. You'll never invite the possibility of that happening."

The alcohol went sour on her tongue. *Jesus.* Was he a mind reader?

"You don't consider me a threat. You think you can play with me and still run when you want to. But deep down, you're a little scared that I might actually get under your defenses."

He tugged on a few strands of her hair, tucking it behind her ear, so she wasn't shielded from his probing eyes. She wanted to jerk forward and pull the curtain down, but the urge to lean into his touch was just as strong.

The warring reactions cancelled each other out, leaving her frozen under his control.

"When you start pushing me away for real, then I'll know I've gotten under your skin. Then, I'm coming after you because I know your heart will finally be vulnerable to me and you'll be mine for the taking. I want your heart, Chelsea. I want it all."

"I don't have that to give. Not to you. Not to anyone."

Threading his fingers through hers, he gave her the same look he'd given her at the psychic reading. The look that said, 'I got you,' and his lasso tugged at her chest, willing her to give in to him.

"We'll see," he mouthed.

It was his promise.

How could she be sure he'd keep it?

Chapter Thirteen

Skeletons

"Antonio, it's me." Greyson made himself comfortable in Matteo's office chair as he phoned home.

"Grey. What are you up to?" Antonio yawned down the line.

Grey checked the time, they'd be finishing up their breakfast after tending to the animals.

"Just checking in before I have to go to class."

"You have to do classes? Like what, how to sift flour?"

"No, smart ass. I'm learning accounting. How are things?"

"Things are fine, if we ignore Papà. He could chew up nails and spit out a barbed wire fence. He hates his brother. *Hates* him. I don't know what uncle Matteo did, but it was unforgivable in Papà's eyes."

"What about Mama?"

"She's been extra quiet."

Grey dug his fingers through his hair and hung his head.

"Lory's been coming around more often. She was broken up when you left. Her brother wasn't impressed."

"You know we were never more than friends."

"I know that, but I don't think she did. And Clay definitely didn't."

"Shit." He pinched the bridge of his nose.

"Yeah, shit."

"Would you look after her for me? Tell her I'm sorry, but she knew I had to go. And, Clay … I'll let him get a punch in next time I'm in town."

"I'll take care of her. Don't worry about it. Just do us proud. Don't fuck things up and you can rub your success in Papà's nose one day."

"Naw. I'm not gonna do that. It didn't help Matteo none. Kiss Mama for me."

He hung up, jerking when he found Matteo standing over him.

"Phoning home?"

"Yeah, sorry."

Matteo's hand swiped through the air, wiping away the apology. "How's your mama?"

"Quiet."

"Hmph." He whipped off his glasses and polished the lenses on the hem of his jacket, grinding his teeth with an audible crunch.

Grey looked a little closer, hoping to unlock Matteo's secrets. "Can I ask you somethin'?"

"That depends on what it is."

"What happened between you and Papà?"

Matteo's mouth pinched and he shut the door behind him before crossing his arms. His eyes flicked to the bookshelf and landed back on Grey as he sighed.

"He's sore because I'm better looking and more successful."

"Isn't that a matter of opinion? The ranch is plenty profitable. Have you looked in the mirror lately? You're no silver fox."

"It's water under the bridge," Matteo spat, reaching for the door handle.

Nuh uh, you're not getting away that easily. "Then why is Papà still mad as a bull?"

"Because his firstborn followed in the footsteps of his wayward brother."

"Nope. It's more than that."

Matteo threw back his head, releasing a barrage of Italian expletives on a gust of superheated air. Grey relaxed back on the bench, letting them wash over him.

"I can't tell you what happened."

Grey's dark eyebrow twitched. "Why not?"

"Because it involves other people, and they don't want the truth revealed."

Matteo stared him down, stumbling forward like he was going to drop the great weight he'd been lugging around on his spine. Whatever the secret was, it was heavy. Grey watched as his uncle scowled at the bookshelf, unfolded his arms, and left.

Crossing the room, Grey studied the shelf. Cook books, business manuals and photos of his family …

His family.

Who else was involved? And why didn't they want the truth exposed?

A thought rammed into Grey's brain and his head cranked towards the door. It must have something to do with him. His leaving the ranch and coming here rattled the old skeletons.

What the fuck were they hiding?

————

Chelsea leaned her chin on her hand and stared through the page of her book as her pencil tapped repeatedly on the paper.

Jenna snatched the pencil and threw it down on the bed, snapping her fingers under Chelsea's nose. "Focus. Exams are next week."

Spinning her desk chair around, Chelsea sighed. "Can we take a break?"

Jenna's jaw dropped like she'd noticed a second head growing out of Chelsea's neck. "We only started half an hour ago."

"Really? It feels like a couple of hours." She spun the chair again, stopping when she heard the snap of Jenna's book shutting.

"If you're not going to study, I'll go home. I can't fail. I'll lose my scholarship."

"Don't go. I'm sorry." Chelsea sprang up from her seat. "Do you want some sweet tea?"

"God, no. I need coffee if I'm going to get through all this." Jenna's hand slapped on the heavy book before checking that her bun was still secure.

"Okay. One coffee comin' up."

Moving down to the kitchen, she prepared the coffee maker and poured herself a cup of sweet tea, sipping while checking through the collection of flyers that had accumulated in a haphazard pile on the counter. With Grey's words still stuck in her craw, she swallowed her tea down like she was trying to wash them out of their foothold. He'd slapped down the gauntlet in the gentlest of ways, and now she had to form a game plan, when she should be more worried about studying. This seemed overwhelmingly more imperative. Like if she didn't take this chance, there was no do-over with him or anyone else.

Hannah waltzed through the front door, dumping her bags and keys on the dining table. "Hey, babe. I hope you're making coffee."

Chelsea put her thoughts aside and removed another mug from the cupboard. "Bad day?"

"The worst." Flopping into a chair, Hannah pulled the elastic from her braid and combed out the light brown waves with her fingers.

"Dare I ask?"

"My professor said I'm going to fail if I don't get a ninety in the exam. I have two weeks to cram my brain with molecular biology facts or I'm done."

Leaning both elbows on the counter, Chelsea pouted her bottom lip. "Oh, honey, I'll just give you the coffee pot once I've poured a cup for Jenna."

"Jenna's here?" Hannah's eyes sparked back to life.

"Yeah, we're studying. But she's threatening to leave if I don't stop procrastinating."

"You …? Procrastinating?" Hannah dipped her head, eyeing Chelsea over the rim of her glasses. "Are you sick?"

She thought about how Grey lingered in her brain cells, waiting to seep into every spare thought. Like an infection.

"Yeah, sort of."

"Mm." Hannah's gaze locked onto Chelsea's, lighting up with mischief. "It wouldn't have anything to do with a cowboy would it?"

Technically, he wasn't a cowboy anymore. "Nope."

"Oh, I see what you're doing. A chef, then?"

"He's not a chef, yet."

"Apprentice chef." She blew a raspberry. "Semantics. You have it bad for the new hottie in the kitchen."

Letting her head fall into her hands, Chelsea groaned. "Ugh. Yes, I do."

"So, take him to bed. Save a horse." Hannah threw in a wink like she needed to emphasize her meaning.

"He's not ready." God, that sounded so stupid when she said it out loud.

"*Pfft*. Honey, are you the Chelsea that I think you are? Because she'd have made it happen."

"I can't force him to want me."

"He already wants you. He's a walking boner when you're near. He's just being stubborn. Seduce him, for Christ's sake."

Watching the dark brown liquid swirl as she poured it into the mugs, she contemplated Hannah's advice. Steam heated her face and clouded her vision, but cleared her perspective. Why hadn't she just seduced him? What man could resist a woman he's attracted to when she makes it obvious she wants to get down and dirty? That guy didn't exist.

"Honey, you're a genius. You are going to kick ass on that molecular bio exam. Grab your coffee and come study with us."

"Okay. Let me have a shower first. I need to cleanse myself of the load of crap I faced today."

She pushed a mug towards Hannah. "Drink the coffee first. You look like you need it. We'll see you in there."

Taking the other drinks, she took the stairs to her room, careful not to spill them.

"Hey."

Jenna's head snapped up, her eyes taking a moment to refocus on her surroundings.

"Wow, you really get into it when you're studying, don't ya?"

"Isn't that the point?"

"Well, yeah. Here's your coffee."

"Bless your heart." Jenna blew across the surface before sipping the brew.

"Listen to you, sounding all southern." A grin tugged at Chelsea's lips.

"You rub off on a person. It's hard not to go 'round saying 'y'all,' after spending a day in your company."

"Y'all is a legit contraction. I don't know why y'all insist on saying 'you guys.' Last time I looked, I didn't have a set of balls between my legs."

"I'll take your word for it."

"Is it okay if another person joins us?"

"Depends on who it is."

"Hannah needs to cram for her molecular biology exam."

Shades of pink rushed over Jenna's cheeks. "Oh. Hannah."

"Yep. Why? Who were you hoping for?"

"I wasn't hoping for anyone in particular. She's doing science? I pictured her more as a philosophy major."

"Ha. Maybe a minor. But she wants to be able to pay her bills, just like the rest of us."

"Which I won't be able to do unless we study."

"Right. Shutting up now."

Jenna put her pen down and relaxed back against the pillow. "Did you hear that Greyson has to work as a server as part of his rotations requirement?"

Chelsea snorted, pulling her glass away from her mouth just in time before she made a mess. "Seriously?"

"Yeah, he's rostered on tomorrow night. I think Matteo is sparing him from the weekend rush. Mainly because it'll hurt the restaurant to put a newbie on a busy night. Dane cackled like a villain when he found out."

"I'm sure he did. Who's Grey buddied up with for training?"

"Who's training? Hi Jenna." Hannah plonked herself and her books on the end of the bed, stretching her legs across, and leaning her back against the wall.

She'd thrown on a pair of ripped jeans and a loose T-shirt—also ripped—that hung off her shoulder, exposing her tattoo.

"Greyson is doing some time in the front of house," Chelsea offered, because Jenna must've singed her tongue on coffee, or something, the way her mouth opened and closed like a fish. And she might've had an eyelash in her eye because she was furiously blinking.

"Chelsea has to train him on how to give service," Jenna's voice crackled out.

Her tongue returns! What had Hannah said about her *gadar* pinging? All sorts of vibes were zipping between the two. Chelsea was probably flushed too.

"I was just telling Chelsea she needed to teach him how to service her. What a lucky coincidence."

Jenna's head jerked back. "I'm sorry, did you just …?" Jenna's timid question accompanied another blush.

"Yes, she means what you think she did. She's worse than me."

"Sex is a natural thing. I don't get why they're dancing around each other. If you like someone and they like you too, you should just be together. There's nothing stopping them." Hannah stabbed a pencil through the messy knot of hair on top of her head and flipped open her textbook.

"I guess so." Jenna's face twisted like Hannah had hit a raw nerve. She started gathering her things. "I'm going to study at home. Thanks for the coffee."

"Oh, okay. Anytime. Do you want me to walk you to the station?"

"No. It's not that far. I'll see you tomorrow. Bye, Hannah." She backed out of the room, hugging her bag to her chest.

Dropping her pen, Chelsea pushed her chair back, ready to follow Jenna out, but Hannah bounced off the bed.

"I'll see her out. I think I upset her."

"Would you mind? Thanks, Hannah."

"Not at all. I'll be back soon. I might take Ryan's car. He won't mind."

"Okay."

Turning back to her books, Chelsea sighed. Now her concentration was shot too. What had upset Jenna? And the coffee aroma was too damn tempting. She figured she'd grab one, since they were in for a long night of cramming. And an even longer period of torture the next night. A whole shift with Greyson taggin' along.

Lord help her.

————

Greyson watched the way Chelsea's ponytail bounced, and how her hips swayed as she weaved through the restaurant, setting up for service. He was one lucky sonofabitch. He got to tail that ass all night. Pity he had to concentrate on his job at the same time.

She handed him an order pad and an apron, stocked with pens and a waiter's friend. "When you write the customer's orders, do it in the sequence in which they're seated. That way you can serve the right dish to the right customer without asking who ordered what. It's more professional."

Shoving the notepad in the apron, he tied it on while following her to the bar. Carafes of water lined the shelves of a fridge behind the bar where Beau was busy restocking the fridges.

"Hey, Beau." Barely missing a beat, she continued the rundown of his duties. "Never let the water run out. Keep an eye on all your tables whenever you're on the floor, because people will want to order drinks. Be careful of dousing the tables in alcohol. Too much will cause you problems. Beau keeps an eye on that too, but it pays to be aware."

Well, hell, there was more to this than he thought. He stopped watching her lips and started paying attention to the words slipping past them.

Following her to the host's station, he couldn't resist a peek at that ass again. "Spread the napkins on their laps after seating, and before handing them the menu. Dane does this, mostly, but you might have to, on occasion. You need to memorize the menu and any special dishes the chef decides to add, depending on his trip to the market. Customers will want to know how things are cooked and what each dish is like. You shouldn't have a problem with that." Her hand trembled as she passed him a menu.

She was nervous. *Well, color me surprised.* He couldn't find enough spit to swallow as his blood pumped harder. Grey shook his head to snap himself out of a lustful haze.

"Chelsea." He touched her arm to get her attention as she marched through the room. "Take a breath."

Peering over her shoulder, eyebrows raised, she finally came to a halt. "Sorry. Am I dumping too much on you at once, sugar?"

She wasn't sorry at all, but the 'sugar' she threw in sweetened her sarcasm and got his pants growing uncomfortably tight. "Definitely." He refused to adjust himself.

Her beautiful blue eyes dropped to his neck, slipping slowly down to his belt, before darting back to the server's station. She cleared her throat and squared her shoulders. "This is where we restock everything."

"How long have you worked here?"

"Over three years."

"Why did you go to a college in Boston? Why not Alabama?"

She fiddled with the silverware before facing him. "Scholarship. But I figured a different experience would be a good idea. I needed to spread my wings before I settled into a fulltime career."

"What if you end up staying here?"

Arms crossed, she leaned a hip against the bench. "That's not gonna happen."

"Why not?" Hooking his thumbs in the top of his apron, he pushed down the lump of unease in his throat.

"Because I have plans."

Why did he feel like he should fall to his knees and beg?

"Plans can change."

"Maybe if nobody is relying on you to follow through, they can. But I'm not letting my mama down."

"I respect that."

He hated it, but he respected it.

Tilting her head, she gave him an amused smile that had his heart forgetting what to do. "Can we get back to work now?"

Exhaling, he memorized the shape of her smile. "Yeah. We can do that."

She turned away from him again. As much as he liked the view, he decided that he didn't like watching her walk away. He'd rather she was running towards him, ready to jump, so he could grab two hands full of that ass and kiss her stupid.

He caught up, watching her add a setting to a table. "Are you going home for Christmas?"

"Yeah. I'm leaving in two days." Her smile stretched her lips and crinkled the corners of her eyes.

Adrenaline swamped him under a tide of want. He had to blink. It was as if the emotion behind her answer lifted a veil, and let him see her, unguarded and real. Excitement transformed her from gorgeous to utterly stunning. His body bunched, ready to strip away her shield and get tangled up with the woman who hid beneath. He could see himself with her, burning brightly together, building an amazing life. Driving each other crazy. Hell if he knew what he'd do when she left for good.

If.

If she left.

Grey knew he was staring, but he couldn't wrench his eyes away.

"What about you? Is Matteo giving you some time off to go home?"

Home? His forehead bunched. Was that even his home anymore? It didn't feel like it, and that made his lungs squeeze a little.

"Are you kidding? I'm the new guy. I have to get through my probation period before he'll let me outta here."

"Don't you get special treatment, being family, and all?"

"No, Chelsea. I have to prove myself just like every other schmuck. What is it with you and the family thing?"

"Nothing. I just thought, maybe since he's your uncle he might want to give you time to see your folks."

"I'm spending Christmas Day working. With my uncle. I will be with family."

"Lucky you. That's great."

"Quit the sarcasm, sweetheart. I am lucky to finally be working where my heart is. I'd rather be here than home any day." He tugged on his apron. "I miss my siblings and my mama and Nonna, but that's where it ends."

Liar. He missed his Papà too. He was just too pissed to admit it.

"I wasn't being sarcastic. I do think it's great. You're fortunate to have an uncle who cares about you and your future. A lot of people don't have that."

"I know."

He watched her thoughtfully as she busied herself, avoiding his eyes.

"What about you? Do you have that?"

"I have my mama."

"No uncles?"

"Nope. Just great friends. Sometimes a girl's gotta pick her own family." Smoothing the table cloth, her shoulders lifted on an inhale before she faced him. "Let's go test your knowledge of the wine list before the doors open."

Her evasiveness ground his patience to a stub. She wasn't like an onion where the layers were easy to peel off ... she was a hundred-year-old tree. If he wanted to get to the center, he needed to wield a saw.

But, it was Grey that felt severed. Here was this woman who'd been raised by a single mom, with no other family to rely on, and she'd gone clear across the country to make something of herself. All she wanted to do was get home and use that knowledge to build something she could share with her mama.

He had a family that loved him and he'd turned away in a selfish search for what? Notoriety? Acclaim? Wealth?

Was it even worth it? Why couldn't he take the experience and knowledge he was going to gain and take it home with him? Make something lasting he could share with his family ... with Chelsea?

If she'd have him.

But he'd still have to get through two years with Matteo. He got the impression his uncle would be as happy about him leaving as his father was.

"After you."

Chapter Fourteen

Did We ...?

Matteo said this was meant to be a slow night. Grey's head was damn near ready to spin off his neck. The entrées had gone out on a few of their tables, with a couple already up to mains, and new parties were still lining up at the door. He was used to being busy. He'd grown up busy. It was putting on a smile and being polite and accommodating that he was having trouble with. Was it so hard for people to say thank you? And what the fuck was it with people clicking their goddamn fingers? He'd pictured herding a few assholes out the door already. At least in the kitchen, he could set his tongue free. Cuss words were cleansing.

There was nothing like spitting out 'fuck' or 'shit', or 'sonofabitch' when things weren't going his way.

Chelsea moved from one task to the next, all with a smile on her face and a hop in her step. She had a way about her that put the customers at ease, and had them enjoying their night before the food even arrived. The service staff held a lot of power in this business. They could make or break a restaurant. He hadn't really thought about more than the food, until now.

Dropping off another order to the kitchen, Grey made his way back to the floor where Chelsea was greeting a new party in their section. He slowed his steps, noticing the stiff set of her shoulders and the clipped tone of her voice, and struggled to keep his own composure. Whatever had her back up, set his hackles rising too.

He tacked on a smile and moved beside her, sizing up the party of four gentlemen in business suits. "Good evening, folks. My name is Greyson and I'll be assisting Chelsea with your service this evening. Would anybody like a drink to get started?" *Motherfuckers.*

See? He felt better just thinking it.

Gold cufflinks winked under the dim light as one of the men adjusted his tie, his predatory blue stare ignoring Greyson and following Chelsea as she retreated a step.

"How is your mother?"

A bit of southern flavored his accent, the words dripping with threat. Grey moved over, shielding her from potential harm. If this guy knew Chelsea's mom, it definitely wasn't on good terms. Grey wasn't real interested in giving him a five-star evening. Maybe a boot out the door. Now, that would be fun.

She stepped around Grey, order pad in hand, smile fastened tight. "You know as well as I do, that's none of your business." Directing her attention to the other members of the party, she licked her lips and poised her pen. "What would y'all like to drink?"

"Uh—"

A chubby guy in pinstripes started to speak up before being cut off by the blond in cufflinks.

"A bottle of Bollinger, on ice. Is she still making those delightful cakes?"

His stare hadn't detached from Chelsea, but she matched it with her own cool blue return.

"One Bollinger comin' right up, gentlemen. I'll let Greyson take any other drink orders while I get you some water and the wine." Spinning on her heel, she aimed for the bar, stopping to check on another table as she went.

Questions jostled for freedom as Grey turned back to the man, pen threatening to snap under the pressure of his clenched fist.

"I'd like a beer." The guy in pinstripes put up a finger, daring to step into the minefield about to blow.

Good, 'cause I'd like to go to the bar, motherfucker. Grey took down the other requests and left them without another word. He wasn't cut out for this shit.

Chelsea had some explaining to do.

Following his tunnel vision, he was sure his boots made tracks on the floor as he traced her steps, finding her behind the bar, filling an ice bucket.

"Who's the guy?"

His question rolled off her shoulders as she kept scooping without sparing him a glance. "Table nine just arrived. Could you go and greet them, please? I'll check on the entrées for seven before taking ten's order."

"Cut the shit, Chelsea. Who is he?"

The metal scoop clanked off the side of the ice bin as she threw it back down. "No, Grey, you cut the shit. We don't have time for this right now, and it's none of your damn business anyways. The customers are waiting. Get your ass moving." Hefting the bucket and stand, she took off.

Once again, he found himself watching her walk away as he ground his teeth together. It was unbelievable how he'd grown to hate that view after just a couple of hours.

"Don't just stand there, man, step on the gas." Beau poured a couple of martinis from a cocktail shaker, adding them to a tray for another server.

"I need a Bud and two shots of Grey Goose for table ten."

Grey collected his own tray and began loading it with a carafe of water and glasses, while Beau made the drinks.

"Do you see the blond guy in the suit looking at Chelsea like he wants to grind her under his shoe?"

"Yeah. Who is he?"

"I thought you might know. You've never seen him before?"

"Nope. Is he a problem?"

"I think he might be, but I don't know. He knows her and her mom. She was real tetchy around him."

"Sorry, man. I don't know who he is. I'll keep an eye on him, though."

"That'd be great, thanks."

Sliding the tray off the bar, he nearly tipped its contents onto Dane when he materialized from thin air.

"For fuck's sake, Dane, stop doing that."

"Tsk. No swearing in the restaurant." Dane held a hand under the tray to help steady it and jerked an elbow towards table ten. "Who's the douche?"

"We'd all like to know." Beau checked out the party of suits with a keen eye.

Dane's eyes were checking out Beau. "You've had your hair cut. Looks good."

"Uh, thanks. Kelly cuts it for me." Beau spun his wedding ring on his finger before he rubbed a hand over his hair.

"Lucky girl."

Grey cut in, "Are you ADHD? We were talking about the douche on ten, remember? What name are they booked under?"

"It's a business name. I checked when I saw our girl drop her happy. Winchester, O'Neil. Don't ask me what they do."

"Could you do me a solid and watch him? I don't like the way he's lookin' at Chelsea, and she's not talking either. Something's not right."

"Sure thing, cowboy." Dane trotted off.

Beau dipped his chin. "We've got you. Better get moving with that tray."

He served the drinks to the table and caught up with Chelsea at the server window in the kitchen.

"I'll look after ten tonight."

"Here, help me with these meals for seven."

Stacking the plates up his arm, he watched her through narrowed eyes. He wasn't letting her dismiss him on this. "I'm serving ten tonight."

"No, you're not. Those guys will be assholes if they smell fresh meat. I know how to deal with them. Just let me handle it."

"Chelsea—"

"Grey … are we doing this again? I said I could handle them. Thanks for your concern, it's real sweet of you. But I'm a big girl." She started out for the floor before hesitating. "Don't forget to greet table nine. The customers don't like to be kept waiting."

He growled at her hasty retreat. It was tempting to frisbee the plates across the room, taking out the asshole who was still staring Chelsea down. But instead, he put on his game face and did his job. Sometimes, customers were pricks. That was part of the job. But the fact that this guy had asked about her mother … that didn't sit right with Grey. Matteo wouldn't want his staff being harassed, and neither did Grey.

The suits were officially on notice.

––––––––

Chelsea yanked her elbow out of a punishing grasp, and turned to face the asshole attached to the offensive hand. It wasn't the first time he'd laid a hand on her. It would damn well be the last. His blue eyes appeared murky with alcohol soaked malevolence. She'd have to cut him off soon. His reflexes were slowing, and that had to be an advantage in her court.

"My chicken is dry and tasteless. Take it back, I want another. And I'll have a glass of your finest whiskey. A double on the rocks."

His diction showed no signs of overdoing it, each word perfectly pronounced. A perfectly polished act to fool the unsuspecting masses. Chelsea knew better than to let her guard down.

"Certainly." *Asshole.*

She noted the guy in pinstripes licking his fingers as he ate the exact same dish of chicken. No way was it fucking dry. She took it anyway, detouring via the bar to order the whiskey. If the asshole wanted to wait even longer until he got to eat, that was his problem. If he was looking to get his meal comped he was shit out of luck. She knew he could afford to pay for the entire restaurant's meals tonight, and her service had been outstanding despite her picturing various ways to torture him with each visit to the table. Sticking a fork in his eye, pouring hot chili sauce in his lap, flipping his table over so that it accidentally landed on top of him ... all fantasies that would never be realized. Such a shame. The asshole deserved it.

Had he known that she worked here and decided to annoy the hell out of her? Probably not, but he'd better not come back.

Grey passed her on his way back from the server's station. "What's wrong with the chicken?"

"Nothing."

"Does someone have his taste buds up his ass?"

"You're not cut out for service, are ya, Grey? And, no, someone has his head up his ass."

She collected the glass from the bar, thanking Beau who looked like he was crunching gravel as he told her, "Last one. I'm cutting him off."

Heaviness jarred each leg as she travelled back to deliver. The asshole was getting under her skin. Her teeth hurt with the effort required to construct a smile for him as she offered the drink. He pulled the whiskey out of her hand before she managed to place it down. Amber liquid spilled over her, and on the arm of the guy sitting beside him.

"Aargh, you stupid girl. What a waste. Go and get me another."

"I don't think so. That was intentional on your part." She sucked the dripping beverage from the back of her hand. "Mm. That's a good drop. Enjoy your drink. It's your last for the night."

"Your mother tried to give me the same line, but I shut her up. Showed her who was the boss."

Red spots burst across her vision and her limbs pumped with strength, ready to deliver a whupping. "Shut your mouth about my mama. You don't get to disgrace her name anymore. Get out of my restaurant."

"Your restaurant? That's laughable. And your mother did a fine job of disgracing her name all on her own, raising a bastard child."

Her nostrils flared as she sucked air in and forced it back out. Her arm twitched with the need to slap him across the room, but she held back. Not only because she didn't want to jeopardize her job, or the restaurant's reputation, but because she knew he wanted to humiliate her. Years of hurt and anger welled in her eyes, poised to spill and feed this man's craving for another's pain. Wrapping her arms around her middle, she prayed for control, blinking back the tears.

"You need to leave." Grey's heavy hand landed on the man's shoulder as his other laid a check presenter on the table. "Here's the bill. Don't come again."

"You must be joking. I'm not paying for anything. The service was atrocious."

Grey leaned down, baring his teeth and spearing the man with molten metal eyes. "I am half a second away from—"

Beau loomed large on Grey's other side, spreading a hand on his chest as a warning to back off before he did something stupid. "If you don't pay we'll call the cops. And we know who you work for. It's your choice."

"Here, take my card." The guy in the pinstripe suit slipped his plastic into the folder as he stood. "I'm done with this evening. Thank you for the delicious food and excellent service. I apologize for my colleague. It would seem he can't handle his liquor."

Oh, he could handle his liquor well enough. It was having his mistakes thrust under his nose that he didn't like. Some things haunted a person forever, no matter how hard they tried to get rid of them.

———

Air vibrated in the back of Chelsea's throat as it whistled through her nose, producing a snore loud enough to wake her. She blinked against the glare coming through the crack in the curtains, and flopped a rubber hand up to wipe away the drool she felt cooling the corner of her mouth. *Gross.* The scent of alcohol and vomit assaulted her nose, combining with the acid taste on her tongue, and she gagged a little. Tentatively, she tried to stretch out her legs, but found one of them trapped under a leaden weight. Levering her head off the pillow, she snapped her eyes open when she saw a muscled male limb bent over hers. Following it up, she discovered a sleepy Greyson curled beside her, wearing only his boxers.

"Holy shit," she whispered, desperately searching her foggy memories for a clue as to how he got there.

And why was she only in her underwear? Wincing, she slid out from underneath him, feeling every muscle groan and her stomach protest as she headed for the bathroom. The reflection in the mirror made her clench her eyes shut and whimper. After relieving herself, she stripped down and showered, scrubbing the heck out of her skin before scraping last night off the inside of her mouth. God, she hoped she hadn't kissed him in the state she was in. What the hell had happened? Last thing she remembered, she was finishing up her tasks and then slipping behind the bar to grab a bottle of Jack, telling Beau to put it on her tab.

Wrapping her body in a towel, she tiptoed back to the room, and found him sitting up and blinking the sleep out of his eyes. Dark, tousled waves framed his scruffy face, caressing his shoulders and chest where they bunched, as he pressed two fists into the mattress beside his hips. His boxer shorts strained where his cock greeted the morning. Her core clenched at the sight of him, and she swallowed down her filthy thoughts.

Tossing her dirty underwear in the laundry basket, she went to her chest of drawers for a fresh set. "Good morning."

"Morning," his voice rumbled out, doing delicious things to her insides.

Down, girl.

Hiding behind her closet door, she slipped on her panties under the towel.

"Thanks for bringing me home. I'm assuming you drove."

She dropped the towel, hooking her bra in place before reaching for a T-shirt and jeans.

"Yeah, I drove."

Mm, that morning voice. She could get used to hearing that.

"Can I ask what happened?"

"You snore."

"I do not."

"When you're drunk, you do."

She bit the corner of her lip. He had her there. "What else do I do when I'm drunk?"

"I need to wash up first, then we'll talk."

We'll talk. What did that mean? Her mind flashed back to a life she'd rather forget. Most of it a blur, thanks to the annihilation of brain cells by alcohol. She remembered enough of it to regret it all.

Rubbing the goose bumps from her arms, she tamped down the rising shame.

Let go of the blame.

Yeah, I'm trying, Beth. I'm trying.

She hadn't been drunk since Beth died.

Until last night.

Chelsea had a damn good reason to get shitfaced. But that was done now. Her father wouldn't be getting through the doors of Abbiocco again. No way in hell would anyone let that happen.

And bless his cotton boxers, Grey had seen fit to make sure she got home safe. He was determined to be her protector. The man was not going to let this go. She had to wonder why she was fighting it so hard when at this stage, it seemed inevitable. If two people were truly meant to be together, wouldn't they figure out the insurmountable and make it happen?

As she turned away from the closet, she found his heavy-lidded eyes watching her in the mirror across the bed. *Shit.* She'd forgotten about the mirror. He'd seen everything.

A thrill rushed through her. There was no challenging the need he provoked in her. There was only submission.

She let it pull her towards him a step, not knowing how she managed to leave any space between them at all. He adjusted his crotch as he stood, brushing close as he passed her on the way to the bathroom.

Sinking down on the bed, fear, lust, and longing, formed a tossed salad of emotions in her head. Desire for him seized her body into a mass of wild fire. She didn't know what had happened between them, the lost time blemishing the moment. But, she wanted him now. She wanted to cement their connection in stone.

He entered the room wearing a towel around his waist, and closed the door quietly behind him. Eyes locked on hers, he came to sit beside her, resting a hand behind her on the bed.

"The bathroom smells like you."

She watched him from the corner of her eye, breathing in the mouth-watering smell of freshly showered man, and checking out the contours of his body. All that smooth, bronzed skin was distracting as hell.

"I'd say you do too, but my soap smells earthy on you, not sweet. Your skin will be as smooth as a baby's butt now." She itched to test her theory with a brush from her fingertips. But maybe she'd already done that? "Please tell me you didn't use my toothbrush."

"I found a spare in the drawer."

Oh, good boy.

She spun to face him. "Did we …?"

One dark eyebrow winged up. "You tried your hardest, but I resisted your charms."

Her spine curved forward. "I was that bad, huh?"

"I prefer my partner to be conscious and in control of her digestive tract when I take her to bed … or in the car …"

"The car?"

"Yeah. You wanted to test out the springs in the back seat."

I'm sure I did. How 'bout you put on a shirt before I do something embarrassing.

She sucked air between gritted teeth. *Oh, shit. What if I—*

"Did I vomit in the car?"

"I grabbed one of the ice buckets before we left. I don't think Matteo will be wanting it back."

"Ugh." She cringed, panic gripping her throat. "Do I still have a job?"

"Yeah, I think you're safe." He moved a damp curl off her shoulder, and pinned her with a stare. "So, that guy last night. You said he got your mama pregnant?"

"Oh, I told you that?"

"Is he the devil's asshole?"

Rubbing her palms on her jeans, she pulled the story together in her throat, preparing to purge it.

"Yes. My ... father. He came to town on a business trip and visited the little bakery my mama was workin' in. She lived in Texas and was only eighteen at the time. He was charming and good looking ... and married. But she didn't know that. He got her pregnant before he left to go back home to his wife in Alabama." Peeking at him, she found thunder in his stare. "He came back to town on another trip, expecting to pick up where they left off. When she told him she was carrying me, he got spittin' mad. He threw a bunch of money at her, told her she had to get rid of me, and that I'd never have his name."

"And your mama told him to go to hell?"

"I'm sitting here telling the story, aren't I? She got a black eye and a cracked rib for her trouble. She nearly lost me."

"I'm guessing that was his plan. Total asshole."

"Devil's asshole."

Grey's hands curled over his knees. "Do you think he came in to see you?"

"No. I think he'd rather forget I'm alive. That's how I feel about him. I'm guessing it's mutual."

"How did you know it was him? I mean, has he seen you since you were born?"

"Ha. Yeah. He came to town a few times while I was growing up. He'd leave flowers for mama on the doorstep; a bunch of pink roses with their heads cut off. Not that we can prove it. He came to the school a few times and watched me from the parking lot. When mama came to get me, she saw him and freaked out. That's when I found out who he was."

"What the fuck? Do I need to worry about him coming back and hurting you?"

"No." She hoped.

Grey's gaze probed for the truth behind her mask of innocence. He wasn't buying it. She wasn't sure if she was either. She'd become an expert at making herself believe she was okay, when the reality was nothing but shitty. The visit from her father rattled her enough to send her to the bottom of the bottle. Maybe it wouldn't be so bad to have someone look out for her. Letting him into her vulnerable center would be so easy, but keeping him at bay was exhausting. Why couldn't she just let go?

"I'm going to worry no matter what you say. If I see that asshole again, I'll rip his balls off as payback for the flowers and as a service to humanity."

"Violence should not be sexy, but damn, you take it there. Especially in that towel. Don't think I haven't noticed you're practically naked." She flicked a pointed finger at his attire.

"I've seen you mostly naked. I think it would only be fair for me to lose the towel."

Her mouth dropped open so she could drag in some oxygen, and her heart went from a steady thud to a riotous beat.

"Do it," she dared.

"Lose the shirt, first." His eyes dropped to where her nipples poked at the fabric.

"I guess I am a ways behind." She pulled the shirt over her head, dropping it on the floor.

His throat bobbed and the towel twitched in response. Rising to her feet, she moved in front of him, unbuttoning her jeans as he watched, riveted. The heavy fabric slid slowly down her thighs, gathering at her ankles. Gray eyes travelled up her length, and he gripped her by the waist, pulling her down to straddle him so he could capture her mouth in a searing kiss. Her hands memorized the lines of his back and tangled in his hair, tilting his head so she could delve deeper, get closer. Maneuvering the towel away with her knees, his erection sprang into place against her wet panties. His grunt and her answering mewl tangled in their kiss, as his hands sank into the flesh of her ass, grinding her down against him.

The sensations crashing over her flooded her system, until she felt she was drowning in him. How long had it been since she'd seen him at that gas station? Months. Months of wanting and frustration. She was finally allowed to feast on the buffet.

He twisted so she fell to the mattress and he climbed over her, tucking his knees into her sides. Warm hands pulled her bra away and her brows popped in surprise. She hadn't realized that he'd undone the hooks. She was glad to see the damn thing get flung across the room, as his mouth sank down on one greedy nipple. Her body arched in pleasure, asking for more. He delivered with each stroke of his tongue and grasp of his palms.

The fever built, until his hands slowed and his mouth pulled away, his silver-flecked gaze locking on to something deep inside her. Some place no one else had ever touched. Her lungs ceased to work. She scissored her legs and pushed against his chest to get some breathing space, and break the hold he had on her. Moving aside, he let her sit up, his face a picture of concern as he watched her struggle for air.

"I'm ... sorry." She couldn't look at his eyes, instead focusing on his legs as they slid into his pants.

"It's okay."

Dropping her head into her hands, she groaned. "Is it?"

"Yes. Do you want to know why?"

"I don't know."

He tugged on her chin, urging her to face him. "It's okay because I finally see you, and you finally see me. When that doesn't scare you anymore, let me know, and we'll finish what we started. But, sweetheart, don't take too long. I only have so much strength."

He dropped a kiss on her head, leaving her to wonder if she was the biggest idiot on the planet, or the smartest woman alive. It wasn't just about getting him out of her system anymore. He pumped through her veins just as surely as her blood did. There was no separating the two.

It was about whether she could take the deluge once she opened the flood gates. She feared she no longer had a choice but to brace herself and hope for the best.

Gathering her wits enough to get dressed she found her cell on the desk, blinking with a message from Dane.

How was it? Is it true what they say about cowboys?

Aw, shit. Everybody was going to be talking about her drunken fall from grace. She was right back to where she was as a disgraced teenager. The gossip hounds loved her. She'd relished giving them a scandal back then, and didn't give a fuck what people would say now. What happened between her and Grey was none of anyone else's goddamn business.

She tossed the phone down without replying. Screw the boots. She had some packing to do. The trip home to Mama couldn't have come at a better time.

Chapter Fifteen

You're What?

Heat blasted from the vents of his truck as his wipers cleared away the falling snow. It was Grey's first white Christmas. Sure, it was pretty, but driving in the frosty weather sucked. His headlights barely cut through the haze, and he had to flex his fingers to stop them from going numb. He'd been too chicken to brave the crowds and buy himself a decent coat. Some things about city life, he could gladly do without. Draped across his lap, his Nonna's old blanket was doing a fine job of keeping away the chill and reminding him of Christmases at home on the ranch. He rolled with the nostalgia, choosing the best memories rather than recalling his hasty exit and his father's contempt. He couldn't have picked a better way to spend his first Christmas in Boston, cooking Christmas dinner for a select few with his uncle. Except maybe if he was coming home with Chelsea beside him, so he could unwrap her and indulge in his wildest fantasies all night. Now that would've been the perfect Christmas. No doubt she was enjoying her time with her mama. Feeling a pinch in his chest, he rubbed his sternum and shifted his attention back to the flutter of white clogging his wipers.

As he pulled up to Matteo's house, the headlights swept across the front stoop where he thought he saw a dark figure huddled against the cold. Leaving the car idling in the driveway, he got out to take a closer look, his boots crunching in the blanket of flakes.

The figure stretched to its full height, draped in a heavy coat with a hood, gloves and boots, he couldn't make out who the mystery figure was until his boot landed on the bottom step and Lory's pale face was revealed.

"Lory! For Christ's sake, you'll catch your death. Come here." Circling his hands on her waist, he carried her to the truck, depositing her on the seat and covering her with the blanket, before hopping in and slamming the door. "What are you doing here?" He punched the button on the garage remote, waiting impatiently for it to let them into the warmth.

"Merry Christmas to you too, Grey." Her teeth chattered as she spoke.

"Sorry, topolina. Merry Christmas. How long have you been sitting there? Why didn't you tell me you were coming? Why aren't you home with your family?" He pulled on the hand brake, but left the car running so they still had heat.

"An hour, or so. I wanted to see you."

"Is everything okay?"

"Oh, yeah. It's fine. Fine."

"Uh huh. Totally convincing. Let's get into the warm house and you can tell me what's going on."

Helping her out of the car, he led her up the staircase, feeling the temperature rise as they went higher into the living areas.

"The bathroom is through there. I'll light the fire and make us some hot chocolate. We've got some Christmas pudding somewhere too. Would you like some?"

"Could I just have some tea and crackers? I don't know if I can stomach anything heavy at the moment."

A crease folded between his brows. Lory loved hot chocolate and Christmas pudding. "Yeah, sure. We should have some tea somewhere."

He got busy heating the water and building a fire while she disappeared into the bathroom.

For a long time.

Too long.

He made the tea and went to check on her, tapping a knuckle on the door.

"Lory? Are you okay, in there?"

"Be—" Coughing cut off her voice. "Be there in a minute."

"Are you sick?"

More coughing, but no answer. Gripping the handle, he jiggled it.

Locked. Damn it.

Going back to the kitchen, he searched the drawers for something pointy that he could use to unlock the door from the outside. Just as he pulled out a safety pin, she shuffled into the living room and sank into a seat beside the fire.

"Sorry. It's been a long day. I guess it all caught up to me."

"That's okay. You had me worried." The pin tinged against the jumble of odd bits and pieces as he threw it back in and slammed the drawer shut. Picking up their drinks, and a plate of crackers, he went to sit on the sofa across from her, handing her the cup.

"Thanks."

Her smile was too tight, skin too pale. She'd lost weight. What the fuck was going on?

"Do I need to ask again?"

"I'm pregnant."

"You're what?"

"Preg. Nant."

He put his cup on the table and leaned back into the seat.

Wrapping her trembling hands around the warm cup, she blew on the hot liquid, dispersing the steam. His mind ticked over as he registered every altered detail between slow blinks. Her pullover hung limp on her shoulders, and her skinny jeans were too baggy. The blood vessels spread a spidery web over the whites of her dull blue eyes. She wasn't well.

Grey's hands clenched into fists, and he shoved to his feet. "I'm gonna kill him."

"Kill who, Grey? Sit down. It's midnight on Christmas Day."

"Jake Johnson. That sonofabitch."

"It's not his."

He plonked his ass back down and fixed a questioning gaze on hers. "Who, then?"

She chomped down on her bottom lip and stared into her cup. "Toni. Toni is the father."

"Toni? As in Antonio, my brother, Antonio?"

Her eyes flicked to his briefly before locking on to the flickering flames.

Shit. "I told him to look after you, not climb on top of you. Holy hell." Locking his hands behind his head, he dragged them down his neck, and shoved out a breath. "Does anyone else know?"

"Toni knows." The corner of her mouth quirked with sarcasm.

"How did he take the news?"

"The same way you did, but with shorter hair."

Dropping his arms, his hands slapped on his thighs and he gave her a rueful smile. "Sorry. It's a shock. He can't have been too surprised. He was there when it happened."

"I was on the pill. We were careful."

Grey let that stew for a while, fixing his eyes on the way she clung to her cup.

"So, it was a matter of wait and see?"

Her head dipped once. "Yes. Neither of us thought it would actually happen."

"Well, it has. So, what's he gonna do about it?"

"What do you mean, *what's he gonna do about it*? I'm the pregnant one, not him."

"He might not be carrying the bun, but he's responsible for putting it there, and he damn well better look after you while it bakes. I can't believe he let you travel in your state. Have you been eating at all? Your family must've noticed." His concerns came barreling out of his mouth in an uncharacteristic jumble.

"I've been busy elsewhere at meal times. Toni doesn't know I'm here."

"You just took off?"

"Kinda, yeah. I told Clay I was coming to surprise you. Toni probably knows by now."

As if he knew they were talking about him, her phone lit up with Antonio's number where it sat on the coffee table.

"It's him," she croaked, eyes flooding with tears.

"I'll handle it. You drink your tea. There's a spare room, second door on the left, up the stairs. Help yourself. It's late."

She nodded, taking her cup with her.

He punched a finger on the answer button, growling into the phone, "What the fuck have you done?"

"Grey. So, she made it there safely. Thank God. Is she okay?"

"No, she's not okay. She's pregnant, you idiot. Do you know how sick she's been?"

"I know. It wasn't supposed to happen."

"Oh, well that's a relief, because if you'd planned it, I'd have to put your balls through the meat grinder."

"That's rich, coming from you."

"What the fuck did I do? I didn't go dipping my stick where it wasn't wanted."

"She wanted me. She wants me. She was finally over you and she wants me. You left her. It crushed her, Grey. You never saw how much she loved you. She had her future all wrapped up in you, but you were too wrapped up in yourself to see it." Antonio paused, huffing a humorless laugh down the line. "I have loved her since we were kids, but our parents had you two pegged from the beginning. I never stood a chance, until you were out of the picture."

His entire childhood replayed in his mind, but with the benefit of a new perspective. Antonio following them everywhere. Antonio coming to Lory's aid when Grey figured she didn't need any help. Grey catching Lory watching him before she shot her eyes elsewhere. Antonio doing the same with Lory. He'd been a blind dick.

"Why didn't you ever say anything?"

"Would you have listened? What would you have done?"

"I never would've carried on with the farce to keep everyone else happy if I knew it was hurting you so badly. I was trying to do the right thing. I told her early on that I had plans, and that I didn't feel that way about her. I thought she felt the same, and we were both just humoring our parents."

"The only person having a laugh was you."

Fuck. Pressing the heel of his hand to his forehead, he hunched his shoulders, squeezing his eyes closed.

"Where is she?" The question was quiet, like Antonio had lost his strength and needed to have her back.

"She's gone to bed. She was exhausted, and sick."

"I'm coming to get her."

Grey folded his body onto the sofa again, rubbing a hand over his chin. "I don't think she wants to see you."

"Fuck you, Grey. You don't get to tell me what to do."

"Just let me talk to her, okay? She obviously needed to get away for a bit, so give her this time to sort herself out. She's making a huge adjustment."

"Yeah, no shit. It's a huge adjustment for the both of us. But I'm happy about it. I want this baby more than anything. I love her so much. Tell her that for me?"

"I'll tell her … Buon Natale."

"Ha, yeah. Merry fucking Christmas to you too."

The call disconnected. Grey placed it on the table, resting his elbows on his knees, and watched the fire flicker for what felt like hours. How blind had he been? How much had he hurt his childhood friend and his brother?

Swiveling his head, he took in the opulence of the room. Worthy of a magazine cover, it was beautiful and pristine. Unlived in and fucking cold. They didn't even have a Christmas tree. It was Christmas night and Matteo wasn't home by the fireplace with his family. He was at Abbiocco, sorting through a mountain of work. Was this what Grey had uprooted his life for?

After sleeping with Chelsea in his arms, he wasn't so sure. He could still feel the echo of her, the way she'd molded to him, deep in sleep and unaware of the unguarded message her body was sending. She needed him every bit as fiercely as he needed her, but as soon as her brain engaged, she backed off, scared out of her wits. Good. He was under her skin where he wanted to be. But now she was across the country in Alabama.

His biggest competition.

Last night, he'd reached for her, finding only cool sheets beside him. Her absence struck his soul, registering a missing piece that needed to be found. Without her, sleep had eluded him, and fatigue now swamped his weary body. His eyes landed on the stairs he had to conquer before he could collapse, his mind thinking of the woman sleeping above. His brother was probably feeling the same without Lory.

Poor bastard …

Lucky sonofabitch.

Grey was going to be an uncle. Lips spreading in a grin, he thought, *now that's something to be fucking happy about*. That's life and that's real.

He had a lot of shit to sort out.

———

"Merry Christmas, Mama!"

Chelsea dashed from her room to give her mom a huge hug, finding her at the range, cooking a delicious breakfast.

"Oh, Merry Christmas, honey. It's so nice to see your face."

Peeking over her mom's shoulder, Chelsea inhaled the aroma of bacon and eggs.

"Yum, but can't we open the presents first?"

"It's always the same with you. Every year. Presents first, stomach later."

"Priorities, Mama." Diving under the tree, she found the presents she'd bought for her mom and placed them beside her on the bench top.

"I don't want to burn the breakfast. You go get your present and open that first."

"Okay."

The branches scratched at her back as she crouched down again, pine needles falling around her, and the bells on the tree jingling. Spotting an unwrapped UPS box, she pulled that out first, curious who it was for. It was addressed to her, the writing strangely familiar.

"What's this?" She held up the parcel.

"I don't know. It came yesterday. It looks like it came from Massachusetts."

"Boston?"

"I think so. Open it."

She took it to the kitchen, finding a knife to slice through the tape. Inside the box was a simple white box with the words *Manolo Blahnik* written on top. Her breath caught and her heart rocketed behind her ribs.

"No," she breathed.

"What? What is it?" Her mom peeked over her shoulder. "Is that a shoe box?"

"Oh yeah. It's *the* shoe box."

Opening the lid, she found a note on top of the tissue paper.

Babe, Merry Christmas.

I'm giving you the benefit of the doubt.

P.S. Express postage is a bitch. You're welcome.

D x

She squealed, tucking the note in the side of the box so she could fold back the tissue paper.

"Ooh, pretty," her mom cooed.

"Aren't they divine?"

"They look expensive, honey. Who on Earth is sending you a gift like that?"

Her gut twisted. Dane shouldn't be spending an obscene amount of his money on her. It didn't matter that he was loaded and only worked at the restaurant to keep himself occupied.

"My friend, Dane. We had a little wager. It was his idea."

Lame, Chelsea. Lame.

The only reason she'd won the bet was because she'd completely freaked when Grey's stare had reached inside her, doing irrevocable damage to the lock on her heart.

She was undeniably in love with him.

Shit, fuck, shit.

Her mama's brows headed for her hairline. "What kind of wager?"

She put the lid back on the box. "It doesn't matter. I wonder if I can return them?"

"Shoes? I'd say not."

"Well, then, I owe him a day at the spa."

"How are you going to afford that?"

"I've been saving as much as I can. It'll be fine. I owe him. Dane is a good friend." She took out some plates. "Are we going to eat? I'm starving."

Her mama loaded up the plates and they took them to the living room so they could eat beside the tree.

"I didn't think you'd be that hungry after your midnight rummage through the cupboards."

Chelsea's jaw faltered mid chew. "Did I wake you? Sorry, I couldn't sleep."

"You always sleep like a log when you come home. What's on your mind?"

The masticated egg may as well have been pebbles the way it went down. She didn't want to think about Grey, or the fact that she'd gone and fallen in love. She especially didn't want to tell her mama about the confrontation with her father, and that she'd gotten so drunk hours of her life were missing from her memory. Lord knows what she'd have done if Grey hadn't looked after her. Her face screwed up at the thought.

"Good Lord, child, is it that bad?"

Yeah. She put her plate on the table and snapped her teeth together, refusing to answer.

"Ya know, I could always tell you were fine when your mouth moved a mile a minute. It was when you buttoned up that I worried. You haven't said lickety split about that fella of yours. I thought maybe I'd get to meet him this Christmas."

"What? No. We're not—" She rubbed two fingers over her forehead, sorting her jumbled thoughts. "We might be. I don't know what we are. I think I've fallen in love with him ... I *have* fallen in love with him. But, we're on two different paths. He's headed for The Big Apple, and I'm comin' home after graduation." Chelsea tossed up her hands in a gesture of hopelessness. "I never wanted anything serious with a man, but I think Grey and I have gone past the point of keeping it no-strings. If I go there with him, I won't be able to let him go, and that means the life I had planned would be gone forever. I'd hardly ever see you, or the Murphys. I can't see how that would make me happy. It's a no-win situation."

Stuffing a piece of bacon in her mouth to plug it up, she chewed fiercely, reducing her dilemma to a masticated mush that she could swallow.

"Ask me how to bake a cake, or how to make a flower out of powdered sugar, and I can tell you. Ask me about men, and I haven't a clue, sweetie." Mama wiped her mouth with a serviette and dropped it on her plate, leaning back. "When you started runnin' around with boys, I just about pitched a continuous conniption fit for two years before I decided enough was enough. And what happened to Beth ..." She paused, raising red eyes to the ceiling to avert tears. "That could've been you. Moving to 'Bama was the best decision I made. I'm just sorry it caused so much upheaval for the Murphys."

"You couldn't have known what would happen, Mama."

"I know. I tell myself that every time I see those kids with their mama. You know how much I love you. You have been my life. Despite how you were conceived, I thank the Lord every day for the gift of you. I've been content not to have a man in my life. And seeing you now, I am thankful I never had to choose between you and the love of a man. But, given my experience, I would have chosen you, honey. Every time. But how can I give you advice on this situation when I've never been where you are? If the right man came along, maybe I would run away with him." A giggle escaped. "Who knows? You know who you should talk to …? Angel. She had to make that decision at a very young age. You talk to her and see what she says. But, I will say one thing. The good Lord placed him in your path twice for a reason. That's something to take heed of."

She nodded. "I will. Thanks, Mama."

"Don't worry about me. I'll be fine doing what I'm doing. I've managed this far."

"Ooh, that reminds me." Chelsea sprang to her feet, retrieving her mama's present from the kitchen and placing it in her lap. "Go ahead, open it."

A beautiful smile tugged up her mama's lips. "Oh, goodness. I forgot all about the presents."

Ripping open the paper, it took her a few seconds to register what she was seeing. "What is this? Is it—"

"Do you like it? I found a graphic designer in Boston who designed the logo for us." Pulling out an apron, she hooked it over her head. "A sweet roll reading a book while sitting in a wingback chair. I thought it was cute. We can change it if you don't like it, it's not set in stone."

"And a T-shirt to match. Are these the paper bags we'll be using too? Oh! How wonderful. Books, Nooks, and Nibbles." She smoothed a thumb over the picture on the bags. "I love them. Thank you, sweetheart."

A tinge of sadness marred the smile on her mama's face before they hugged.

"I am coming home, Mama. We will do this together."

"Okay, honey." Nodding, she took a seat, crossing her flannel clad legs. "Tell me all about this man. I think he'll be an important part of your future, no matter what you decide."

I think you're right, Mama.

———

The dining room at the Murphy's held so many of Chelsea's best memories of growing up. Every Christmas, since that first one in Alabama, she and her mama had been invited to join the Irish brothers and their brood around the big antique table in the dining room. Thirteen people fit easily. Given the size of the Murphy men, that was a spectacular feat. Everything about the home was huge, including the craic when this group got together. The house had been passed down from Angel's mother's side, but the Murphys made it their own.

Harvey Murphy, the youngest and loudest brother, licked cranberry sauce from his thumb. "That was delicious, Angel. You do your mother proud."

Angel fussed with cleaning Addy's little face, but the little girl squirmed, reaching for more stuffing, and then dropping half of it in her lap. Angel's five cousins were seated at the other end, taking turns cooing over Angel's son, Harrison, who sat quiet and wide eyed, taking it all in.

"Thanks, Uncle Harvey."

"Now, where's Mary's puddin'?" He spread his hands over his belly and winked at Chelsea's mom.

She blushed. "There is no end to your stomach."

Harvey coveted her mama's puddings since he first tasted one. His red-bearded face was a regular fixture at the bakery where she worked.

"It ends where I'm sitting, but I empty it on the regular, so I can fill it all I want." He clinked whiskey glasses with his brother, Harry, who sat across from him, snorting with glee.

Chelsea joined in. She never failed to leave these gatherings without sore cheeks from laughing too much.

"Harvey. The children." Angel's aunt, Dulcie, elbowed her husband in the ribs, turning the color of beetroot. She'd married the man. She should be used to his humor by now.

"When are we going to see the opening of your place?" Angel's Dad asked from the head of the table.

"It'll be a while yet, I think." Her mama's eyes landed on hers briefly, doubt in their depths.

Chelsea's throat squeezed, knowing she'd put it there. "Hopefully in a few years, depending on the finances, and if we can find a suitable place. I've scoped out some bakery equipment places. We should be able to get some quality second-hand equipment for a decent price. I have the numbers of the contractors you recommended to fit the shop. I'm getting all the figures and information together so I know what it will take to start up. Once we have the money and the space, we need to find a designer. Mama will have to work with them on the plans. But first thing's first, I have to find a job."

"You'll have no trouble there. A woman like you would be an asset to any business."

"Thanks, Hank. Let's hope you're right."

If only she knew in which city she should start searching.

Chapter Sixteen

Now She Was Getting It

After lunch, the party moved into the parlor, and Chelsea pulled Angel aside, dragging her to the library.

"What is goin' on, Chelsea?"

"I need your advice."

"Okay, so ask instead of ripping my arm from its socket." Angel rubbed her shoulder, glaring daggers.

"Sorry. I don't know my own strength. Could you please help me make the biggest decision of my life?"

"Sounds ominous. I'll do my best. Shoot."

They took a seat at each end of one of the sofas.

"Fuck, it's cold in here."

"I wasn't expecting to use this room, so I didn't light the fire. Take the throw off the back of the armchair. And stop stalling."

Chelsea tugged the blanket over their legs. "I've fallen in love with the tall drink of water from the gas station."

"I'm sorry, what?" Angel pinned a stare on Chelsea from under her eyelashes. "The guy you met at the diner after you forced me to drop you off, leaving you in possible peril?"

"I'm not proud of my actions, believe me. I'm sorry I did that to you. It turns out he was headed to Boston to work for his uncle, my boss. He's training to be a chef."

"Wow." She raised both hands, spreading her fingers wide.

"Yeah, wow. He can cook. I mean he can really cook. No offense, honey, but his turkey leaves your turkey in the dust." Chelsea wrinkled her nose, all contrite.

"So it should, if he's going to cook for a living. What's the problem?"

"The problem is, he's got New York in his sights and I'm headed back here. Lord, we're not even dating and I'm thinking of forever with him. How stupid is that?"

Angel shrugged. "It's not stupid if you're in love with him. You don't have to be dating someone to fall in love. It's gonna happen if it's meant to be, without the help of candlelit dinners and walks on the beach."

"I thought I could keep him at bay, but he got in under my defenses and now I'm in this goddamn situation where I want to ride him cowgirl style, but I can't because I'll never be able to leave after that. I can't let Mama down. I can't picture a life anywhere but here."

"Can't or won't?" Her friend tilted her head and lifted a brow.

Pushing her hair off her face, Chelsea trapped the air in her lungs as Angel watched through sharp green eyes.

Can't or won't?

She let the question sink down into her heart in search of the truth. Hadn't Grey said that she didn't think she deserved the love of a man? She'd written that part off as trash talk, but maybe he was right. Her own father hated her existence. Had tried to make sure she was never born. And then with what had happened to Beth ... And the reason Chelsea wasn't there to save her.

Chelsea spent years holding all males in contempt. She unashamedly played them before they could play her. The truth was, she craved their affection, starved for something she saw every other girl receive, and not herself.

Hank had done his best as a surrogate father of sorts, but he wasn't hers. Chelsea wanted someone she could claim as her own. Someone who would take her, faults and all. But she had to believe that she was worthy first. That he wouldn't leave her because she wasn't good enough. And she needed to be able to take the huge leap of faith to call Boston home, leaving her mama behind.

"Won't." Dropping her hand, she twisted her mouth to the side in a rueful smile. "How hard was it for you to decide to drop everything to be with Aiden?"

"Easiest decision of my life. I didn't want to leave, but it wasn't a choice for me. I would've found a way to get us back here. I would've fought for us with every breath. I'm just sorry he couldn't do the same." Angel's mouth twisted as she dropped her eyes to her lap.

"Aw, babe. We don't know what that sonofabitch did to him. Don't lose faith in what you had. It was real."

"Then, where is he now?"

"I wish I could tell you." Chelsea paused, shuffling her legs and contemplating whether she should share her other bit of news. After a couple of seconds, she sat up, unable to hold it in. "I saw my sperm donor."

"What!?"

"Yeah. He came into work. I had to serve him. He's still a prick."

"Is he living in Boston now, or just there on work?"

"I didn't get his particulars, Angel. He's a fan of Bollinger, if that helps?"

"Who was he with?" Angel's hand gripped the blanket, her voice trembling with the tentative question.

"Work colleagues. Sorry, hun."

She dipped her eyes again, fiddling with the blanket. "Does your mama know?

"No, I didn't want to tell her. She doesn't need to know. It'll only upset her."

"True. Should I be worried about him returning to hurt you?"

"I don't think so. Grey would have his balls." She smirked at the recollection of his promise.

"He'd protect you against a man like that? He's a keeper, honey. Pure and simple." She reached for Chelsea's hand, giving it a squeeze. "I can't wait to meet him."

She tried to picture Grey here in her world, surrounded by all the people she loved, and damn it, the vision was clear. He would fit right in. But would he be happy being stuck back in a podunk town, with no bright city lights and glory on the horizon?

Boston was big, but New York was massive. Would she be happy living as a speck of dust in an anonymous pile? She pushed the blanket off her legs, feeling claustrophobic and out of control. Sitting on the cusp of change sent ants crawling under her skin. She needed to leave.

"Thanks for the talk, hun. I miss you, ya know? Would you mind dropping me back home? I just need some alone time."

A crease folded between Angel's brows as she searched Chelsea's face. "Sure thing. We'll look after your mama."

Chelsea nodded. "Thanks."

Maybe if she hid somewhere ... she'd never have to choose. Wow, she was screwed up. Hiding wasn't her style. She'd always hit things head on.

Maybe that was exactly what she needed to do.

————

Chelsea hustled to the server window at the sound of the bell letting her know meals were ready. Grey dominated her vision, arms spread wide and taut on the counter as his dirty silver gaze fixed on hers. Two weeks away and his effect on her had not diluted one bit. Her body responded, nipples puckering, core clenching. She had to remember to breathe.

"Table seven's up. Welcome back."

Uhn, that voice stoked the fire licking along her skin. She was so screwed. Angel was right. There was no choice.

Hit this head on.

"Thanks. Merry Christmas and Happy New Year."

He bobbed his head in acknowledgement. "We'll talk after closing. I'll give you a ride home."

A shiver trickled down her back.

"Great. I look forward to it."

Pushing back, he kept his eyes on her as she collected the plates.

The dishes wobbled in her arms. Gulping against a dry throat, she tottered off on liquid legs. Lord, getting through this night without self-combusting was going to be a challenge if she had to see him at the window every time.

Two hours later, she was proven right when she ached all over, not from the work, but from wanting to go to him, her body priming itself every time their eyes clashed.

"You seem nervous. What is going on?" Dane intercepted Chelsea on her way to the bar.

"I'm absolutely fine. And loving my new boots, thank you. Did I say thank you?" She loaded a cold carafe of water onto a tray.

"Only fifty times."

She fumbled, trying to stack glasses for her table. "Good, good. Let me know when you want to go to the spa and I'll book it in, 'kay?"

"You don't owe me the spa, babe."

"I want to do this, Dane. I never should've agreed to that stupid bet in the first place."

He shrugged. "It's your wallet. So, what actually happened after your drunken night of shame?"

She narrowed her eyes, unimpressed at his dig. "Grey was a complete gentleman. He told me he held my hair back while I defiled an ice bucket. Thankfully, I don't remember."

"I know all that already. Grey was tight-lipped about the rest. I know there's more, babe, don't bother denying it. You can't wake up next to that without wanting a taste."

"We may have seen each other partially naked."

"Partially?"

"Grey was in the buff. I still had panties."

"Oh, be still my heart. Please tell me he's all that I think he is."

"He is, but I freaked, and he left before we got to the best part."

Dane clutched at his chest as if he was having a heart attack. "You kill me, woman. What is wrong with you!?"

"Dane, stop holding her up, she's got tables to serve." Jenna rolled her eyes at Dane's dramatics as she stalked past on a mission to the kitchen.

"Yes, Jenna, my love." He called out before leaning into Chelsea. "What is hiding inside that bun, I'd so love to know?"

"It's where she stores her tips."

"I heard that."

"Love you, hun." She grinned at Jenna, blowing her a kiss.

"So, are you together now?"

"Not exactly." She saw one of her customers waving her over. "I gotta go, I'm being summoned."

"We'll talk later."

"Maybe." She raised an eyebrow as she left him behind. "Go answer the phone."

"You're going to leave me hanging, aren't you? Cruel, cruel woman."

Beau gave her strange looks every time she slurped down a cool water to quench her dry mouth. The extra tips were a bonus. She'd never done so well. Apparently, the customers liked their servers ready to go. She hoped she hadn't given out any inappropriate signals, although there had been a couple of napkins with scribbled phone numbers. Lord, was it that obvious how desperate she was?

After the final parties left, she got to work bussing tables, Jenna helping with the flatware while Chelsea took the dishes. Plates and silverware clashed together as they collected them, raising their voices in order to be heard.

"Some guy gave me tickets to the game on Valentine's instead of a tip."

"Seriously?"

"Yep."

"Who's playing?" Chelsea took her loaded bus tub to the next table over, with Jenna trailing her.

"Celtics versus Bucks."

The soft music drifting from the overhead speakers changed to a pumping rock beat to get everyone fired up for the cleanup. She didn't need the beat to get pumped, she'd been hyped all night.

"How many tickets did you get?"

"Four."

"Tickets to what?" Dane came over, wheeling a bus cart.

"The basketball. Would you like to come?"

He recoiled, screwing up his face. "Ew. No, thanks." Smoothing his fingers over his eyebrows, he regained his composure. "I only watch sports if the uniforms consist of tight pants."

"What about you, Chelsea?"

A game at the Fleet Center? Possibly her last unless she came to visit. Yeah, she'd be in that. "Sounds great. I have the night off, for a change, and I don't have any plans."

Jenna smiled like Chelsea had never seen her smile before. "Okay. That's all the tickets."

Wait, what? "Who else is coming?"

"Grey said he was interested, but he wanted me to ask you too."

Did he, now?

"That's my boy," Dane chirped. "Who's the fourth?"

"Hannah loves basketball. I thought maybe Chelsea could ask if she wants to come?"

Chelsea inclined her head and hummed. *Hannah?* Yeah, there was definitely something going on between those two. "Sure, I can do that. Can I give her your number in case she needs details I don't have?" *Because I'm pretty darn sure she'd kill for it.*

"Mm hm. That's fine." The words stuttered from Jenna's throat.

"Great."

Well, that's a gentle shove in the right direction for Jenna and Hannah. Now, what was she going to do about the cowboy in the kitchen? Chelsea's smile was all caddywonked.

Valentine's Day with Greyson and friends ...

Was this supposed to be a double date?

———

Placing her hands against the vents in Greyson's pickup, she rubbed them together to stop the insistent tremble. The cold wasn't the only culprit. Being alone with him and the anticipatory ambience had her nerves jittering. He'd walked her out of the restaurant, holding her hand, and now, he reached for her again, tugging her hand until it rested on his thigh.

That was not helping, at all.

"How is your mama?"

"She's great. Same as always." Chelsea bit her lips, fire coursing up her arm from where they touched.

"You're quiet tonight."

"Last time we saw each other, we were naked." The thought fired from her mouth without her thinking if it was a good idea to bring that up.

"I was. You weren't." He sent her a heated look, clearly remembering every detail of that night.

She swallowed and licked her lips. "A pair of lacy panties hardly constitutes clothing, Grey."

"Tell that to my cock."

Oh, damn. He just threw her control out the window. Fuck, he looked sexy as that word came—

Oops, lost my train of thought.

Her fingers flexed, aware that they were a mere two inches from said cock. "I would, but he wouldn't listen."

"He is perfectly tuned in to you. Hell, he'd hang on every damn word."

She smirked. This conversation had just ventured into the ridiculous. "Are we talking about your cock like he's a separate entity with a name and birth certificate?"

"No, he's all me, sweetheart. Feel free to give him a name, though. I'd like to hear your suggestions."

Her hand crept higher so she could feel the outline of him straining at his pants. "Sir Comes a Lot?"

He widened his legs as his lip quivered.

She rubbed along his length. "Master Baiter?"

That drew out a snarl. "Hell, no."

"Heat Seeking Erectile?"

He groaned, tapering off to a grunt as her hand kept moving. "It just gets worse. How about Dick?"

She gently squeezed and shook her head. "Dick? Dick is boring. Dick wears glasses and spends hours on YouTube watching how-to videos."

"How to get it up?"

"No, that would be porn."

"Dick definitely watches porn." His hand covered hers.

"Does he?"

"Yes." His hips flexed into their combined grip as his answer hissed out.

"Do witches watch porn, as well as sleep naked?"

"They might."

He glanced down at her, taking his eyes off the road for a beat so she could see the need in his gaze. "Will I get to find out, first hand?"

"You, or Dick?" A grin overtook her face.

"Both."

It was the strangest foreplay she'd ever engaged in, but fuck, it was erotic. "We still have five minutes until we're at my place. If it wasn't so freezing, I'd ask you to pull over so I could ride you like I've been dreamin' about."

"We've waited this long. What's another five minutes?"

Pulling her hand up to his lips, he kissed a trail from her knuckles to her wrist. She moaned, feeling a tug at her core and a flutter in her heart. He'd just taken it from lighthearted to real in the space of two seconds. The man was lethal to her defenses.

"Open the glove compartment."

What was he up to? "Is that where you stash your porn?"

"No, honey. That's what the internet is for."

She popped the latch, finding a box wrapped in shiny red paper sitting on top of an old map and a torch.

Pulling it out, she shot him a questioning look.

"Merry Christmas." He grinned.

She bounced on the seat, her face pulling up in a huge smile. She loved presents. Giving, receiving, it didn't matter. She practically shredded the paper to get to what was inside.

"A Witch's Guide to Baking." She slid the book off the pile. "The Good Witch's Book of Sweets. And a pair of long, stripy socks." She dangled the blue and white socks. "All I got you was a toque blanche with your name embroidered on it."

"You got me a chef's hat? I love it. The books are to start your collection at Books, Nooks, and Nibbles. The socks are for sleeping in because I wouldn't want a witch to get cold, sleeping naked."

She smacked a kiss on his cheek, unable to contain her delight. The man was sweet *and* sexy. She loved her presents. She loved him. Clutching her gifts on her lap, she stared at him while he pulled up to her house, picturing all the things she wanted to do to say thank you. Her chest heaved, her muscles braced for impact, but she held back until it was safe.

He turned off the engine and she dove for him, the presents falling, forgotten, on the seat.

"Fuck, I want you," Grey growled, catching her.

Slamming her mouth on his, her body slid out of the truck as he dragged her with him, tucking her into his side so he could lock the door. Gripping her ass cheeks, he encouraged her to jump up and wrap her legs around him before he walked them to the front door.

He broke the kiss, grunting, "Keys."

The door opened, a burst of heat and light engulfing them.

"I got it. Have fun." Hannah stepped aside to let them pass before shutting the door and going back to the TV.

They grinned at each other as he ran up the stairs with her still in his arms.

"She is the best roommate."

"Yeah, she's cool." He kicked her bedroom door shut behind him, and threw her on the bed with the pair of socks landing beside her. "Get naked, but wear the socks."

When did he grab those?

Grey flicked on her lamp, bathing the room in a purple haze of light. They whipped off their clothes, watching each other's strip show as they fumbled with sleeves and buttons. Picking up the socks, she started to put them on, but he took them from her and knelt on the floor at her feet. Picking up one foot, he kissed it, slipping the fabric over her toes, and licking a trail up her leg, the sock following his tongue up to her knee. He did the same with the other, lighting a path of fire in his wake. She curled her hands into the edge of the mattress, unable to stop a moan.

He licked across her lips, sinking in deeper for a slow kiss before rising to his feet. "Stand up for me."

Chelsea shoved to her feet, eager to obey his command.

"Turn around." Circling a finger in the air, his gaze mapped her naked body down to her socked feet. "Damn, you are a sexy witch. On your hands and knees."

The sting of a slap landed on her butt cheek as she crawled forward, before she felt the bed dip at her feet. Heavy hands spanned the small of her back and she arched, reveling in their weight.

"When we're together like this, I'm in charge. Do you understand?"

The demand should've chilled her to the core, but it sent a gush of liquid pooling in her center. With any other man, she would have bolted out the door if he'd tried that tone on her. But with Grey, she didn't have to question his motives. It was completely natural to let him take control. A welcome relief. She was exhausted from holding it together. She needed him to just take it all away.

Oh, yeah. "Perfectly."

"If you don't like something I do, speak up, but I am going to test your limits as I learn what you like."

"Okay." Her answer squeaked out through a clamping throat.

Another slap, this time on the other side, and she reared forward in pleasure. "Good. Rest your cheek on the bed."

Oh, sweet Jesus. Her mouth dried up as he took charge, pulling her hips up higher, and delving two fingers into her center. Bucking at the delicious invasion, she whimpered when he spread the moisture over her folds, rubbing her clit. His tongue licked it away, circling her entrance before dipping in and repeating the path his fingers had taken.

Chelsea's hips started a slow rhythm to match his movements as her senses came alive. Clenching the sheets in her grip, she watched his intense mask, heady with pleasure and the power rising between them. He'd give her everything she desired, and take what he needed, without compromising her in any way. That was how it was supposed to be.

She heard the rip of a plastic wrapper before his shaft slid through her folds, driving her pleasure higher. She pushed back, trying to get closer, and received another slap on her ass.

"Greedy girl."

"I take it back. Dick is not boring. I want him."

He pushed into her entrance. "Like this?"

She moaned, her head rising off the bed as she curled her spine. "Yeah, just like that."

"Head down. I want to see your face."

She faced the other side. "Then turn me over."

His hips slammed forward, plunging into her to the hilt, and he smoothed a hand up her spine to grab a handful of her hair. "I like you just where you are, for now." His other hand came around to pinch her nipple, as his hips jerked in short, sharp strokes. "Rub your clit, sweetheart."

She did as she was told, setting off a barrage of tiny quakes that grew closer, merging into one unstoppable, excruciating bliss. They both panted as their frenzied movements built a need on the brink of pain, before fireworks exploded from her center, and her screams accompanied his grunts of ecstasy.

Their hips slowed, bodies collapsing to the bed, still connected intimately. He threaded his fingers through hers where they clutched at the sheets, and kissed the back of her neck.

"Round one," he rumbled in her ear.

Her hips jerked, stomach clenching.

She was right when she feared there'd be no going back, that she'd be lost to him. He'd mastered her body and wrapped around her soul, making her his, completely.

She wasn't done. Not even close. She would never get enough of him. "I want to take you slowly next time. I want to savor your flavor, and the way you smell and sound. I want you to feel me deep within you, as deeply as I feel you in me."

Her eyes dropped closed and she dragged in a breath, pushing down the spike of fear that accompanied the swelling of her heart. God, what this man did to her.

"You still scare me."

"That's how you know it's real."

He rolled to the side, taking her with him so he curled around behind her.

She tilted her head, speaking over her shoulder. "Grey?"

"Yeah?"

"What's going to happen when we have to go our separate ways?"

A heavy hand landed on her hip. "Let's just worry about what's happening now. You're here for another six months, right?"

"About that, yeah."

Pushing her hair off her neck, he placed a kiss on her nape. "We'll enjoy the time we have. Who knows what's gonna happen down the track?"

"If New York becomes a real possibility, are you going to go?"

"I don't know. It sounds great in theory, but I'd have to think it through before committing to Matteo. He wants things his way and I'm the same. We're too alike. I don't know how that would work."

"Yeah, he's a real pain in the ass."

His fingers came up to pinch her nipple, the pain shooting down to where they were joined.

"Ah. What was that for?"

"Are you saying I'm a pain in the ass?"

"I don't know. We haven't tried that yet."

"It can be arranged, dirty girl."

The chuckle died in her throat when he pumped his hips, his cock growing hard for more.

"Are you ready for round two?"

Dark pupils almost swallowed the metal of his irises as he took in the way she licked her lips.

"Ready when you are."

"Nice and slow this time, sweetheart," he promised before dropping his lips to hers for another taste. She sank in, letting him take her to another place where only the two of them existed. Right now, it didn't matter what was in their futures.

———

Grey followed Chelsea down the stairs to the kitchen, greeted by the sound of Hannah's applause.

"Stellar effort, you two. Four hours. Seriously, I had my headphones on, but you breached the sound barrier. That deserves pancakes. Or an egg on toast, at the very least. Grey, you should definitely choose the egg. I think you might need to replenish your protein stores."

"God, Hannah, don't be gross." Dakota threw her toast crust back on her plate.

"Dee's just grumpy because she got no sleep. I'm happy for you. It's about time, but maybe gag her next time."

Grey raised a brow, pulling the frying pan from a cupboard. He'd forgotten someone else was in the house. There was no way he'd be gagging Chelsea. Hearing her screams made him want to beat his chest and yodel like Tarzan ... the louder the better.

Hooking an arm around Chelsea's waist, he planted a kiss on her lips. "Do you like your eggs sunny side up?"

"Perfect, thank you." She stole another kiss and started the coffee. "Mornin' Ryan."

"Hmph," he grunted from the sofa.

"Sorry if we kept y'all awake. It won't happen again."

He should smack her ass for making a promise she couldn't keep.

Grey thought he heard Ryan mumble, "Fucking hope not," under his breath before he shoved another spoonful of oatmeal in his mouth.

He couldn't blame the guy. Grey would've done the same thing if he was in Ryan's position. Living under the same roof as Chelsea and not being able to have her ... It would suck. If he had his way, she'd be under his roof, not Ryan's.

"I've been looking around for my own place. I think I might've found a studio apartment not too far from here." He watched the whites of the eggs solidify into color, waiting for Chelsea's reaction.

"That's great. When do you know if you've got it or not?"

"I should know within a week."

"Do you have any stuff to furnish it with, or do you have to go shopping?" She popped some bread into the toaster.

"I'll need to buy a bed, and a table and chairs to start with. It comes with a fridge and a communal laundry in the basement."

"I know a place where you can get furniture on a budget," Dakota offered.

"That's great. Thanks, Dee." Chelsea smiled at her friend.

"You're welcome." Dakota dumped her bowl in the sink, brushing past him on her way out. "I'm going back to bed. I don't have class until this afternoon. Nice to see you again, Greyson."

"Yeah, have a good sleep."

Her eyes lingered on Grey a little too long, before she disappeared around the corner. He didn't trust that girl. Something about her chafed.

Hannah leaned her elbows on the breakfast bar, waiting for Chelsea to pour the coffee. "We'll help you move in. Won't we, Ryan?"

Ryan protested around a mouthful of oatmeal. "What is there to move? He just said he didn't have any furniture."

"There's more to moving in than just shifting furniture. You helped Chelsea move in. Remember all the boxes?"

"I'm sure he can handle it."

Grey added salt and pepper to the meals. "I'll be fine. Chelsea and I should be able to get the job done. Thanks anyway."

Hannah's eyes lit up as Chelsea poured their coffee. "Holler if you need me, okay?"

"Absolutely, sweet pea. We appreciate it." Chelsea smiled, pushing a steaming cup of java across the bench.

We.

She was finally talking like they were a couple. Now she was getting it.

Grey's heart thumped harder as he pictured them together in his new place. Scrubbing a palm across his chin, he bared gritted teeth. He had to snap himself out of it before he burned the eggs.

"Grey's going to drop me off on campus, do you want a lift, Ryan? You've got an early class, right?"

"I'll just catch the T. Thanks." Ryan smiled tightly, darting his eyes to Grey as they moved to the dining table to eat. Vacating his spot on the sofa, he excused himself and stomped up the stairs.

The guy needed to get his head out of his ass, Grey thought. Chelsea didn't want him. He thought they'd made that pretty clear last night. Ryan didn't have to be a moody prick about it.

Chelsea watched Ryan go, worry lines etched around her mouth. Grey leaned in and kissed them away. "He'll get over it. Don't worry about him."

"Yeah, I know. Ryan and I have had a tumultuous relationship. Maybe now that I'm clearly off limits, he'll chill out and be a friend."

"If he's a problem, let me know. I don't want my girl in a bad situation."

She scraped her nails through the scruff of his chin. "I can handle him, but you're sweet to care."

Hannah sighed from her spot at the breakfast bar. "Ugh, new love. It's sickening to watch. I'll take my coffee in my room. Enjoy your day, guys."

"Bye, Hannah." Chelsea spun in her seat, shrugging her shoulders. "We cleared the room."

Good. He liked having her to himself. "What are you doing after class?"

"I have to chase up some things for the function center. Do you want to come with me?"

"Yeah, I'd like to know how it's coming along."

"Slowly. We've secured the lease for the building next door, but that's where we've stalled. Matteo is a stickler for perfection. He's changed the plans about twenty times already. I don't mind so much. We have to get them right. But he keeps switching up the style he's going to go with for the center. I think it should capture the same ambience we have in Abbiocco, but with a more intimate feel. He's going for more flamboyance. I'm leaving the designer to argue with him on that one. Until the plans are finalized, we can't apply for the building permits. Lord knows how long that process will take. I'll be long gone by then. He's going to have to find someone else."

Grey's body revolted, wanting to fold in on itself as the words lanced deep. He took a bite of toast to cover his reaction. Dry crumbs, rolling around his tongue with nowhere to go, because he couldn't swallow the reminder that this was finite. He'd only be allowed to have her for a few beats of his heart ... before it would be crushed.

No. This was meant to be a forever kind of thing. He'd wear her down. Keep sawing until he got to the center. Because he was pretty sure that when he got there ... he'd find his home.

Chapter Seventeen

Gino

Through the snow whipped windshield, Chelsea took in the TD Banknorth Garden sign on the huge sporting arena. "Since when did the Fleet Center change its name?"

"Since last year," Jenna offered.

"Everybody still calls it Boston Garden though, right?"

"The Garden. Mostly."

"Nice night for it." Hannah quipped. "Thanks for driving, Grey. You're a brave soul. I don't think you'll be fighting for a parking spot."

Grey pulled his truck into North Station Garage, giving them a reprieve from the storm. They all piled out and made their way up to street level, where they paused to watch winter in its full glory through the glass doors.

"I estimate about fifty feet between here and the entrance. How're we gonna do this? Are we all going to huddle up like penguins and hope we don't get blown away?" Chelsea tucked her chin deeper under her green scarf.

"That could work." Hannah pushed open her door, inviting a frosty gust of wind into the station headhouse. "Fuck. Brace yourselves."

Keeping close together, they made it inside, shaking off the white stuff before heading to their loge.

Chelsea turned to the girls. "You guys grab the seats, Grey and I will get the food. What do you want to eat?"

"A lobster roll."

"Make that two."

Her eyes flared "Mm, that sounds good."

Grey's lip curled in disgust. "It sounds good, but it'll be shit. I can make a better lobster roll."

She patted him on the chest. "Honey, you could make Brussels sprouts taste good. Let's go."

They weaved their way through the meager crowd in search of their supper.

"Is it just me, or does it seem a little empty for game night?"

"Numbers are down, for sure, due to the snowstorm. I've only been here once before, but that was to a Bruins game. There were way more people with less than an hour until start. Wanna bet on a baby boom in nine months?"

If he had the option to be home in bed with her, he'd take it.

Grey tucked his hand into her elbow, pulling her to a stop. "Hey, before we go in, I got you something." He pulled a small box out of his back pocket, handing it to her. "Happy Valentine's Day."

She held it like it was a hot potato.

"Open it, Chelsea. It won't bite."

Popping the lid, she let out a snort when she saw the silver earrings depicting a naked witch riding sidesaddle on a broom. "Aw, thank you. You know, for someone so serious, you have a wicked sense of humor."

"I thought you'd appreciate them. Did you think it would be an engagement ring?"

"No, don't be silly." She swatted a hand through the air.

"So, you wouldn't freak out if I gave you the spare key to my apartment?"

A flicker of fear darkened her eyes before she hid it with a smile. "You got the apartment? That's great." Licking her lips, worry creased her forehead. "Are you asking me to move in with you?"

"No. I'm asking you to hold the spare key in case you ever want to drop by, or rescue me if I lock myself out. But, if you wanted to keep some stuff at my place, I wouldn't complain."

Sinking her teeth into her lip, she gave him a shy look from under her lashes. "I'd be happy to hold the key for you."

The expression seemed so foreign on her face, like the sassy, confident woman had gone into hiding under a layer of doubt.

"When are you moving in?"

"In a couple of weeks." Running the edge of his thumb down the side of her face, he touched his nose to hers. "Are you taking me shopping?"

"Mm hm." She nuzzled his neck before pulling back, any doubt wiped away by the return of her mischievous streak. "I got something for you too, but it's back at the house."

"What is it?"

"Uh, uh. I'm not telling." She placed a finger on her mouth in a provocative move that had him hankering to race her home and throw her back on the bed.

"You told me about my Christmas present before you gave it to me." He took her finger and gave it a playful bite.

"My bad. I'm not spoiling this one." She feathered her touch along his lip, dipping inside his mouth a little. "I'd rather show you."

A bolt of lust shot to his balls. He put his lips up to her ear, drawing her body into his. "Does it involve getting naked?"

"Not entirely."

"But, partially? That's good enough for me. Let's blow off the game and go back to your place." He took a step towards the exit, taking her with him.

"Whoa there, cowboy." She patted his ass and leaned away. "We're here with friends."

"Right. Damn it." He grimaced. "Let's go get the crapster rolls."

"Don't be a food snob. The fast food is a big part of the fun while watching live sports."

"Whatever you say."

———

"Yes! We're back, baby." Jenna jumped out of her seat. "Pierce is making all the difference after his comeback from injury."

The half time buzzer sounded and the players cleared the court for the entertainment to take over.

"I had no idea you were such a fan." Chelsea had never seen Jenna so fired up.

"Born and raised Bostonian. It doesn't matter that my parents are Asian. Sport is in my blood."

"Well, all right then."

"This is going to put an end to their eighteen-game losing skid. I can feel the luck of the Irish. We'll be seeing Gino tonight, ladies and gentleman."

"Who's Gino?" Grey asked.

"*The* sporting icon in Boston. You'll see." Jenna balanced her tail on the edge of her seat.

Hannah pushed her glasses up her nose, smirking at Jenna's enthusiasm.

"Babe, you can't call it when we're only four points up and we've been behind for most of the first half."

"I call it as I see it." Her hand popped up to check her bun before she took her seat.

Grey rested an arm along the back of Chelsea's chair as they watched the scantily clad dancers do their thing. Some guy in a leprechaun suit did a forward somersault off a mini trampoline, snatched a basketball from a player's hands while upside down, and slam dunked it through the hoop.

Chelsea whooped and clapped. "That hat must be glued to his head."

"Probably," Hannah conceded.

The Jumbotron, suspended above the center of the court, captured footage of the crowd enjoying themselves and the shenanigans happening down below. Kiss Cam flashed up in large letters on the screen as the cameras searched the arena for possible lovers, framing them in a love heart. Grey grinned at the surprise on people's faces when they realized they were in the spotlight, until his face appeared with Hannah's in the frame. His jaw went slack, eyes widening. Hannah laughed beside him, turning to her other side to lay one on Jenna as the camera followed and the crowd cheered wildly.

Chelsea's face filled his vision, blocking his view of the screen.

"You want to join them?"

He didn't have time to reply before she pressed her lips to his, making him forget all about the damn cameras and the lobster roll that was sitting heavy in his gut. He wrapped his arms around her and dragged her half onto his lap, tongue probing between her lips for a taste.

"I like your style, cowboy."

"I can't resist your witch's charms." Cradling her head in his palm, his eyes traveled over her beauty.

"We're gonna get in trouble if we take this any further. I think Dick wants to come out to play."

Grey's lips tipped up. "Heat seeking."

"You do realize we can hear you." Jenna's face twisted in disgust.

"I thought we were whispering." Chelsea climbed back in her seat, threading her fingers through Grey's on his thigh. "Since when did you two happen?"

Hannah rested a hand on Jenna's. "Since you went to get the lobster rolls."

Grey smiled at the pair. "Happy Valentine's Day, ladies."

Things sure were different up here in Boston. Snow storms, and studio apartments. American Bandstand dancers wearing too tight shirts, and kiss cams. The world was opening up.

And he wanted to share it with her.

———

Chelsea bounced into her room after a shower and searched her underwear drawer for her witch socks, wanting to surprise Grey. He was moving in to his apartment, and she was planning on *helping* him for a few hours after class. She turned over scraps of silk, lace and cotton in varying shades of color, but couldn't see the blue and white stripes she was looking for.

Snapping the drawer shut with a frown, she went through all the drawers and the bottom of her closet, before rifling through the laundry basket.

Nowhere, damn it.

She knocked on Dakota's door, hearing a faint, "Yeah?" on the other side.

"Hey Dee? Have you seen a ridiculous pair of blue and white striped socks anywhere?"

"No. I think I'd remember something like that. Sorry. Ask Ryan. He's home."

Calling out thanks, she travelled further down the hall and tapped on Ryan's door. It was slightly ajar, creaking as it moved on its hinges.

"Ryan?"

No answer.

She pushed the door open enough to poke her head through, shocked to find it in immaculate condition. He'd even made his bed, the grey comforter pulled taut and crease-free. The desk under the window had a neat stack of books, and one notebook left open as a resting place for an abandoned pencil. Beside his bed, an end table held a novel with some sort of spaceship on the cover, and a lamp. That was it.

She didn't realize he had it in him. She started to turn away before hesitating, eyes drawn to a hint of blue poking out from under his pillow.

Pushing the door open all the way, she went to investigate. As she tugged on the blue fabric, the striped socks emerged from their hiding place.

"Ryan, you sick bastard. What are you doing with my socks?"

She turned to leave just as he came in through the door.

"Hey. What are doing in my room? Did you need something?"

Remain calm. Remain calm.

She drew in a breath through her mouth and released it through her nose. "Why were my socks under your pillow?

"Fuck knows. Do you seriously own those? Ugly." He shuddered and walked to his desk so he could dump his backpack on the chair.

"You've never seen these before?"

"Nope. I'd probably have thrown them out. They don't belong in my space. My space is pristine."

"Yes, I see that. Why are you so shit at cleaning up after yourself when you've been eating on the sofa?"

"Everybody else eats in the living room. Why should I care if I leave a few crumbs?"

"Ryan, you leave half-eaten packets of crisps all the time." She shook her head. "Anyway, that's not the point. The point is my socks."

"Are butt ugly. Throw that shit out before I do it for you."

Tucking the socks to her chest, she snarled at him. "Sometimes you are such a cock."

"I am *the* cock, babe."

Ugh. She turned away, shutting him in his room where he belonged, and went back to her room to get ready to leave. She had better things to do than worry about him being a nosy douche bag.

———

"Just put it down against that wall, thanks fellas." Chelsea directed the delivery men where to place Grey's new bed in his tiny apartment.

His bedroom was in the corner, separated from the living space by a gauzy curtain and a stepped bookcase. It was kinda cozy in there behind the curtain. With the addition of books and pictures in the case, and maybe a rug on the floor, it'd be a great place to relax and unwind after a busy night at work. A small square table sat next to the kitchen, but other than that, the place was bare.

Grey tipped the delivery men, seeing them out the door before turning back to her with a wicked grin.

A frisson of excitement zipped through her veins, and her feet twitched, wanting to run so he could chase her. If she had anywhere to go she would, but he had her trapped.

Coming at her, he scooped her up in a fireman's hold and threw her on the bare mattress, with her squealing all the way.

He slapped his hands on either side of her, grinning as he crouched over her on the bed like a lion with his prey.

"My first place." His kiss was firm but fleeting.

"You're on your way."

"Yes, I am." He dropped his body to the side, rolling on to his back and spreading his hands on his chest. Smiling at the ceiling, he looked like he'd landed in a dream.

"Do you ever miss ranch life?"

"I miss my family. Mostly. Seeing the new calves after they're born, that's something special I'd like to witness again. I miss seeing the land meet the sky for miles without obstruction."

God, yes. She missed that too.

"I don't miss the scratch of hay on my skin, or the stench of cow dung. And I sure don't miss copping a lungful of dust."

Bumping her arm to his, she joked, "Naw, exhaust fumes are so much better."

Grey turned his eyes on her. "There aren't any exhaust fumes in a kitchen."

"Only grease, and steam."

"Grease and steam I can handle."

Propping up on an elbow, she placed a hand over his firm stomach, feeling it rise and fall as he breathed. "What does your family think of your career change?"

"My brother thinks I'm nuts. When Matteo left the ranch to come to the city, Nonno and Papà didn't take it well. They lost respect for him because he abandoned the legacy Nonno was building. He thought his sons would build the ranch into a dynasty to rival our neighbors, the Carters." Forming a pillow with his palms, he huffed. "My papà hasn't spoken to Uncle Matteo since he left. Nonno disowned his eldest. Actually, Matteo wasn't the first born. Nonna had a stillborn son before him. They named him Antonio, after my Nonno. My brother got the name passed down to him."

"So, you have a brother. Younger or older?"

"Younger brother. And two younger sisters, Marianne and Sofia."

"How come your younger brother got the family name and you ended up with a name like Greyson?"

His jaw did a shuffle before he answered. "My mama's father was English. His middle name is Greyson. She liked it and fought Papà for naming rights."

"What is your middle name?"

"I have two. Matteo and Lucca."

"Greyson Matteo Lucca Agrioli. Good Lord, your wife will have a mouthful to say on your wedding day." She loved the way it sounded on her tongue.

The ache she felt inside every time she thought of having to leave him reared its head, a snake coiled around her heart ready to strike. His name was her mouthful. She wanted to be the one to join him at the altar. And, yeah, she'd give up the uninterrupted horizon to suck down exhaust fumes, if it meant she got to have the real thing with him until they parted in death.

Sinking onto her back, she stared at the ceiling, eyes frozen wide.

Whoa. Where the hell had that come from?

———

Grey was careful to maintain a poker face, but he was damn near suffocating with the need to punch something. She was so determined they were going to go their separate ways, when he'd known she was meant for him the minute he sat at the table in Abbiocco and recognized the woman from the little diner in Alabama. The good

Lord wouldn't put them across each other's paths twice, from opposite ends of the country, without there being a fucking good reason.

He just had to have faith.

It would work itself out. It had to.

"What's your middle name?"

"Rose. I keep dissing Mama that she should've picked Thorn instead."

"I think Rose is perfect. A flower to be admired for its beauty and its many layers, but one that commands you to handle it with respect, or you'll get pricked."

"I've never thought of it that way."

No, it seems she hadn't seen herself clearly, at all. But maybe, with his help, she was starting to wipe the fog from the mirror.

"Are you hungry? I don't have much kitchen stuff, but I bought some groceries to cook a basic dinner."

"Starved." She rolled off the bed, disappearing into the tiny kitchen on the other side of the room.

He followed, pulling out the necessary pot, pan, and kitchen utensils he'd bought, and the ingredients to make ravioli.

"There's barely any bench space. Where are you going to work?"

He pointed to the table.

After cleaning the work surface, he roughly measured out the flour, scooping a well out of the middle with his hands so he could add the eggs and extra yolks. Chelsea took a seat, watching him whisk through the yellow goo with a fork, as he pushed the surrounding flour into the well with each swirl until the sticky dough was formed.

"They don't do it like that in the restaurant. You look like you've done this a hundred times."

"Probably several hundred. Pasta was a regular on the menu at home. It's much quicker with machines."

"Did your mama teach you?"

"A little. It was Nonna who taught me how to make the best pasta. Mama likes cooking, but Nonna rules the kitchen back home. We were merely the assistants."

"Did your brother and sisters learn too?"

"My sisters did. My brother wasn't interested. He loved tinkering with the farm equipment. He can fix any machine."

"He'd get along with my friend's daddy. He and his brothers own an auto shop where they build cars from scratch. They restore old classics too."

"Antonio would love to visit, I'm sure." He scraped the sticky dough off his fingers, adding it to the ball taking shape. "This is going to take a while because the dough needs to rest for an hour or more before I can roll it out. And my sauce needs to simmer. Do you want to make garlic bread while I do the rest?"

"You want me to cook?" She sounded so incredulous he had to laugh.

"I don't expect you to bake the bread from scratch. I bought a ciabatta loaf, you just have to crush some garlic, chop a few herbs, and mix it into the soft butter and olive oil."

"Er. Okay. But don't complain when it comes out burned and tasting like I threw in weeds from the garden instead of the good stuff."

"Don't be scared. Cooking takes patience, timing and love. It's a pretty easy recipe. Use the timer and your nose, and you should be all right."

He talked her through how much of each ingredient she needed, and how to chop and crush as he kneaded the dough, wrapping it tightly in plastic to rest. Joining her in the kitchen, he started on the sauce and the stuffing for the ravioli.

She spread her finished butter mixture onto the halved ciabatta loaf and slid it into the pre-heated oven, wearing the widest grin on her beautiful face.

"I did it."

"Let's put the timer on so we don't end up with charcoal."

"Oh, right. How long?" She crouched down, fiddling with the timer dial, exposing the top of her ass in yoga pants.

"Fifteen minutes should be enough. We'll put them under the broiler for a minute or two, to finish them off before we eat."

"My mouth is watering already."

He splashed some wine and water into the makings of the sauce, letting the alcohol burn off a bit before reducing it to a simmer. "Would you like a glass?"

"Absolutely. Where are the wine glasses?"

He opened the cupboard above the miniscule bench, finding only the four tumblers he'd bought the day before. *Shit.* "These will have to do. I'll add wine glasses to the list."

She took the wine and tumblers, pouring drinks for them both.

"Don't bother. I'll get them for you as a housewarming gift." She held up her glass. "Here's to starting out on your own. Cheers."

On his own? Not with her here sharing his first meal, and if his luck held out, sharing his bed for the first night in his new place. She was what made this place a home. It didn't matter where they were standing. If he knew for sure that she'd be staying long term, he'd ask her to move in with him. He didn't give a shit if anyone thought it was too soon.

"To new beginnings."

He reached for the keys he'd thrown on top the fridge, and took the spare off the keyring, handing it to her.

"When you bring over my glasses, make sure you bring a spare toothbrush too."

"What about tampons? Are you gonna be okay with tampons in your bathroom?"

"Whatever you need, sweetheart." He stirred a wooden spoon through his simmering sauce, dipping his head to draw in the aromas. Tomato, basil, garlic, bacon, onion … *Delizioso*.

"Really?"

"That's what I said."

She took a swig of alcohol. "You are too damn tempting."

"Wait until you taste my ravioli." He took the drink out of her hand, placing it next to his, and grabbed her by the hips. "Are you going to help me make them?"

"Do you want me to ruin them?"

"You won't ruin them. Just follow me and it'll all be fine."

She bit her lip, eyes too big for her face, like he'd asked her the million-dollar question.

Finally, she nodded. "Okay."

Something told him he'd broken through another of her defenses. The ghost of hope in her eyes, or the way the tightness in her shoulders eased, and her body seemed to relax into him.

Slipping his hands under the fall of her hair, he cradled her head, covering her lips with his. Their soft tongues curled around each other, and the heady flavor of wine enticed him to taste deeper.

Her hands wandered up over his shoulders, down to his ass, searing his skin as they went. He wanted them everywhere. The heat in the kitchen had nothing on the fever working its way through his muscles and down to his groin. Circling his arms around her, he pulled her closer so they didn't have a lick of space between them from chest to knee. His mind started flickering with a slide show of Chelsea's naked breasts. Her legs, the dip of her stomach where it met her navel. He wanted her naked. In his kitchen.

Pulling back, he flicked off the oven before a command rumbled from his throat, "Get naked." His fingers were already working on helping her out.

She stepped out of his reach, deciding to tease him with the slow drag of fabric down her legs, and a wicked grin on her face. He reached for her, impatient to get his hands on all that bare skin, but she skipped to the side.

"Uh uh. Patience is a virtue, Greyson."

He liked his witches naughty. His cock grew painfully hard before he wrenched the pants off her legs, picked her up, and plonked her on the flour-covered table.

"I don't have any virtues, Chelsea. Get it off, now." He tugged at the bottom of her shirt, teeth clenched, and eyes probably wild enough to induce fear.

She wasn't running away, though. Her face was flushed with a mask of desire, chest pumping as she ripped the shirt off the rest of the way.

Grey reached around to discard her bra before whipping off her panties, feasting his eyes on the tastiest buffet he'd ever seen.

She leaned back on her hands as his palms landed on her thighs, travelling their way down to her ankles. Grabbing on, he lifted them so her feet were poised on the edge of the table. His eyes roamed her contours and her delicate pink folds, glistening and ready for him. She was all his for the taking.

Running his fingers from her shoulders down to cover her breasts, he played with her tight nipples. Her chest surged as she whimpered at the sensation. Her responsiveness cranking up the beat behind his ribcage. He dipped his head down, unable to hold back from having a taste any longer. With his tongue wrapped around her nipple, his palms squeezed her soft tits, reveling in the contrast. She was hard and soft. Strong and vulnerable. His salvation and his downfall.

A cloud of flour puffed up from under her as she let her back fall flat on the table, hands finding purchase on his biceps. Grey tugged off his shirt before slapping his palms in the sticky, powdery mess beside her head. Diving in for another kiss, their stomachs dipped and pushed against each other as they fought for breath.

It wasn't enough. He wanted to get inside her.

Surging up, he got rid of his pants, grunting at the momentary relief as his cock sprang free. He started to lean down again before mentally slamming on the brakes.

Shit. Condom.

It took Greyson two seconds to fix the problem before he wrapped his hands around her thighs and put his tongue where he wanted his cock.

He wanted a taste first.

Chelsea's legs clamped around his head, and her hips circled, as her fingers threaded through his hair. He nipped, and licked, swirling his tongue over her clit until she screamed out her release.

The grip of her pulsing body wrenched a moan from his lungs as he slid in deep. *Ah, shit.* She felt so good. He wasn't going to last much longer and he'd only just begun. He was completely at her mercy.

Chelsea lifted her hips to meet him stroke for stroke. The force between them built and swirled into an undeniable power. Lust and desire thundered through his veins and gathered in his center, ready to deliver him to ecstasy. She dug her heels into his ass, locking her gaze onto his, and he was done for. He wanted to keep his eyes open, stay trapped in her sights forever. But he had to clamp them shut as his body was seized in a barrage of sensation.

He could still see that look, though. Her big, blue eyes telling him he was right.

He'd found his home.

He'd like to think she'd found her home in him too.

Chapter Eighteen

Who's The Father?

Bounding up the stairs in Matteo's house, Grey found his way to his old room to collect the last of his things, the noise of his heavy boots echoing in the large expanse. He shivered a little in the stark, cold space. After the novelty of the experience had passed, it didn't seem like such a great place to be after all. It was no wonder Matteo was never home.

Clearing out the last few things in the closet and the bureau, he headed back out to the hallway, pausing before he reached the top of the stairs when the door to the spare room opened behind him.

"Grey?"

He dumped his bag, turning fully, resisting the urge to rub his eyes. "Mama? What are you doing here?"

She shuffled out in her nightgown and slippers, looking like he'd interrupted her beauty sleep, but happy to see him nonetheless. Engulfing her in a hug, the full extent of how much he'd missed her hit him like a truck. He probably squeezed her a bit too tightly, but she didn't complain. She never did.

Stretching up on her toes, she pecked him on the cheek. "It's wonderful to see you. You look happy."

"You too. Why didn't you tell me you were coming?"

"I wanted to surprise you for your birthday. I had to come and check out the shoe box you'll be living in. I guess you've moved in already, since you weren't here when I arrived last night."

"Yeah, I'm just picking up the last of my stuff. So, that was why Uncle Matteo left early last night. He didn't breathe a word."

"I'd have tanned his hide if he did. Happy birthday."

"It's not until tomorrow."

"I was in labor with you by this time twenty-three years ago. That's good enough by my calculations. You were well on your way." She combed her fingers through her tangled hair. "What are your plans for today?"

"I was going to hit the shops to get some things for the apartment."

"Sounds fun. Do you want some company?"

"Yeah, okay."

"Let me clean up first. A girl has to look her best."

Grey waited for her in the living room, scanning the book shelves while she did her thing. He'd never taken the time to look around Matteo's things before, since he had been too busy with his commitments. Running his finger along the spines of the books, he reckoned his uncle had a thing for thrillers. Political thrillers, mostly, but the horror genre came in a close second. Row upon row of DVD's took up the bottom shelves, while on the top shelf, he recognized a photo of him when he was a baby, and one of Matteo with his arm around Grey's mama, and his papà standing awkwardly at her other side.

What the fuck?

And where were the photos of his siblings? Why was it only Grey's baby photo on the shelf? The questions dangled like a loose thread, able to unravel his whole life if he dared to pull. He was leaving that shit right there in Matteo's living room.

"Okay. I'm ready. Let's go."

Putting the brakes on his runaway thoughts, he smiled at her. "You look beautiful, Mama."

Offering her his elbow, he led her out.

———

"You're all business when it comes to shopping, huh Mama?"

They stacked the back of his pickup with bags of everything a guy could need for his first place. Sheets and towels, plates and an ironing board. For some stupid reason, there was a vase hidden somewhere in one of the bags.

"I don't muck around. You should have everything you need now."

"I didn't need a vase."

"Yes, you do. Flowers brighten up the place."

He turned the radio down, switching to the country station. She loved country music. "When you see how tiny my place, is you'll wonder where to put the thing."

"I'll make it fit."

"Do you want to stop in at the restaurant? I'll bet you've hardly seen Uncle Matteo since you've arrived."

"We talked last night. He said he was spending the day at the restaurant but would be home to cook for us all tonight. I'd like to see the place though. Is that okay?" Flipping down the sun visor, she checked herself in the tiny mirror.

"Absolutely. I'd like you to see where I'm learning my craft."

Grey pulled in to park behind the restaurant. "You go on ahead, I just need to do something, real quick."

"Okay."

He took out his phone, watching the backdoor to make sure she made it inside as he sent Chelsea a text.

Hey sweetheart. What are you doing tonight? Come for dinner at Matteo's. There's someone I'd like you to meet.

Who is this?

Very funny.

;P Who am I meeting?

My mama's in town for my birthday.

He stared down at his phone, scrubbing a hand across his chin when the screen went blank.

You want me to meet your mama?

You've met my uncle, what's the big deal?

Your mama is a way bigger deal.

She's harmless. Are you in?

His nerves endured another torturous minute before her answer came.

Yes.

He grinned like a clown as his heart beat a frantic rhythm. That yes held more meaning than three letters should carry. That yes was as long as the whole alphabet. It was more than the two months they had left together. It was the key to unlocking the future. It was the hammer that smashed the stopwatch keeping their countdown.

She'd said yes to becoming a bigger part of his world.

That meant everything.

Sending her a message saying he'd pick her up at seven, he snapped the phone shut and jumped out of his truck. He picked his way through the hustling bodies in the kitchen to the office, pushing his way through the door.

"… know who the father is—"

His mama silenced her tongue and spun around looking like she was staring down the barrel of a gun. She gathered the front of her shirt in a tight grasp and tried to compose herself.

"Grey. You all done?"

Greyson's eyes took in the frustration and disappointment on Matteo's face as he watched her, before tracing the thread of secrets trailing through the room to his mother.

"Yeah. Who were you talking about? Lory told me the father was Antonio."

"Funny how history repeats." His uncle's eyes drilled into the back of his mama's head.

"Matteo," she snapped, spearing him with a look over her shoulder.

"He deserves to know. Let's sort this out once and for all."

Grey's questioning gaze landed on his mother as she turned her back on him, shaking her head at his uncle. He feared the loose thread had followed them here, and was about to unravel whether he was ready for it or not.

Matteo set his sights on Grey, resolve firm on his face. "Have a seat Greyson."

"I think I'd rather stand."

"Suit yourself."

"Please don't," his mother interjected.

Matteo pushed on. "Before Lucca married your mother, she and I were a couple."

His mother took a seat on the bench beside the door, putting her head in her hands in silent surrender.

"We were in love, but I wanted to leave. She couldn't see herself living the city life so she turned me down when I asked her to come with me." He turned to the bookshelf, dragging out a large book. "Two months after I came here, she phoned to tell me she was pregnant. But by that time, my dear brother had moved in and taken my woman."

"You left. I wasn't your woman anymore."

"I loved you. I still love you," he gritted out before scrubbing his hands over his face and emptying his lungs in a rush. He turned to Grey. "Nelle doesn't know who your father is."

Grey's neck cracked as his eyes snapped down to watch his mother softly crying, her head bowed.

"I was forbidden to set foot on the family property; first by my father and then by my brother. I've been forced to watch you grow from afar only. Apart from the few times I managed to visit town, these photos were all I had of you." He opened the large book, revealing an old photo album. "Until you decided to follow in my footsteps."

"You might be my father?"

"Yes."

His mother's watery gaze fixed on his. "The man who raised you is your father. It takes more than biology to be a parent."

"You never gave me a chance," Matteo objected.

"You had no room in your plans for a wife or a family. We wouldn't be sitting here if I hadn't let you go. I would've hated every second of this life. I'm sorry, Teo. I still choose Lucca."

"Lucca. *Bastardo.* How does he like the fact that his sons have done the same thing that we did? How is he handling watching his son grow into a man from afar? And what about the fact that it's me who's nurturing that growth, huh? How does he like it?"

"Matteo, don't be cruel."

"Just returning the favor, tesoro."

Grey pelted daggers across the desk, pissed that a man who was supposed to love his mother would dare disrespect her like that. His inner beast awoke in answer to Matteo's outburst, matching his uncle's anger and resentment with his own, bringing it to the surface. What she'd done was wrong. Matteo had a right to know if he was a father or not, but that didn't excuse his contempt.

"Watch how you speak to my mother. Do you actually care about being a part of my life, or are you just on some sick revenge kick?"

Matteo's body seemed to deflate. He dropped down on the chair.

Setting his mother in his sights, he tried to swipe the ire from his face, replacing it with confusion. "And, what are you talking about? Antonio and I haven't done the same thing. Lory and I were never together like that."

"No?"

"No."

"But she loves you."

He shook his head, pursing his lips, and joined her on the bench. "No. We talked. What she felt for me was infatuation, not love. She loves Antonio. Lory was scared about what he would think of the baby, but he's happy about it. I didn't know he'd always loved her. You were wrong to push us together. But don't worry, Papà still gets his merger with the Carters." He couldn't stop a bit of resentment from creeping into the conversation.

His mama's head reared back as her eyes popped. "Is that what you thought our motivations were? A merger?"

Matteo grunted from his bunker. "I wouldn't put it past my brother."

"Hush, Matteo. You're as ruthless in business as he is. That's one of the long list of things you both have in common." Resting a hand on Grey's knee, she raised her tired eyes. "That's not why we wanted to see you together, Grey. It was always Lorelei's wish to be with you. She fell in love with you when she was just a little girl. You always protected her like she was yours. I didn't know there was nothing beyond friendship in your heart."

"She's moved on. We've both moved on."

It would seem his mama had moved on, but Matteo hadn't. Poor bastard. Grey's mind whirred, seeing things from Matteo's perspective. He wondered if Matteo would've left if he had known about the baby. Did he leave, not because he was chasing a future, but because he was escaping a past? If Grey'd loved Lory, and she'd chosen to be with his brother, there'd be no tolerating seeing them every day. Hell, no. He understood why Matteo was hurting. Why he poured all his love into the restaurant. Why there was no Christmas tree at his home.

If Matteo was his father, they had a lot of catching up to do.

"How do we go about getting a DNA test? I need to know."

"I'll organize it. I'd like to finally know too."

"Good." He nodded at his uncle …? *Father?* Grey's head imploded as the reality of the situation sank in.

Nine months ago, he would've secretly been glad to discover there was a chance he was Matteo's son. Now, knowing how stubborn and selfish Matteo could be, he didn't want to model himself on that kind of example. He'd learned his lesson from Lory and Antonio. Being so involved in your own ambition and drama blinded you to other people's needs and wishes. Selfishness had the potential to harm. Grey wanted to do better than that.

Chi troppo vuole nulla stringe.

He who wants too much does not get anything.

"I've gotta go. Sorry about dinner, mama, but I've lost my appetite. I'm sure Matteo will be happy to take you home. I'll see you tomorrow, okay?"

Chapter Nineteen

Stay

Chelsea bolted down the stairs at the sound of insistent pounding on the front door. It was two hours before Grey was supposed to pick her up and she was doing some last minute studying before getting ready to meet his mama. Or was she delaying? She reckoned if she was late, she wouldn't have to spend as much time with the woman, and maybe she'd survive the meet and greet without tasting her foot.

The thumping intensified, shaking the door on its frame.

"Calm your damn fist or you'll be paying for a new door," she yelled as she stomped through the living room.

"Open the damn door and I won't bust it down."

She twisted the lock and yanked it open. "Gre—"

His mouth swallowed the rest of her words as it took her with a desperation born from need. His hands grabbed at her shoulders like he was a drowning man and she was the life boat. She stood there and took the storm that raged out of him, waiting for the calm to follow as his fight drained.

He loosened his grip, trailing his hands down her back as he rested his forehead on hers.

"Sorry. I missed you. I needed you."

"Glad I could help."

"Can we get out of here? I know it's early."

She balked, looking down at her loose T-shirt and shorts. "I am not dressed to meet your mama."

He flattened his lips, shaking his head. "There's been a change of plans. How does takeout at my place sound? Just the two of us."

"Is everything okay?"

"I'll explain later."

"Yeah, that sounds perfect. I'll grab my pocketbook."

He tightened his grip as she started to move away. "You won't need it."

"I don't go anywhere without it. I'll just be a second."

She dashed up the stairs, wary of leaving him fidgeting by the door for too long. She'd never seen him this worked up. Something major had obviously gone down, and she was the one he'd turned to. Lightning bugs were doing all sorts of stunts in her belly at that thought. She had to help him. Whatever he needed, he thought she was the one who could give it to him. Chelsea hoped he was right.

When she returned, she found him staring through the front window, rocking on his heels.

"All set."

He clasped her hand in his as she followed his hurried steps to the truck. Grey sat in stony silence on the drive to his place, while circling his thumb over the back of her wrist. He was a lion waiting to pounce on his prey, the thrum of pent up energy pulsing in the small space. She didn't dare ask him what was eating him, or what caused the play of emotions hidden deep behind his steel eyes. He would tell her in his own time. His thumb and his silence spoke volumes. He just needed her company as he sorted through the turmoil churning inside.

The truck did a sudden jerk to the right as he yanked on the wheel. Chelsea's hand flew to the side, bracing her arms against the door. Pulling into a random, dark, underground carpark, he switched off the engine and threw off his seatbelt, turning his molten, hooded gaze on her.

"Get in the backseat."

Her throat cramped and her pussy clenched in excited anticipation. That commanding voice could order her to do anything and she'd obey.

"Pardon?" She mouthed the protest, barely a noise passing her lips.

"Now." He didn't raise his voice, but his tone brooked no further argument.

Who was she kidding? She didn't want to argue, anyways. She wanted to throw off her panties and mount him.

He unclipped her belt, impatient, before she climbed through the gap. His hand landed a stinging slap on her ass while it was trapped between the seats, drawing out a squeal and sending a bolt of lust through her system. Getting out of the car, he climbed in the back, finally unleashing the wild animal as he pounced on her. Devouring her mouth with his hungry kiss, he tugged up her tee and pulled down the cups of her bra, licking his way around her nipples before drawing them in to fill his mouth. His hands worked her shorts and panties down her legs, while she rubbed his hard shaft through his pants.

"Take it out."

"You mean Dick?"

"My cock. I'm not playin' around, sweetheart."

She snapped her mouth shut, undoing his jeans and reaching in to set him free. He was hot and pulsing in her hand. He lined himself up and drove in deep, both of them arching and gasping as they joined together. Grey started a punishing rhythm, squeezing and pinching her breasts as he watched his cock pound into her. She grasped at the seat, holding on as Grey consumed her.

His eyes were locked onto hers, laying bare his soul. Pain, anger, his battle with his demons. He needed her to take it all from him. Chelsea moved against him, letting him know that she could take it. That she'd be there the whole way. She gripped onto his forearms, fearless and matching his strength. Undulating hips, fingers digging deep, the sensations grew in ferocity, refusing to be tamed. Grey released a grunt, his movements turned jerky before he slammed his hips forward one last time.

Chelsea's view captured his heaving chest and shoulders hidden behind his T-shirt. She crept her fingers up his abs, inching the shirt higher until she could place a kiss over his racing heart. Grey dropped his eyes to watch, his throat bobbing as she rested her head back on the seat, sending as much love through her smile as she could gather from her spiraling emotions.

He sucked his thumb to moisten it before pressing down on her swollen folds, his shaft still seated to the hilt. Slicking through the wetness, he circled and dipped his thumb until she writhed underneath him, on the verge of falling apart. With a pump of his hips and added pressure on her clit, she broke apart, losing herself somewhere in bliss. Somewhere in the back of her mind, she realized he was taking care of her, careful not to be selfish with the pleasure.

Hooking her legs behind his back, he picked her up, and sat on the seat with her straddling him. His hands guided her head to rest on his shoulder, as his arms folded around her, molding her body close. All she could hear were their harsh breaths and the distant sounds of traffic.

"Sorry." The word rattled up through his chest.

"Don't be." She kissed his neck.

A long, slow breath cascaded over her hair before he pulled back and kissed her lips.

"Thank you."

His gaze feathered over her features with such reverence her toes curled. She ran her fingers through his hair and over the scruff of his short beard, wanting to feel him, melt into him, comfort him.

"Anything you need, honey."

Strong arms drew her back in, as his mouth sought hers in a passionate kiss seeking entry to her heart. "You. I just need you. Let's go."

They fixed up their clothes and climbed back in the front before taking off again. Picking up some Mexican takeout on their way, they spread it on the table when they arrived. Grey sat, eyes glazed over, picking at his nachos.

Chelsea called on what little patience she had while letting her brain think up all sorts of tragic scenarios. Surely if anyone had died he'd have said so, straight out. Shit, did he lose his job? Had a customer been poisoned? Had he been notified that he needed to vacate his apartment? What the heck was wrong? She wanted to scream, but kept her lips sealed, reaching over to hold his hand instead.

His eyes re-focused as he came out of his trance. "My mom used to date Matteo. It's possible that he's my father. She doesn't know who my father is. How screwed up is that?"

Her eyes widened as the information hit. *Wow. Go Mom.* That was pretty intense, but it wasn't shattering. At least he'd had some sort of relationship with both of the men who were the possible candidates. "It's a shock, but it's not all that bad, is it? He's a good guy."

He pulled his hand out from under hers as his brows slammed down, turbulence churning behind his stare. "They've kept us apart almost my entire life. I love my dad, but he tried to make me into something I wasn't. We've fought over it for years. How different would my life have been if I'd been allowed to have a relationship with Matteo? I would've felt accepted. He would've let me follow my passion years ago, instead of the goddamn struggle I had to go through. My father kicked me out. He told me not to come back."

Oh. She bit her lip as her heart tore a little for him. Being told you were unacceptable—having your own father kick you out of his life—that was a story etched into her skin. You couldn't scrub something like that off. It wasn't a stain. It was a scar. Evidence that someone who should have loved you made you bleed instead. Turning your thickened skin into armor.

"I didn't know. That's awful. I'm sorry you had to endure that. But, you're here now. You made it to where you wanted to be without your father's blessing. He's made you stronger. Someone willing to fight for what he wants instead of having it handed to him. Doesn't that count for somethin'?"

His eyes made a slow study of her face, the stormy gray settling as silver flecks shone with clarity. "You're right." Pulling her wrist up to his lips, he placed a kiss on her pulse, making it jump. "You get me." One corner of his mouth quirked, and he smirked down at the table, shaking his head. Flicking his eyes back to hers, they trapped her in their uncharacteristic vulnerability as he breathed the plea, "Stay."

Yes. Jesus, it was on the tip of her tongue. Looking at him now, and after what they'd just done, she didn't want to walk away from him. Ever. But if she stayed, she'd be laying her heart at his feet, unguarded. And that would be breaking the promise she had made to herself.

Chelsea groaned. "Lord. You make it so hard. You weren't in my plans. I thought I had everything worked out, and now … I don't know what to do with you."

"You know what to do with me. We just demonstrated that in the back of my truck, and again, here at this table. You know me. You know us. You just don't want to give up the last of your defenses. I get it. But, sweetheart, we have a fire between us that can't be put out. When I try and think of a life without you, I can't imagine it." He tapped a fist over his sternum. "You're in too deep now. I fucking love you, Chelsea."

Her jaw fell slack as euphoria flooded her system, scrambling her brain and weakening her muscles. If she hadn't been sitting down, she'd have fallen to the floor. He couldn't have made a more perfect declaration. It was raw and real, and it shot straight to her soul, stitching together the cracks that her father had made.

Picking up her jaw, she lined up the appropriate reply on her tongue like tiles on a Scrabble board. "I fucking love you too."

"Then why are you so fucking far away? Get over here."

She shot to her feet so fast the chair clattered to the floor, but she barely took notice, her attention all on Grey. He picked her up by the thighs, hooking her knees at his sides as they tangled tongues. The Mexican spices lingered, making his flavor even more heady. She heard his zipper, and felt the shock of cool air that hit her ass as he pulled her shorts and panties to the side, and lowered her onto his eager cock.

"Ah, God. I love your tight pussy. I know you deserve better, but I need to be inside you."

Her muscles tightened around him.

"Totally fine by me."

Gasping as she pumped up and down, she took her pleasure as much as she gave it to him.

The room tilted as he moved them to the bed, laying her down. His palms hooked around the back of her knees, and he folded her legs up so he could slam into her with long, deliberate strokes. Gripping her calves, she cried out, chasing oxygen with shallow drags into her lungs. Her head slipped off the edge of the bed, his driving force pushing her along the sheets. He didn't stop. Shoulders following gravity, she reached over her head to brace her hands on the floor before they both ended up in a heap. Lifting her ankles to lock onto his shoulders, she met his force with a rock of her hips, and he gripped her ass to pull her in tight.

She didn't know how much longer she could hold on. The drag of his hard flesh through her slick inner walls unbearably arousing. With a long, keening cry, she let go. Pulsing waves of ecstasy burst from her center, and she lost her purchase on the floor as she let her elbows go lax. His hands clamped onto her hips, keeping her tethered to him as his cock pulsed his seed inside her.

"Fuck, yes," Grey growled, following the curse with a gritty groan.

Blood rushed to her head, pounding in her ears, and the room shifted again as he pulled her back to horizontal.

Her body settled, and her thoughts cleared after several minutes.

That's about when she realized they hadn't used a condom. Not in the truck ... and not now.

Fuck.

Chapter Twenty

Not Again

The lights of Fenway Park turned night into day as the Sox hosted their arch enemy in pin stripes. Thousands of simultaneous conversations around the stadium beat like boxing gloves against Chelsea's ears. She sat stewing over the fact that it was two thirds of the way through April, and her period should've been and gone by now.

She flinched at the crack of the bat and the roar of the crowd when The Red Sox got another one past the home plate. A Yankees fan sitting two rows down yelled a foul remark, and Ryan returned it with a "Yankees suck!" at the top of his lungs.

Why the fuck had she agreed to this, anyways? She knew nothing about baseball. Nada. But Dakota knew how to turn her big, brown, pleading eyes into a weapon, that's why Chelsea found herself here. On a double date with Ryan, for frick's sake. Her friend had reminded her they hadn't been on a night out together since Halloween, and she just about withered into a puddle of remorse. What a shitty, neglectful friend she'd been. She was spinning too many plates and they were all in danger of crashing down. It wasn't ideal, putting Grey with Ryan and Dee in the same place. But she was a have-your-cake-*and*-stuff-it-in-your-face kind of a gal. Two birds—one stone …

Dee managed to wedge herself between Ryan and Grey, with Chelsea on Grey's other side in the aisle seat. Slouching in his chair beside Dee, Ryan kept his eyes glued to the play on the diamond rather than trawling over Dee's legs, exposed in tiny shorts. Apparently, she'd taken to borrowing Chelsea's clothes without asking, because she was wearing the halter top Hannah had borrowed the night Chelsea moved in.

Grey pulled his elbow in tight so he didn't encroach on Dee's space, his other hand resting on Chelsea's thigh as it agitated like a washing machine. She stuck her thumb nail between her teeth and proceeded to do a manicure by mastication. *Shit.* She hadn't chewed her nails since freshman year. Funny thing about it was, she was doing it for the same reason. Tearing her hand away, she gripped her knee, ordering up a dose of calm the fuck down.

"What's up with you tonight?" Dakota leaned over Grey to speak to Chelsea,

His shoulder pushed her sideways as he attempted a getaway, and she twisted, twining her arms around his neck to pull his body back into hers.

I think I'm fucking pregnant, that's what.

"It's gonna be real hard to catch up if we have to lean over Grey to talk." Chelsea patted Grey's chest. "How about we switch seats, honey?"

Dee frowned. "I thought you liked the aisle seat?"

"Great idea." He pushed to his feet, giving Chelsea a view of his ass in jeans as he slid past her to the stairs.

That ass was what got her in trouble in the first place. Shifting over, she shamelessly ogled the view again before he took his new seat. She may be in a shitload of trouble, but she wasn't dead.

"You're acting weird. What's going on?"

"The bottom of the fifth. Isn't it? Who's hungry? Do y'all want some food?" Chelsea took out her wallet, fiddling with the zipper.

"I'd love a hotdog." Ryan scooted back in his seat, perking up at the mention of sustenance.

"It's the top of the third. You haven't even noticed who's batting. What's going on?"

Short answer? She'd been sucked into a time warp, back to when she was fourteen and too damn stupid for her own good. Beth's face drifted into her head and she swatted it away. Things were different this time. She hadn't put anyone in danger. She was in love with a good man. Everything would turn out okay. Chelsea kept telling herself that so she didn't fall apart.

Grey's hand warmed her thigh and she clung to his anchor, replaying the scene at his apartment a couple of weeks before. They loved each other. She hoped it was enough to stop a repeat of the hell she went through as a rebellious teenager.

"Honey, all I know about baseball is that all the players want to get a homerun, just like the rest of us. What do you want to eat? I'm paying."

Dee frowned, unhappy with the brush off, but didn't push it further. "I'll have a hotdog. Mustard and ketchup, no onions, no cheese."

"I'll have mine with the lot. Do you want me to come with you?" *Aw, Ryan.* He looked at her with wide, hopeful eyes, half out of his seat already. He just wouldn't give up.

"I got her." Grey led the way up the stairs.

Chelsea sent Ryan an apologetic smile before she hustled behind. Grey pulled her aside before they got caught up in the people milling about in search of food and drink.

"Why are we here, Chelsea?"

"Because I felt bad that I've hardly spent any time with them lately. And because it's my last chance to come to Fenway Park."

He dragged a hand through his hair and let his arms fall loose by his side as he stared, exasperated. "You're still talking about leaving."

"God!" She pushed her hair off her face before slamming her hands on her hips. "I don't know, Grey. I have to go where the work is. There are no guarantees here. I made a promise to my mama, and I'm still going to fulfill that whether I'm there or somewhere else. I owe that woman my life."

"I understand that. I do. I just don't want to lose you. I signed on for a two-year apprenticeship." He stabbed a finger towards the ground. "I feel like you're writing us off before we've even begun. I swear to God, Chelsea, if this is because you're lumping me in with that piece of shit father of yours, I'm gonna get mad. I'm never going to treat you like you don't mean everything to me."

She emptied her lungs and sank her teeth into her lip, folding her arms around her middle. "I'm late."

"Late for what?"

One blonde eyebrow winged up before she flared her eyes.

His jaw loosened and his tongue swiped across dry lips. "You're late, as in *late*?" Shoving his hands deep in his pockets, he rocked back on his heels. "Have you done a test?"

"No. Not yet."

"Is there a drug store around here that'll be open?"

"I'm not stopping at a drug store on the way home. Ryan and Dee will ask questions. It's better to do the test in the morning, anyways. I'll get one tomorrow."

"They won't ask if you come home with me."

"No. I have classes tomorrow and then the dinner shift. All my stuff is at home. If I go to yours, the only change of clothes I have are a pair of stripy socks and the lingerie I bought for Valentines."

"Don't forget the blindfold."

"Yeah, that too."

"You look amazing wearing all that."

"For your eyes only, honey."

"Damn straight."

She narrowed her eyes, taking in his lascivious smile and the spark of silver in his gaze. He wasn't scared, or angry. He was … turned on.

"You're not running away."

"Nope. Did you think I would?"

"Maybe."

Tugging on her ponytail, his mouth pinched in annoyance. "Didn't you hear me when I said I fucking loved you?"

"I heard you."

"That means I plan to make you my wife and the mother of my children. If it happens sooner than we thought, then we'll deal with that."

Her heart stopped dead for a couple of seconds, her hand flying up to clutch at her chest. Oh, God. She wanted that. Wanted him so badly. Maybe he didn't realize it, but he was offering her the world.

"You're serious."

"Deadly." Gray eyes bored into her.

"I've never met anyone like you."

"Ditto, sweetheart. Ditto."

Her lips quirked up as the tension left her body. This incredible, sexy, talented, thoughtful man really loved her. He wanted her in his life, always. He kept saying it, but somehow, it refused to sink in. If she turned her back on him because she couldn't get over the fears she'd held on to since she was a kid, then she didn't deserve him. She owed them a chance. Chelsea needed to speak to her mama. There was no way she'd be leaving Grey. Especially not if she was pregnant.

How had Grey's mama gone all this time not knowing who Grey's biological father was? The burden must've been hell to carry.

She grasped the lapels of his leather jacket, pulling him closer. "I never got to meet your mama. What happened?"

"She went home early. She was too angry with Matteo to stay. I guess she thought she could keep it a secret forever. Maybe she doesn't want to know because she wants Lucca to be my father, and if the results show that it's Matteo … it would complicate things." Grey paused, his eyes far away. "Matteo and I sent off our DNA samples. We're just waiting for the results. I don't know if Papà knows the secret's out."

"Do you think he treated you differently all these years because of it?"

"Maybe. The eldest has more expectations placed on their shoulders. I guess that explains why I didn't get Nonno's name."

"I like your name. Four names. Good Lord, I guess I'm going to have to practice that mouthful. For the future. Way down the track."

"Not that far away, sweetheart." He put his palm over her stomach. "And not if my baby is growing in here. I want you to have my name before we have children."

"Is that a proposal?"

Smiling, he brushed his thumb onto the cushion of her lip, eyes riveted to the movement. "No. When I propose, it will be a moment you'll never forget."

Unh. She caught the moan before it escaped, but she could imagine what Grey's proposal would be like. In her dirty mind, it ended up in a whole lotta naked. Her mouth started to water.

"I'm hungry."

He coughed out a laugh. "Then let's get some vomit dogs and go back to your shallow friends."

"They're not that bad."

He took her hand and led her into the milling crowd. "The hotdogs, or your friends? If she bumps my thigh one more time, I'm gonna spill my drink on her so she has to go change into some real shorts."

"Poor Ryan. Dee doesn't seem to like him anymore."

"That's because he's in love with you."

Her eyes flipped up to his. "No, he's not."

"He thinks he is. Poor shmuck."

"Oh? Is it such a torture to love me?"

"Sweet, sweet torture." He smacked a kiss on her temple and hooked an arm around her shoulders, steering her towards the hotdog vendor.

"Ditto, babe. Ditto."

———

Grey spent the night tossing around until the sheets tethered him like a strait jacket. He couldn't stop obsessing over the possibility that he'd gotten Chelsea pregnant. Finally giving up on sleep, he'd driven around the streets of Allston, just wanting to go back and crawl into bed with her. What if she was pregnant? He'd have to get a place big enough for all of them. There was no way his family wouldn't live together under one roof. She wouldn't want to fight him on that. She'd lose.

How had Matteo dealt with being so far away, being outcast, and not knowing if he was a father? Greyson pushed down the anger still simmering at his mother's revelation. She'd been scared, he understood that. Given the choice between what Lucca offered and the life Matteo was building, a life that had no place for her and a baby, she chose stability and family rather than fame and fortune. Hadn't Lory made the same choice? Not that Grey had given her a choice.

He rubbed the back of his neck, unease trickling down his spine when he thought about his childhood friend and how oblivious he'd been.

The urban landscape zipped past the windows, a blurry background, as his mind rehashed his morning wake-up call. Or rather, text.

The results have arrived. I'll expect you shortly.

He didn't know what result he was hoping for. Before he moved here, he would've been rooting for Matteo. But now? Yeah, he didn't know.

Chelsea had peeled off the emotional filters from his childhood memories, allowing him an unobstructed view of his father for the first time. Greyson was the man he was today because of *both* his parents ... because of both the good and the horse shit.

Arriving at Matteo's, he'd stood on the threshold, staring at his keys in his hand, wondering how the fuck he'd gotten there. Then, his uncle had expected him to sit through a meal before they ripped open the truth. That had maniacal laughter bubbling in his throat, ready to spill out his frustration. But he held back, and sat silently through the culinary torture.

The garlic and chili from Matteo's spaghetti with shrimp still zinged on his tongue, as Greyson rinsed the suds out of the sink after cleaning up. The envelope taunted from its position on the coffee table while Matteo stalled for more time.

What the fuck was he waiting for?

Maybe Matteo didn't want to know, preferring to maintain status quo rather than accept the responsibility. But then why did he bring it up in the first place? It would have remained a secret forever if he kept his silence.

Or maybe he did want to be his father and he was afraid. The chance of an heir to his fortune, erased by the black ink on the page in that envelope.

Greyson poured another glass of wine, a viable companion to his turbulent emotions, and joined Matteo in the living room.

Dangling the test results between his fingers, he watched Grey through sharp eyes. "Before we open this, I want you to know I'm proud of the work you've been doing. Albert said he sees me as I was twenty years ago, when he looks at you. I tend to agree. I have big plans for you."

Grey's hands itched to snatch the envelope from his uncle before the statement filtered through his impatience, making him pause.

"What plans?"

"After a few years as Butcher Commis, we might promote you to line chef. Eventually, you'll be the saucier."

"You want me to wait *years* to become the saucier? I want to have my own restaurant by then."

"Why would you want to start from scratch when I've already built a reputation that will eventually be yours?"

"Is that what Nonno said to you when you told him you wanted to leave?" Grey flattened his palms on his thighs and shook his head. "Why did you disown your family's legacy? Because you wanted to build something you could call your own, right? Because you knew you could make something amazing, and stamp your name on it. That's what I want. Abbiocco is awesome, but it's yours, not mine."

"It could be ours."

"On your terms and your timeline. Not gonna happen. I didn't come here to hang on your coat tails. I came here to learn my craft, so I could make something of my own. I appreciate the offer, but it's not what I want."

Matteo let out a hiss of breath. "That's disappointing, but I can respect where you're coming from. We're a lot alike. I've always hoped that you were mine. I wish things could've been different."

He leaned forward, ripping open the letter. Furrows creased his brow as his gray eyes scanned the page, fingers gripping the paper before letting it drop. He pushed off the sofa, and left the room without giving Grey another glance or word.

Grey snatched the letter off the sofa, curling his body over it like it held the key to healing his past. His eyes flicked back and forth, scanning the page for the answer to the twenty-three-year-old mystery.

The alleged father is excluded as the candidate for paternity.

The sheet fluttered to the floor as Grey hung his head, staring at the facts in print. He was the son of a cattle rancher. His pulse thudded as conflicting emotions smudged together into an unrecognizable mess. He'd almost been convinced that his whole life was a lie. That the reason he didn't fit in on the ranch was because different blood ran in his veins.

But knowing Matteo as he did now, he saw that the brothers weren't so different. They both had his future mapped out for him, without considering if it was what he wanted. Stubborn bastards. He thought his father was the one who'd gotten the raw deal, being stuck on a ranch, neck deep in cow shit. But his papà had it all. A family who loved him despite his heavy-handed rule. A successful farm, and the love of a good woman. What did Matteo have, really? A big reputation and an empty house. He was chained to the restaurant, a slave to its demands on his attention, and his unwillingness to delegate. Were the financial rewards enough to compensate for what he'd left behind?

He'd bet good money that it wasn't even fucking close.

————

The muscles in Grey's legs burned as he jogged along the streets, shaking off his claustrophobia. He needed an outlet to redirect the nuclear buzz he had going on under his skin, pulling it too tight. He didn't want to admit it, but after growing up not being able to see where his yard ended, the four walls of his tiny apartment were closing in real fast.

Grey's phone pinged in his pocket as he unlocked his door. He took it out, scowling at Dane's number gracing the display.

What the fuck have u done to Chelsea?

Grey's hand flexed around the phone, nearly crushing it as his gut dropped to his boots.

What's wrong? Where is she?

She sent a text saying she was sick and couldn't work. I thought she'd be with u.

Fuck. The baby.

If there even was a baby.

He wanted to have a family with her. Saw it so clearly it was already his reality.

He tossed the phone on the bed and jumped in the shower. As he toweled himself dry, his phone rang. Snatching it up, he checked the number to see if it was Chelsea.

Goddamn it, Dane.

He threw it down again, impatient to get moving. The persistent ring hammered his ears as he tugged on some clothes, and he punched the answer button before he'd gotten both arms in his shirt.

"What?"

"Where is she?"

"I'm going out to find her. For fuck's sake, stop calling ..." He blew out a breath, slipping his arm into the sleeve before pinching the bridge of his nose. "Sorry. I know you're concerned. I'll look after her, you don't have to worry."

"You'd better, cowboy, or I'm going to do horrible things to you while you sleep. Starting with your eyebrows. I know how to pick a lock."

"Pfft. Whatever, Dane. I know how to hogtie an animal twice your size. I'll text you when I find her."

"Good. I'll be waiting."

The guy was a pain in the ass. He did friendship like the mafia did family.

They were damn lucky to have Dane on their side.

––––––

The side of his fist throbbed from bashing it on the wood. No one was answering the damn door. Chelsea wasn't answering the phone either. He was almost tempted to call in Dane's lock picking abilities, but he shimmied up the drain pipe and onto the porch roof instead. The neighbors probably saw shit like this all the time. He didn't think he'd be hearing sirens anytime soon. Just in case, he'd spin some bullshit story to set them straight. If they didn't buy it, he'd swallow jail time. He needed to be sure that Chelsea was all right.

Tiptoeing to the last dormer window, he crouched down, cupping his hands around his face to see through the crack in the curtains. The room was empty. Anxiety twisted his stomach and fucked up scenarios stormed his brain. What if her asshole of a father had found her and screwed with her mind? He tottered on his toes, ready to jump off the roof and chase the sonofabitch down, before he reigned in his thoughts and realized how crazy that sounded. Chelsea could've gone to see a doctor.

He pressed an ear to the window, hearing a faint coughing before the sound of water running filtered through the glass. Testing the window, he inched it up and crept inside, his brow creasing at how easy it had been.

The purple comforter was in a heap on the floor and the sheets resembled the messy bed he'd left. Taking off his boots, Grey headed for the bathroom where the noise was coming from. Someone *was* home.

"Chelsea?"

"Grey?" He barely heard her as she rasped out his name.

She *was* sick. His instincts had his hand turning the door handle before he thought to ask if it was okay. Curled on the floor in front of the sink, wearing an oversized T-shirt and panties, she presented a ghostly mask, blending into the pale tiles.

"Don't come near me." The words strained through raw vocal cords, like she'd been hurling for hours.

"Shit." He knelt beside her.

She flopped a hand to ward him off, too weak to hold it up. "No. I've got both ends playing exorcist, and I don't want you in the line of fire. Get out," she gasped, trying to get her breath back.

Her skin burned through her shirt as he scooped her up and took her back to bed before searching for some supplies. This wasn't morning sickness. If she was pregnant, he hoped to God the baby would be okay. She'd picked up some bug, obviously, and her body was hell bent on getting it out. He'd helped his mama look after his siblings enough to know what to do.

An hour later, he had her sponged down and her temperature under control. She'd managed to keep down a few sips of water, but she shooed him off at every turn, screwing up her nose. The woman was the worst kind of patient. Completely adorable, with a side of pain in the ass.

He left her sleeping and headed to the kitchen to make himself some dinner, skidding to a stop when he found Dakota studying in front of the TV.

"Dakota. How long have you been home?"

Her head popped up, all dewy-eyed. "Not long. I didn't know you were here. How are you?"

Her sugar-coated facade might have fooled him if he didn't know better. His truck was parked right outside. If she'd only just arrived, she would've seen it.

Folding his arms across his chest, he sent her a pointed look. "Did you see Chelsea this morning?"

"No, she was tossing her cookies in the bathroom so I left her to it."

"You knew she was sick?" *And you didn't give a shit.*

Shrugging, she shifted her book to place it beside her. "Yeah. I thought she was just hung over. Is she still barfing?"

"I had to break in. I found her damn near passed out on the bathroom floor. Why didn't you call me?"

"I didn't think she was that bad. Do we need to get her to the doctor?" Getting up off the sofa, she reached for the phone, a picture of concern. "There's an after-hours clinic not far from here."

"I've got her settled for now. I think she's over the worst of it." He narrowed his eyes, assessing Dee as she stood with the phone poised in one hand, constructed integrity shielding something he couldn't put his finger on. "Thanks."

"Let me know if I can help." She smiled, evidently satisfied that she'd done enough, and went back to her books.

"Yeah. Sure."

Any decent human being would be checking on their friend right about eight fucking hours ago. Dakota was officially on his shit list. Was she just too wrapped up in herself or was she up to no good? He didn't know, but he'd damn well find out.

After downing a quick toasted sandwich, he returned to the bedroom to find Chelsea curled on her side, sobbing as she clutched her stomach. His hasty dinner turned to a block of ice in his belly, and he wished he hadn't bothered with the goddamn food.

"What is it? What's wrong?" His hands fluttered over her form.

She wiped her cheeks, shaking her head. "It's just like last time. I know it's not the same, but the cramps … the pain. It feels the same. It's stupid. I'm being stupid. Sorry."

"You're not making any sense. If you're in pain, I can't give you any more medicine yet. Maybe a heat pack will help. My sisters use them for …" *Oh.* Some of the puzzle pieces fell into place and he shifted to sit on the edge of the mattress. "Did you get your period?"

"Yeah."

Disappointment nearly barreled him over, the force of it surprising him. Scraping his fingers over his chin, his face tightened as he stared at the wall. He wasn't set up to support a wife and child. This was a good thing. Right? He'd keep repeating it until he believed it.

Burying his face in her neck, he dropped a kiss and rubbed a hand on her sore tummy. "I guess we won't be needing a test."

"No."

He smoothed a palm over her hip, replaying her words. Some lose puzzle pieces still niggled at his curiosity.

"What did you mean, about last time?"

Dropping her lids shut, she rolled on her back and then looked at him with sad eyes. "Do you remember the witches' circle in Salem? How we had to speak the name of our dead?"

His head bobbed. "Yes. You said Beth."

She dipped her chin, her throat jumping with a swallow. "You remember. You've never asked me about it."

"I figured you'd tell me if you wanted me to know."

Her eyes fixed somewhere over his shoulder as she continued. "It's hard for me to talk about her. She was my friend. I did her wrong, Grey. I was so stupid and I wasn't there for her when she needed me."

Her face caved in, her hands flying up to provide a screen for her pain and a moment to pull herself together.

"Before Mama moved us to 'Bama, Beth and I were inseparable. We used to get in trouble together. We were the party girls, getting drunk and missing curfew. Mama grounded me all the time, but I'd sneak out and carry on. I was angry. Mainly at my father for preferring that I'd never been born. Mama was the best mother I could have asked for, but I'd see other girls with their daddies and I'd get spittin' mad."

She grunted, rubbing her tummy as she pulled her body up to sit.

"Beth had her own troubles. Her daddy was a mean drunk. He beat on her mama. Beth wanted to run away. I think she looked for any opportunity to get away, and Lewis Mitchell was the guy who offered an escape. He was a senior. His family owned a car dealership in town."

Folding her arms around her legs, she tucked her face into her knees, falling silent for a few moments. Grey resisted reaching out for her, as he watched her shoulders shake and heard her sniffles. He moved to his side, resting an elbow on the bed, and his head on his palm.

She continued, her voice muffled as she spoke into her knees. "We went to a field party on the Mitchell's land. I lost track of how many beers I'd had, and ended up foolin' around with Lewis' friend in the back of his truck. I was just learning about boys, and I liked him. It went a bit further than I had anticipated. I don't remember much, but I know I only did it to try and please him. When I got back to the party, Beth had disappeared. Lewis told me she took off with some other guy. But, she never made it home. Two days later, they found her floating face down in the Mitchell's water hole. A few weeks later, I discovered I was pregnant. I never told Lewis' friend because he wouldn't even look at me, let alone speak to me."

Her blotchy, red face rose to meet his, and his heart shattered in his chest. Some fucking asshole had used her and gotten her pregnant. Same as what happened to her mother. Those motherfuckers should be shot. Now he got why she'd thrown up so many walls. The sassy, self-sufficient woman was only protecting the wounded girl hiding inside.

A small part of him struggled with knowing she'd been pregnant with another man's baby, his possessive side rearing its ugly head. He batted it down, wanting to gather her in his arms and reassure her that he was going to look after her now. That as long as blood pumped through his veins, he would do everything in his power to keep her happy and safe. She'd never need to question whether she was worthy or wanted ... ever again.

He circled her ankle in his tender grip. "You lost the baby?"

"Yes. I didn't want the baby, but I would've loved it because it was a part of me. I thought the miscarriage was my punishment for not looking out for my friend. She died because of me."

"No, Chelsea. That's not true. You were both in too deep. If you were responsible for her, then she was responsible for you too. You were lucky you didn't end up dead."

"The police said it was an accident. That she went for a swim, but was too drunk and drowned. I always suspected that Lewis had something to do with it. I didn't trust him, and I left her alone with him. So fucking stupid. I will never abandon a friend like that ever again, especially if they've been drinking."

"Why did you invite me to the diner after we'd just met?"

"I guess I was hell bent on proving my theory that I could enjoy the attentions of a man without needing any attachment. It sounds stupid, but I was fortifying the walls of my heart by keeping things superficial and on my terms. I think we've established that I have daddy issues. You were passing through. I knew it would be nothing more than a bit of fun. And I couldn't keep my eyes off your ass in those jeans." Her mouth trembled in a weak attempt at a smile before she sniffled again. "You blew my theory to hell."

He crawled up to sit beside her, enveloping her in his arms. "Come here, sweetheart."

She scurried over, and tucked herself into his chest, where his heart drummed a steady rhythm, all for her. He threaded his fingers into the mess of gold strands spilling down her back, loosening the knots from her fitful sleep. There was no doubt in his mind that she was the most precious thing he'd ever held. He'd moved across the country to follow his heart and he'd found it, not in the kitchen, but at this woman's feet. He could cook wherever, whenever. He'd never find home anywhere but with her.

Chapter Twenty-One

Who the Fuck is She?

Chelsea ducked into Matteo's office, avoiding a collision with Albert as he hustled his way to the mixers with a huge bag of flour. Her boss had called her in early for a discussion. He'd better not be thinking of railing on her for calling in sick. Four years she had worked for him, and she'd always shown up on time.

"Chelsea. Good to see you're feeling better. Have a seat."

She dropped her butt on the bench and reigned in the glare she had prepared for him. "What's this all about? I thought I was in trouble."

"Greyson assured me that you were unfit for duty. I wanted to talk to you about the function center."

"Have you found someone to take over as Project Coordinator yet? We're running out of time, Matteo. You know I'll be graduating next month. I'll need a bit of time to do a thorough handover. The contractors are due to start in July. I know it's not ideal, since we're heading into peak tourist season and all. But if things go well, we should be ready for Christmas. Thanksgiving, if we're lucky. This must go as smoothly as possible. Ooh ..." She jabbed a finger in the air, as if pinning the idea that just rushed into her head. "You should host a Christmas Gala as the grand opening. Make it a fundraiser, and get all your corporate contacts to buy a table, and spread the word. We could deck the place out to look like the North Pole threw up in there and—"

"If you'd give your mouth a rest for two seconds, I'll tell you what the plan is."

"Okay." She pinched her lips shut and clasped her hands on her lap, bouncing in her seat.

She could do as she was told. When she had to.

"I want you to continue doing the job as coordinator, and I'd like to promote you to the position of Events Manager for the function center. It needs a better name. That's your first task as manager."

Her eyebrows headed for her hairline as her mouth popped open. The offer wiped her brain clean. She was not expecting that. At all. Matteo leaned back in his chair, steepling his hands as he trapped her in his stare, and waited.

"Do I get to think about it?"

"Do you really need to?"

Chelsea huffed. "Yes, Matteo. That is a huge detour from the path I had mapped out."

Resting his clasped hands on the desk, his shoulders bunched as he tilted forward. "I was under the impression that you had changed your plans about returning home."

"Please, tell me you're not offering me this position because I'm dating your nephew."

"Not at all. I never wanted you to leave. I think it would be a huge loss for my business, especially now that we're expanding into bigger things. You have the vision to make them happen."

"Oh, well, thanks. It's nice to be appreciated."

"So, you'll take the offer?"

Of course, she'd take the offer. Who was she kidding? The only thing holding her back at this point was the promise she'd made to her mama. But maybe she could organize things from Boston and fly back regularly. Yeah ... That's what business people did, right? She could stuff down the cake and keep the plate full at the same time. It could be done. She just needed to break the news to her mama before accepting.

"Can I have a few days to think about it?"

"You have until tomorrow."

"Jeez, Matteo, you're such a hard ass."

"And your mother didn't smack yours enough. I don't know why I let you get away with your loose tongue."

"Because I'm good for business. We'll talk about it tomorrow. I've gotta get out front, or Dane will start making Beau sweat."

"Tomorrow. And Chelsea, I haven't told Greyson about the offer, but I will use him to persuade you, if I have to."

"Duly noted. Thanks, boss."

He didn't need to use Greyson. The man had already done a stellar job of convincing her to stay with his lethal charms. His tight ass was a bonus. But his heart. That big, beautiful heart hidden under the hard exterior. That was what finally did her in.

———

Quarter to one on a Sunday morning, and the Boston street life was just starting to wane. Laughter preceded people spilling out of nearby venues on their way to their next destination. The night air carried a slight chill and the threat of rain, but none of that could dampen the buzz of excitement under her skin. Chelsea secured the strap of her pocketbook higher on her shoulder while she flagged down a taxi. She wanted to surprise Greyson.

Still amazed at how everything had fallen into place, she hoped Grey hadn't influenced it in any way. She needed to know that she'd earned the position all on her own, and not by throwing her heels in the air for the boss's son ... or nephew. Did he know the results yet?

"Chelsea."

Her head wrenched around, as her name was released like a curse from her father's mouth, sending a spray of needles up her neck. Dressed impeccably in a wool suit, he managed to look down his nose while smiling like a salesman before he takes all your money.

"What are you doing here?" She measured her words, not wanting him to know he'd set her off balance. Again.

"Looking for you."

"Just reassuring yourself that your nightmares are real?" She couldn't resist letting a smirk form on her face. After all, he was the one that'd taught her the art of the nasty barb.

The muscle in his cheek ticked and his mouth pulled tight. He paused before gathering his composure.

"Not at all. When I found out you'd moved out of that sleepy little backwater, I checked up on you. You're making something of yourself. I'm impressed. Maybe you're more like me than I thought."

"Christ! You're not gonna convince me to drink the Kool-Aid."

"I'll ignore your insolence since you didn't have the benefit of proper discipline while growing up. I have a proposition for you, something that would be mutually beneficial. I have connections, Chelsea. I'll help you rise to the top of corporate America, and you could help me. The long-lost daughter taken by her spiteful mother. I could bring you into the family fold, and you'll help me on my way to congress."

She barked out a laugh, feeling anything but amused. His offer stoked the fire of hatred she'd harbored since she was old enough to remember.

"That is priceless. It truly is. You're assuming you know what I want and that you, of all people, are the one to give it to me. You could offer me a billion dollars to pose as your daughter, and I'd throw it in your face. And if I want to make it in the business world, I'd do much better not being associated to you. Ever."

"You're passing up a huge opportunity in favor of your pride."

"Damn straight, my pride comes first. I'm not letting you take anything more from me."

"You think you're going to be satisfied working in a little café with your mother? I don't think so. You're more like me than you want to admit. We're motivated and ambitious. Natural leaders. We're built for power."

"Everything that I am, I am because of my mama. Ambition is no good without heart and purpose. So, you can take your offer and shove it up your ass."

Spinning on her heel, she stomped off in search of a taxi, air surging in and out of flared nostrils. As riled as she was, it had been strangely cathartic, finally dumping her feelings on his head. It didn't matter what he thought of her, or her mama. He was about as important to her as the dirt crunching under her shoes.

"Your mother raised a slut. But then, what else would anyone expect from a whore?" From afar, his words brushed at her back, as useful as a ball of cotton thrown at a wall.

"Thanks for sharing!" She injected as much sweetness into the dismissal as she could muster.

The nerve of him. What a complete ass wipe. Her hands itched to scrub herself clean, but no amount of scrubbing would erase the mark he'd left on her. She shared his DNA. And that was the most damning fate she could've suffered.

Admitting that she'd been just like him tangled her gut into a painful knot. She didn't target the vulnerable ones, conning them into loving her like her father had done. She'd only been with men who were after a good time, same as she. And she hadn't slept with all her conquests either. As soon as they hinted at wanting more, she ran. But still, it had been a cruel game. Until Greyson called her out on her bullshit, she hadn't seen what she'd become.

If she had to spend the rest of her life proving she was nothing like that sack of shit, she would. Money, power, they weren't her motivation. Her mama taught her that giving people a little piece of sunshine in their day was the greatest reward in life. To make a positive difference in some small way.

It's what Greyson did with his cooking.

Her heels clicked on the sidewalk as she waved down a taxi. Getting to Greyson and ending her day on a high was at the forefront of her mind.

———

Rummaging through the paraphernalia in her pocketbook, she beamed a triumphant smile when she found the key to his apartment. Chelsea slipped off her shoes, holding them in her hand before she tiptoed through the door. She inclined her head when she found a dim light bathing the room. As her eyes tracked their way to the table, the ground gave way under her stockinged feet, her vision tunneling and warping as she tried to make sense of the scene.

Grey had company. A beautiful blonde with her stomach swollen in pregnancy, a diamond sparkling on her finger, and the ring box sitting between their steaming mugs as they shared a mid-night beverage. It was her future played out before her. Or what could've been. Because it wasn't her sitting beside him. It was her doppelgänger.

What the fucking fuck?

"Chelsea."

She held up a hand, silencing him, as she pinned her eyes on the blonde. They were both in their pajamas. As far as she could see, Grey hadn't gone out and bought another bed. He didn't even have a sofa yet.

"Nice engagement ring."

"Y—yes. It is." Her twin blinked, caught under the sting of Chelsea's gaze before she flicked her eyes to Grey.

He pushed his chair back, starting to get up. "Chelsea, don't—"

"Greyson, if you know what's good for you, you'll shut your damn pie hole before I smack it shut."

"You're way off track." He rose to his feet, ignoring the warning.

"Oh, am I? Is that a ring box on the table?"

"Yeah."

"And did you purchase the ring that came in that ring box?"

His fingers dove through his hair. "Yeah, but—"

"Alrighty, then. Have a nice life. And, hey, congrats." She waved a finger at the obvious baby bump, before sprinting out the door and down the stairs, his shouts following her down.

The taxi still sat at the curb, evidently on a coffee break.

Lucky me.

She dove in, barking the address to Jenna's place, knowing that Hannah would be there tonight too. She needed their shoulders, and she sure as hell didn't want to deal with Ryan. She didn't question why Dee wasn't on the list, she just knew who she wanted. If her mama and Angel were here, it would be the quadfecta. And, of course, Dane, as an honorary female, was included in her inner circle of powerful women. See? She had a gaggle of girls who could get her through anything. Who needed men, anyways?

Clipping her seat belt, she held on to her composure by a fingernail, until she saw Grey bolt out the door, hands flying up to grip the sides of his head as he watched the car pull away. Unable to hold it any longer, tears gushed down her face, an ungodly noise barreling from her mouth. She folded over, wracked with pain as her heart ripped from her chest, landing on the sidewalk, still caught in his lasso.

She didn't need men.

She just needed him.

Chapter Twenty-Two

You Will Never Be Her

Holy fucking hell, what just happened?

Grey shuffled back into his apartment, closing the door behind him with a click.

"You didn't catch her?"

"Obviously, Lory, or he'd be kicking us out so they could make up." Antonio scrubbed a hand over his buzz cut, jaw stretching wide with a yawn.

Frozen solid and numb, Grey just stared at the worn carpet under his bare feet.

"Hey. Come and sit before you fall over." Lory carefully herded him onto a chair, patting him on the shoulder.

His brother had the cheek to grin. "Oh, man, you're so sunk I'm surprised you're not fixin' to rent a tuxedo."

"Toni! Not now. Have a little compassion."

Antonio tugged on Lory's hand, guiding her to sit on his lap. "Sorry, sugar. But I know exactly how he feels. It's different seeing it from the other side, huh, Grey?"

Grey watched his brother's mouth move, but his words were white noise, on a different frequency to where he was tuned. Incomprehension, shock, and now anger, brewed one hell of a storm.

Why the fuck did she run without letting him speak? All he had to do was pull back the curtain so she could see his brother out cold in the bed, and the camping cot wedged next to the bathroom, where Grey was bunking for the night. She didn't fucking trust him enough to even let him explain.

Yes, the ring box was his. Lory was returning the engagement ring he'd bought her. It was worth a wad, and she reckoned he'd be needing to pawn it off for some cash one day. There was no point in her having it anymore. And Antonio said he wanted it out of his sight. *Understandable.* Now, he zeroed in on the thing, wanting to sling it down the street after the taxi. Who knew that trying to keep everybody happy would come back to bite him on the ass repeatedly?

"I have to go after her." He launched to his feet, heading for his keys.

Lory heaved herself up, belly first, pushing off the table as Antonio helped her. "Don't, Grey. You shouldn't drive when you're worked up like this. Tony, go with your brother."

Grey dialled Chelsea's cell while his guests debated what he should do to stop his life from derailing.

"Your call could not be connected. Please try again later."

Pulling the phone from his ear, he scowled at the screen.

Tony spoke through another yawn. "Shouldn't he let her calm down a bit first? That's what he told me to do when you ran off to Boston."

Lory's head cranked around to face Grey. "Right. She's not going to listen to you. Maybe wait until morning?"

Shaking his head, he bent over his phone, dialing her number. She'd turned off her phone, damn it. Glaring daggers, Grey punched in a text message.

Her name is Lory. She's my EX-fiancée and is engaged to my brother. It's his baby.

He had to try.

Eyeballing his family, he clenched his keys in one hand and the phone in the other. "Thanks for your help, but I'm going. Get some sleep. Sorry I woke you."

In a rush, he was out the door again, breaking the speed limit to get to her place, and shoving past a bleary-eyed Ryan as he answered Grey's rude awakening.

He made it to the kitchen before Ryan pressed a palm to his chest.

"Whoa. Dude, what are you doing busting into the house in the middle of the night?"

"Where is she?"

"Who? Chelsea?"

Stony faced, Grey homed in on the jackass getting up in his grill, daring him to leave his hand where it was.

Ryan got the picture and snatched it away, putting an extra foot of space between them. "She's not here."

"I'd rather see for myself." Stepping around Ryan, Grey took the stairs three at a time and stalked to the end of the hallway.

Pushing through the door, his chest burned when he saw an empty room. She'd discarded her bag on the floor beside the desk, still packed full of her books. Dirty clothes clogged the corner near the hamper, and one closet door stood ajar, an empty hanger hooked over its handle.

Damn it. Where is she?

Like a fucking madman, he stomped to the bathroom, checking that she wasn't hiding. Light spilled through Ryan's door, left open from his dash down to let Grey in before he woke the entire street. That ruled that out. Not that he thought for one second that she'd be in there.

Ryan appeared on the landing. "She hasn't come home. I told you. What have you done? Is she hurt?"

Grey ignored him, continuing his search. The poster of a woman in a yoga pose clued him in to which room was Hannah's. He didn't bother opening her door. Deep in his gut, he knew Chelsea wasn't anywhere in the house. He didn't feel the pull in his blood, giving him that zap of energy whenever she was near.

"Did you guys split?" Ryan's tone held a little too much glee.

Beyond the final door, he assumed Dakota was asleep. Grey wanted to bang on that wood about as much as he wanted a brick to the head, but if she had any information on Chelsea, he needed to pluck it from her mind and squirrel it away for his own selfish needs.

He rapped a knuckle on the door, and balled his hands, beginning a mental countdown as he pictured himself bashing the barrier down. He made it to two before the door swung wide, and Dakota draped herself on the frame.

"Grey!"

His eyes narrowed to slits, not only because of her enthusiasm, but because of what she was rubbing in his face. He counted for an extra two seconds to pull back some 'what the fuck?' before speaking.

"Where is Chelsea?"

Dee's smile faded as she tossed her head. "I haven't seen her for days." Letting go of the frame, she struck a pose, showing off the blue and white striped socks she was wearing. "You like? She didn't want them anymore so she gave them to me."

Bullshit. "Has she called? Sent a text? Anything?"

"Aw, has she given you the flick?" Pouting her bottom lip, she latched on to the door frame again, nudging closer. "It was only a matter of time. She does it with all the guys. Don't be upset. It's not you, it's her."

He scowled, dropped to his haunches, and ripped the socks from her legs. If she hadn't had a grip on something she'd have toppled over.

Hauling his ass up, he shoved the socks under her nose. "I don't know what game you're playing, but you will never be her. Jealousy looks ugly on you, Dee." Eyes straying over her shoulder, he spotted a photo, stiffening in rage.

Charging across the threshold, he snagged the picture, studying the way the two halves were taped together. Hannah and Greyson were on the left of the divide, Dakota and Ryan on the right, all dressed up for Halloween. Chelsea was absent, sliced out of existence.

He spun around, fighting back the need to roar. The Wicked Witch of the West lived and breathed in Allston.

A perplexed Ryan had heard it all. "Was that you that put Chelsea's socks in my room?"

Her eyes flickered with guilt. "I don't know what you're talking about."

"Have you been trying to get rid of her?" Ryan leaned against the wall, his arms hanging loose. "You know, Dee, I've had it with your two faces. Pack your shit."

Butting in to their tiff, Grey snapped at Ryan. "Call me if she shows up."

"Why the hell should I help you?"

"Because I know you care for Chelsea, and you want her to be happy, even if it's not with you. Isn't that right?" he challenged, knowing Ryan only gave a crap about himself.

"Whatever. Just leave already."

Greyson's boots pounded on the steps as he growled at all the time he'd wasted with the narcissist twins. Wracking his brain for ideas on where she might be, his stomach hollowed out at the only answer he got.

If he wanted to chase her, he had a fucking long trip ahead.

"Have some coffee." Jenna placed a warm mug in Chelsea's hands while Hannah rubbed soothing circles on her blanket covered back.

Gripped by uncontrollable shivers, Chelsea gratefully accepted the offer. Taking a gulp, she spluttered as the burn trekked down her esophagus. "Shit! How do you call that coffee?"

Jenna propped her backside on the arm of the sofa. "I may have added alcohol. It'll help warm you up."

Chelsea wrapped a hand around her neck, eyes watering. "My throat is on fire."

"Excellent. If you see him, you can blow it in his face." Hannah grinned.

Her brow bunched, thinking of that diamond ring. "So stupid. So fucking stupid to trust a man." Turning her face up to her friends, she grimaced. "Did I mention she was pregnant?"

"A few times, yes." Jenna placed a hand under the mug, lifting it back to Chelsea's lips. "Drink some more."

She knew this was a bad idea. It never helped. Drowning her sorrows in alcohol only plunged her deeper into her shit. Dropping her gaze to the hot drink, she shrugged through another shiver, and tipped more spirits into her system. *Fuck it.* She was in a wallowing kind of mood.

"Why can't I stop shakin'?"

Jenna opted to give a scientific rundown, keeping a tight hold on her own emotions. "It's called an adrenaline rush. You perceived a threat and your body responded with the fight or flight reflex. You chose to flee."

Chelsea snorted. "Why couldn't you have said, 'because your boyfriend's an asshole'? See? I feel better hearing it." Glancing at Hannah, Chelsea added, "If both of us gang up on Jenna, she might loosen up and let her hair down."

"She lets her hair down with me in private. He's lucky you didn't pick the fight reflex, because he'd have come off second best. I'd be happy to pay them a visit if you want. I know you'd do it for me."

"You are a woman after my own heart, but no, thank you. There is one thing you can do for me."

"Name it."

She handed the mug back to Jenna, already feeling her stomach turn and her legs start to numb with the effects. "Could y'all help me pack up my room and get out of here?"

"What about work? You had another two weeks until you were supposed to leave." Jenna's face paled.

Oh, shit. She'd forgotten about the job offer. Matteo wasn't going to be happy. He'd be furious with his nephew—son—*whatever*, when he found out why she ran. Abandoning him went against every one of her moral fibers. She felt the sting of them shriveling at the thought. But how the hell could she possibly wait and train her successor, with Grey working next door? She wouldn't compromise her sanity for any Agrioli man. She'd get Jenna to drop in all the information she'd gathered. It was all laid out and categorized in logical order, so anyone could figure it out easily and take it from there.

"I can't." Choking back a sob, she coughed and managed to swallow after a couple of attempts. "I'm going to miss y'all terribly, but I can't stay. I need to follow through on a promise I made years ago. It's what I've been workin' towards. I lost sight of that, but now it's back in focus. It's where I'm meant to be."

"We'll do whatever you need, hun."

Her face crumbled as she dissolved into more tears, crying for what she had lost. Her friends engulfed her in a group hug, giving her strength to get through what she had to do next. Chelsea squeezed them back, thanking the heavens for sending her more angels than she deserved.

———

"So, that's it? You're moving out?"

Stacking a few more books into a box, she closed it up, the rip of the tape gun declaring it sealed. "I am. I was only supposed to stay until graduation anyway, Ryan. You knew that. That's what I signed up for."

He tucked his hands into his armpits, mouth turned down as he shuffled his feet. "Yeah, but I thought you'd changed your plans."

"No, honey. I'm goin' home. Why are you so upset?"

"I thought Greyson and Dakota were driving you away. I didn't touch your socks, I swear."

"What in the Sam Hill are you talkin' about?"

"Greyson came looking for you last night." Ryan pointed up and down the hallway. "He was tearing through the place, didn't believe me when I said you weren't here. Did he hurt you? Is that why you're leaving?"

She paused, stomach rolling as she was buffeted by an emotional storm. What had he hoped to achieve by chasing her? How did blondie feel about him running after his girlfriend? Maybe he hadn't hurt her physically. But emotionally, he'd crushed her. Not that she would ever breathe a word to Ryan.

"No."

"Is it because of Dakota's sick games? She came out of her room wearing those butt ugly socks you love so much, claiming you'd given them to her. I figured maybe you thought I'd taken them."

Her eyes levered wide, unsure that she'd heard him correctly. "She wore my witch socks?"

"Witch? Oh, that explains the ugly stripes."

"What did Grey do?"

"He tore them off her legs."

Good. Nobody touched her fuck socks. Chelsea fumed. Dakota was in a heap of trouble.

"Where's Dee?"

"I kicked her out. She's been playing me this whole time. I found out she slept with four other guys while we were together, including Cameron. That's not all. Grey found a photo that she'd sliced, cutting you out. I guess she's just not happy unless she's the center of attention."

Abandoning the packing, Chelsea aimed for the room next door, ready to tear it apart if need be. "Has she packed up all her stuff? I need to search her room."

"Go for it. She hasn't been back to collect it yet."

Rifling through the closet, she found several items of clothing Dee had 'borrowed' from her. That was no surprise. The photo Ryan mentioned lay discarded on the floor. And in the trashcan, several more versions of herself in print. Her own exclusive cutting room floor. More disturbingly, they were accompanied by a name and phone number hastily scribbled on a scrap of paper.

Her father's name and number.

It all made sense now.

He had gone to find her at the restaurant.

Or maybe Dakota had found him. He'd probably paid her a fortune to keep quiet.

Jesus. You never truly knew a person, even when you lived together.

The last drop of her sanity drained as she let the paper flutter back into the trash.

She needed to curl into a ball and cry for a week.

She needed to go home.

J.M. ADELE

Chapter Twenty-Three

Sweet Home

"Honey, I appreciate your concern, but if you mention that name again, I'm gonna march your ass out the door. I seriously don't want to talk about him, so quit your prying and help me choose the layout for the shop. Mama can't decide."

She didn't know why she'd been able to spill the details of Gre—his betrayal to Hannah and Jenna, only to clamp down on her tongue when she arrived home. Maybe it was because Chelsea had left Boston behind, and that included Gre—him. Alabama won the fight, hands down.

She just wanted to start fresh, move on, and ignore the constant hollow agony she carried behind her ribcage.

Angel joined her as they moved through the abandoned shop that used to be Mama Berry's BBQ, stepping over loose carpet tiles and rubbish scattered on the floor. Charcoaled grease and hickory sauce exuded its odor from where it had seeped into the building's pores. The place needed a good blasting with a steam cleaner.

"You don't have to bite my head off. I'm just worried about you. And so is your mama."

Chelsea opened one of the ovens, snapping it shut when the stench almost knocked her on her ass. Skipping back a couple of steps, she waved a hand in front of her face. "Did she put you up to this? It's not like you to push."

Arms akimbo, Angel looked about ready to pitch a fit. "Maybe you need pushing. You're working eighteen-hour days. Your clothes are hangin' off you. And Mary said she heard you pacing the floor in the middle of the night." Angel clapped her hands together, pleading for Chelsea to listen. "You can't keep up the hard-boiled act because one day your shell is going to crack, and you'll find out your insides aren't so tough after all. It's gonna be messy. And honey, you know what I went through because you were there for me. I'm just returning the favor."

"I know what you're doin', but your situation was a bit different. You were pregnant, for one."

Her throat grew tight and her hand involuntarily covered her abdomen as deja-vu hit her.

She recalled befriending a devastated Angel as she'd grown huge with child, and had no idea where the father was, or even if he was okay. Not long before that, Chelsea had lost her own baby, but at that time, it had been a blessing.

Racing forward in time to blondie with the swollen belly, and again, Chelsea's womb was empty, after possibly losing a baby. She didn't even know if she'd been pregnant with Gr—his child. She cursed herself for not doing a test. But, it was probably better not to know.

But the look on his face when he'd covered her stomach, and told her he wanted her to have his name, had struck so deep it stopped her heart.

Now ... that would never happen.

Get over it. Move on. Keep busy. Her walls were rebuilding brick by brick. Mantra by mantra.

"And your man wasn't already hooked up with someone else. I need to deal with this in my own way. Just leave me be. I'll holler if I need you. I promise."

"Be sure you do. I don't want to have to organize an intervention." Dropping her arms, Angel motioned to the windows streaked with dirt, and still advertising the old restaurant. "And the counter should go to the side, where there's more light. You want the reading space to be cozy with warm lighting, and the counter space to be brighter. It also fits in with the access to the kitchen better, I think."

"You're right. Thanks, hun. I'll let Mama know."

She didn't need an intervention. She was fine.

Just peachy.

———

Chelsea crept into the kitchen, switching on the light over the range instead of the fluorescent, so she didn't blind herself. Pulling a glass from the kitchen cupboard, she paused when she spotted her mama's chicken mug, swapping the glass for the apron-wearing fowl. The mug was as old as she was, privy to all those moments when she'd poured her heart onto the kitchen table for her mama to patch up and put back in its rightful place. Lips twitching, she rubbed a thumb over the chip on the bottom edge, a memento of her first attempt at drying the dishes, little hands not quite strong enough.

"You know …"

Chelsea jerked at the sudden intrusion. Her fingers tightened, barely managing to avert poultry annihilation.

"… when I found out I was pregnant with you, I couldn't have been more thrilled."

Her mama was wearing the bathrobe Chelsea had bought her for Mother's Day three years back. Her blonde hair, pulled up in a clip, like it hadn't touched a pillow for hours. It was bad enough that she couldn't sleep, now she was keeping her mama awake too. She put the mug down and reached for two glasses, heading for the faucet to fix them some water.

"I knew I was too young, but I felt ready. You and I had a connection right from the start. Maybe even sooner." Mama took the glass with a polite nod and put it on the bench. "Maybe I was drawn to your father because you were meant to be, honey. I would go through all of it again because I learned a valuable lesson. That a person can survive through a hell of a lot if they believe in themselves enough. That good things can come from bad … And you were the absolute best thing that ever happened to me."

She wanted to beg her to stop, not ready for the patchwork to begin. Gazing at the kitsch mother hen, Chelsea crossed her arms, bunching her shoulders. Throat cramping, the withering organ in her chest hiccupped, in an effort to restart and get on with her new reality.

Her mama ran a hand down the side of Chelsea's face, hinting at a smile, her eyes watery. "I also learned that in order to let things go I had to get them out of my system.

Holding it all in does a lot more damage than you think. I'm here if you want to tell me what happened. I'll always be here."

Well, shit. Score one, Mama.

The tenuous hold she had on her emotions evaporated, releasing as all the hurt, anger and betrayal in a deluge of sobs. Her mama cocooned her inside a warm hug she never wanted to leave. Chelsea burrowed into the spongy material of the robe, soaking its fibers with her tears. This is why they made robes so soft and comforting—and absorbent. Perfect for moments like this.

She'd have to buy one ... or five. One for each of the women in her inner circle, and one for her. She reckoned her mama might need a backup, if tonight was any indication. And ... one day, she might have a child of her own, just not with him. He already had fatherhood covered.

Keeping her face firmly planted in her mom's shoulder, she croaked out her pain, "He's engaged and about to become a daddy."

Her mama's arms went taut around her, before pulling away so she could look at Chelsea's face. "He what now?"

"Pregnant fiancée, Mama. I saw them sitting at the table together after one in the morning, in their pajamas."

"What did he say when you saw them?"

"He said my name, like he'd been caught red-handed."

"Doing what?"

"Two timing. Now I know how it feels being the other woman. Awful."

"No, baby girl, what were they doing at the table?"

"Having a hot drink, talking, I dunno. Maybe the baby was kicking and it woke her up, so he made her a hot drink to help her back to sleep." *Because that would be the kind of husband he would be.*

Ugh. Her throat shrank as she blinked away a fresh bout of tears.

"Sounds innocent."

"What?" She focused on her mom, pricking her ears. "I didn't see a spare bed anywhere. There's only one bed, Mama."

Her mama's brow skipped up. "Did you walk around and have a look?"

"No. It's a studio, with a bathroom in one corner. There's nowhere to hide."

"So, he sleeps in his living room?"

"No, the bedroom is partitioned by a curtain and a bookshelf."

"Sounds like somewhere to hide."

Chelsea frowned, the cramp in her throat traveling higher to lodge behind her eyes.

"What else did he say?"

"He told me I was way off track, and then he admitted that he'd bought the engagement ring."

"That doesn't make sense."

No, it didn't. But she couldn't believe anything that came out of his mouth when he was sitting in his damn pajamas with a woman who looked so much like her, and was pregnant with his child.

"Was that all he said?"

"Yeah. I told him to shut his pie hole before I smacked it shut."

Her mama bit her lip, eyes crinkling before she smoothed away her amusement. "Maybe you should've let him explain. Honey, you tend to do things in a fever. Maybe she was a neighbor locked out of her apartment."

"How do you explain the ring then?"

"Right." Her chin bounced and she dropped her hold, crossing her arms. "I can't. But, baby girl, he can. And you should let him. When a person is being unfaithful, there are always signs. They work late, or go away for days. They act shifty, and you know in your gut that something isn't right, even if you don't want to admit it. None of that was happening, was it?"

"Er. No."

"Then why didn't you trust him enough to give him a chance to explain?"

Fuck. Shit. Fuckity, fuck.

"Because when it comes to men, I act first and think later."

"Maybe you should call him."

"And say what?"

"Ask him to explain what was going on. You love him, Chelsea. Don't throw it away because you let your pride get in the way. And don't think ill of him because of the equipment he has dangling between his legs." Her mama tutted, blushing. "Oh, goodness, you are a bad influence on me. Forget I mentioned his equipment. The point is, not all men are like your father. There are some genuinely good ones out there. You just have to find the right one. I think you have already." She tweaked Chelsea on the cheek. "Call him. But get some sleep first, sugar. Love you lots."

"Love you too, Mama."

Slumping in a recliner, Chelsea propped her elbows on her knees and her head in her hands. Her pulse pounded inside her skull, as her heart hiccupped along.

What if she'd jumped to the wrong conclusion? Thrown away the love of her life in a rash, knee-jerk decision.

Oh, Lord. What had she done?

Chapter Twenty-Four

Country is in My Blood

Grey wound down his window as the truck trundled along the bumpy road up to the ranch. A trip so familiar it was like slipping on his favorite pair of jeans. Watching the horizon stretch over the contours of the land, he took his first deep breath in months. He realized he wasn't as citified as he thought.

With the house in view, he narrowed his eyes, searching the front porch for any sign of life. The door swung open, and his mama rushed to greet him as he pulled around the front.

"Greyson!"

Lifting a hand in a wave, he stopped the car and jumped out.

"Hi, Mama."

Hopping up on her toes, she twined her arms around him. "Ah, it's so good to see you. Matteo called last night. Why didn't you tell me you were coming?"

Shocked at the defined ribs under his arms, he cursed himself for causing her so much grief. "I had my head full of troubles and my phone battery died about three states ago. I don't know where my car charger is. Sorry, I should've phoned before leaving."

She let him go, taking his elbow to lead him up the steps. "It's okay, you're here now. Come inside and bring your bag."

"I'm not staying. I just wanted to visit on my way through, and talk to Papà if he's around."

"But … Where are you going?"

"I'm heading to Alabama. I managed to transfer my apprenticeship to a place owned by one of Matteo's friends."

"He didn't tell me that part." She dropped her hold on him, her face stricken.

Way to go, Grey. Asshole. Spinning his keys around his finger, he looked at the ground, waiting for it to cave in and swallow him up. He didn't know if he should hug her again, or if that'd just make it worse.

Slipping his keys in his back pocket, he scratched his chin, offering up a consolation. "It's only about a 6-hour drive. We'll be able to visit all the time."

"We?"

"Yeah. *We*. Didn't Antonio fill you in?"

"He told me what happened. So, you're going after her?"

"Yeah. I can't be without her." Jamming his hands in his jeans, he rocked on his heels. "I can cook anywhere. Uncle Matteo didn't get it."

"Teo will never understand." Grey's papà came up behind them, placing a hand on his wife's waist and dropping a kiss on her cheek. "Come inside. We'll talk."

Grey couldn't stop the reflexive clench of his fists. The last time he'd seen his father, he told Grey he was no longer welcome in his home. Now he'd been invited in to talk.

Stretching out his fingers, he sighed and followed his parents onto the porch. Scanning back and forth between them, he couldn't believe it'd only been ten months. His papà's proud posture was now stooped. The rifts in the family, pushing him over. Time had sped forward by years, not months. Both of them had lost weight.

Despite the evidence of stress, Greyson smiled. Papà's arm wrapped tightly around Mama as she leaned into him. Grey hadn't seen them so united since Nonno died, just before he met Matteo. Maybe now that they knew the truth, they could finally move on.

He took a seat at the dining table, seeing the experience through a surreal haze. He'd grown up eating every meal at this table, surrounded by family. But the memory of his last meal threw up an eclipse, darkening the good times. He struggled to let it go in the awkward silence, in a room intended for eating, laughing, and recounting their day. With only the three of them present, Grey fidgeted in his chair, waiting for one of them to start speaking.

Papà cleared his throat. "It's good to see you, son." Dark brows descended over weary eyes as his father picked invisible crumbs off the cloth. "I'm sorry about how we parted ways. I may have been too hasty in my decision, forbidding you to come home." His metallic gaze locked onto Grey, pummeling his point at the target. "You understand, it was hurtful to me, you turning your back on us. All a father wants, is for his children to be happy. To help set them on their way, give them a leg up. I thought I was building something for all of you to share, like my papà did for us. A legacy. I wanted you to choose *my* legacy, not Matteo's. You were always my son in my eyes. And now we know it's true."

A crease formed on Grey's brow. Didn't the brothers realize how their grudge had affected the rest of the family? Selfish Agrioli men, bred for generations. He appreciated his brother all the more, knowing Toni wasn't like that. Grey had to step up and break the mold.

"Why didn't you do the test when I was born?"

"I didn't need a test. You were mine. End of story."

Grey relaxed back in his chair, the certainty in his papà's words blowing away decades of hurt in one breath.

"No doubts?"

"I was meant to raise you as my son, whether you had my DNA or not. I was always your father. Do you understand?" He jammed a finger on the table.

"Yeah, I think I'm getting it now."

"*Bene.*"

"I was born to cook."

"I understand."

"Do you?"

"*Sì.*" Nodding his head, he leaned forward on his elbows. "But you were also born to be a part of this family. Boston is too far. Your mother can't cope with her bambino so far away. And your nephew needs an uncle."

"Nephew? Did Lory have the baby?"

"Early this morning. Congratulations, Uncle Grey." His mama clasped a hand with papà, beaming at the proud Nonno.

"Looks like I'll be stopping by the hospital on my way through. What did they name him?"

"Jack Lucca Clay Agrioli." His father's chest puffed up as he spilled the mouthful.

Mouthful.

Good Lord, I guess I'm going to have to practice that mouthful. For the future. Way down the track.

Well, looky here, it's down the track. The future has arrived. He hoped she'd practiced.

"Papà, Mama ... I'm sorry. Sorry for everything. I love you, but I have to go. I promise to visit as soon as I can."

He kissed them and jogged back to the door where his Nonna was waiting with a bag of food, the home cooked aroma hitting him square in the chest.

"*Molte grazie,* Nonna." Dropping a kiss on each weathered cheek, he grinned. "I'll be back. Often."

————

Chelsea grunted as she scraped up another filthy carpet tile, soaked in God knows what, and dumped it on the mountain of rubbish. Slicking the sweat off her forehead, she sat back on her haunches, cranking her neck to watch her mama scrub out the oven. They'd drawn straws. Her mama got the short one. Although, looking at how much more Chelsea had to do, and with the stench coating the inside of her nose, she reckoned hers hadn't been much longer.

"How's it lookin', Mama? Is it salvageable?"

"This one, yes. The other one, no. It's dead and gone."

"Okay. That's okay, we'll deal with it. I've got an equipment place lined up. How about the cold storage?"

"Pete's going to look at it for us tomorrow."

It was amazing how quickly things moved when you worked for the mayor. Luckily, the man had a sweet tooth, and a soft spot for Mama's cakes. His wife also happened to run a book club and had been instrumental in putting a firecracker under the necessary people to get things rolling.

Yep, everything was hunky dory. All her plans were falling into place like dominoes. Except for one huge missing piece in the middle that screwed up the pattern. A miserable, gaping, Greyson-shaped hole. Chelsea stretched forward, attacking the next tile with the scraper, her mind thousands of miles away. He'd turned his phone off. *Touché.* Why the hell would he take her calls when she'd so successfully smacked him where it hurt?

Heaving her frustration behind the tool, the glue underneath gave way too easily, tumbling her forward. Her other hand snapped out to break her fall, slicing along the sharp edge of the scraper. A nasty sting shot up her arm.

"Fuck ...!" Hissing in a breath, she cradled her injured limb, watching the red blood well up and spill down her wrist. "Sorry for cussin', Mama. Would you throw me a dish towel, please?"

"Ooh, dear. Blood ... I ..."

Her mama's face looked like it had been whitewashed, before her eyes rolled up and she slumped sideways on the floor. Good thing her mama didn't have far to fall.

Chelsea snorted. As she got to her feet, the air thinned out the higher she got. Apparently, a preclusion to fainting was hereditary. The room swayed as her vision flickered with a bokeh effect. She could barely register the sounds from the street as her hearing faded out. Bending forward, she tried to get the blood flowing north before she completely disgraced the Gilbert name.

Cool cotton enclosed her hand as she was tugged down to sit on the most uncomfortable chair she'd ever sat on. She shuffled her butt as her vision cleared, the drop in altitude working its magic.

"You'd better stop doing that, or meeting your mama is gonna be real embarrassing."

That voice.

Jolting, she twisted and found Greyson's hooded eyes fixed on her. Instantly, her heart thumped steady and strong, hiccups cured. Her vision sharpened on his lips, not so far away. She could just tip up her chin and …

Purposely, she wriggled her bottom again, watching as those lips curled and revealed his smile.

Grey lowered his head, and his mouth connected with the shell of her ear as he whispered, "I know what you're thinking, dirty girl. Save it for later. I think you're going to need stitches." He pressed harder on the cut, making her whimper with the pain.

"Ow, you're hurting me."

"Hold still, I'm trying to stop the bleeding. What were you doing on your hands and knees with a sharp object?"

"I was doing my job … What are *you* doing here?"

"I'm finding my home."

The moisture evaporated from her mouth, but she tried to swallow, anyways. Scared to ask the question trapped in her throat, she forced it out on a whisper.

"Did you find it?"

"I sure did."

"Where?"

"I'm looking at her."

Heat rushed her face, as her whole body hummed in recognition. She knew exactly what he meant. Home wasn't a place. It was flesh and blood, and soul. Souls meeting and connecting, acknowledging that they were meant for each other.

She wriggled out of his lap and turned to face him. Grey didn't let go of the pressure on her hand, raising it higher. But Chelsea didn't care about the cut anymore. She needed to make things right between them.

"I'm sorry. So damn sorry for not trusting you. I should've let you explain. It's hard for me, I've never done this before—"

He cut her off, pressing a finger to her lips. "Chelsea, honey? I know you're sorry. I got all your messages when I finally charged my phone. I'm guessing you got my messages too, or you wouldn't be apologizing. But I need to get you some medical attention, and your mama has been awake for a few minutes now, waiting politely for you to remember she exists. So how 'bout you shut up and jump in the truck?"

Clamping her mouth shut, she threw a sheepish glance at her mama who returned it with a smirk.

"Go on, before you bleed to death and I pass out again. We'll talk over supper. Nice to finally meet you, Greyson."

"You too, Mama."

He called her Mama.

Greyson stretched to his full height, offering up his hand, and reserved seating for her heart and soul. Buoyant with love, she took it, happy to sign up for a lifetime.

Her knees buckled as the force of reality hit, and his arm came around to keep her steady. She thought she'd lost him. He'd picked up his life and plonked it back in the middle of nowhere to be with her. Mouth ajar, she blinked up at him in wonder, understanding how much she stood to lose.

Holding all the promises she wanted to make in her eyes, she hoped he'd see.

"I found my home too."

"Only you, sweetheart." He gave her a chaste kiss, aware of their audience, no doubt. It had her hankering for more.

Reaching the truck, she waited for him to unlock the door, still afloat on some surreal dream.

He nudged her out of her daze, helping her into the truck with a hand on her ass, his body blocking her mama's view. "Later, sweetheart. Later."

Slamming her door, he hustled around to the driver's side, making sure she was buckled in and still putting pressure on her hand.

"Have you been practicing?"

"Practicing what?"

He leaned closer. "My mouthful."

Oh, damn. His answer tumbled out on a bed of gravel and reeking of sin. She squeezed her thighs together to relieve the ache he'd started.

"Greyson Matteo Lucca Agrioli." She enunciated each name, tasting how it felt in her mouth. Her pulse thundered in her chest, core clenching, injured hand forgotten.

"Sweetheart, my name was made for your lips. You'd better get used to saying it, because I'm putting a ring on your finger as soon as I can."

That was one promise he'd better make good on.

Epilogue

Sitting in the yard of the Murphy's house, the last of summer's heat clinging to their skin, Chelsea spread her wedding planner out on the wrought iron table to show Angel.

"Can I be a flower girl?"

Chelsea combed her fingers through Addy's midnight tresses. "Of course, sweetie. And Sonny will be a page boy."

"Do I have to?" Sonny screwed up his tiny nose, pinching his mouth shut.

Chelsea winked at Angel who grinned at his distaste over the rim of her glass of sweet tea. She didn't think he'd go for the position, but Chelsea had to try. "Nope. You can be my special witness, if you like."

"Do I have to get up in front of people?"

"No, baby. But you get a front row seat."

He narrowed his eyes, giving it some serious thought as he tossed a baseball up, catching it in an oversized mitt. "Okay."

"Do I get to sit up front?" Addy tugged on Chelsea's arm, eager for her say.

"You can stand next to me."

Addy didn't even blink before moving on to a more pertinent question. "Who gets to drive the car with ribbons?"

"Your granddaddy will drive me, and your granduncles will drive you and your mama."

"Do I get to drive?"

Angel coughed. "Not for a long time."

"Aw. But granddaddy lets me sit behind the wheel of his Chevy. I even started the engine once."

"Well, that's as far as it goes for now. You have to be able to see over the hood to be able to drive."

Addy's little face fell. "Aww, but that's gonna take ages."

Angel beamed. "Yep."

"But how am I gonna win races if I don't practice?"

Angel clanked her glass on the table, sighing. "Oh, Lord. I pray that this is just a phase. Imagine my baby racing cars. I feel like pitchin' a conniption fit just thinkin' about it."

"Dinner is ready," Grey called out from inside the house.

The kids dumped their baseball gear where they stood before darting off after food.

"Those two are bottomless pits, I swear." Angel gathered her drink and packed away the mitts, shaking her head. "I'll see you inside."

"Are you coming?"

Chelsea snapped the planner shut before Grey saw the contents, diamonds surrounding a ruby sparkling on her finger.

"Yeah." She smiled a wicked smile, brushing close as she passed him. "Are you?"

His eyes lit up and he snagged her around the middle, pulling their bodies in tight. "You're such a tease. I can't get enough. Let's disappear into the yard while they eat."

"Tempting. But I think I'll make you suffer for a while before I have my way with you."

"Fuck," he growled in her ear, placing hot, open-mouthed kisses over the jumping pulse in her neck. "Marry me."

Her hand slid into the back of his jeans to grab a handful of flesh. "Almost a done deal, honey. Later."

"Promise?"

"I do." She winked.

Titles by J. M. Adele

Coming Home Series

Shattered Home
Remembering Home
Finding Home
Leaving Home (Coming 2019)
Coming Home (TBA)

Sensing Series

Sensing You
Convincing You (Coming Soon)
Indulging You (TBA)

Bloodlust Series

Ashes and Dust
Ember and Flame

Excerpt from

Remembering Home

Chapter One

Self-hatred was the purest thing Aiden Thomas had felt in years. He stood in the bathroom of his hotel room, harsh, fluorescent light casting unforgiving shadows over the angles of his face. His shoulders wrenched up and down as each breath grew harder to drag in. The face reflected in the mirror twisted with shame and a fierce disgust. Black eyes bored into the mirror and back again in an infinite battle of wills and intimidation.

The news he'd discovered ten minutes ago was the baseball bat to the head he needed. A wakeup call after more than a decade of numb oblivion, isolation and ignorance. Aiden had let everyone down, including himself. He'd never see Hank Murphy again because he'd been behaving like a chicken shit, little boy. His teeth made a horrible grinding sound as he clenched his jaw.

The urge to destroy proved irresistible. He pounded his fist into the grim reflection, the shattering of the glass deafening in the small space. A satisfied smile crossed his face as he inspected his shredded knuckles. Aiden flexed his hand watching red spill down between his fingers, coloring the shards in the sink. It hurt like a bitch, and it felt fucking awesome.

The pussy in the mirror was gone. Aiden Thomas was awake and determined to make things right.

————

Almost a day later, he stood deliberately separate from a huddle of black sorrow, listening to the somber tones of a man of God eulogizing and offering prayer. A summary of the life of a man who meant so much to him, the one a young Aiden wished had been his real father.

The intermittent breeze carried away the murmurings of the minister, stirring the rich smell of freshly dug soil mixed with the more delicate scent of the floral adornment on the coffin. He sucked in the smells and the moisture in the southern air, grateful for some relief from the heaviness of his guilt. Beneath a makeshift bandage, his throbbing hand reminded him of the task ahead.

Aiden surveyed the crowd, recognizing most of his fellow mourners, although they were much older now. As a boy, he'd thought of them as his family until his father had disabused him of the notion, called him a foolish leech, and taught him that the only person he could truly rely on was himself.

He belonged to nobody.

All utter bullshit. He *had* belonged to Hank, his true father in every way that counted. He knew that now. Now that it was too late.

Jesus, Hank. I'm so sorry.

He set his jaw to prevent an agonized shout from escaping, as his eyes locked on the coffin. He forced them away, tilting his head side to side to loosen his neck. The pain from flexing his fingers allowed him to center his torment as far away from his heart as he could get it. It was welcome relief, however brief.

Aiden absorbed the poignant words, and looked around the gathering once again. A petite woman across from him drew his eyes. The only points of color were her red lips, and the green leaves and stem of a white rose visible through a curtain of raven hair. Each tear caught on the corner of her mouth before it trickled down her chin and fell to the earth. Her gloved hands clasped those of a fellow mourner's, obviously her close friend. They presented a striking contrast, a dark crown beside platinum blond. The women rocked slightly side-to-side, alternating between supporters and supported.

Something about the brunette pinched at his distant memories, imploring him to remember a familiarity long forgotten. Aiden's feet wanted to move of their own accord, to circle the huddle to get to her with some amount of stealth. He locked his knees refusing to bow to their demand, dropping his gaze to take in the grass beneath his feet. That'd be a good start. Embarrassing himself the first time he'd seen these people in fifteen years, and at the funeral of one of the town's most loved. His shoulders dropped as he pushed a long breath out, before raising his eyes once more.

The woman stood trembling, staring straight at him, barely holding it together. She was beyond beautiful, although agony etched her features. Her distressed state tugged at his protective side more than it should have, drawing the corners of his mouth down. Her big, doe-shaped eyes blinked through her tears, draining more rapidly now. Mouth quivering, her distress seemed to grow as she watched him. Jesus, she looked like she was going to collapse.

Aiden's right foot lifted and he stumbled forward slightly, catching himself before he could go any further. A prickle of awareness caused his stare to shift, taking in the narrowed gaze of her friend as she gripped onto her companion around the waist. He schooled his features, and quickly turned away. What the hell did he think he'd be able to do for her anyway?

Once again facing the Minister, he joined in the last prayers for his dear friend. "Rest in peace, old man," he said to himself, letting his grief wash over him once again. The minister finished the service and the coffin was lowered. A tepid breeze carried some dry leaves to join his friend in his final resting place in the ground.

Aiden watched as the woman broke away from her friend to throw a folded piece of paper and the rose onto the coffin. She made her way straight to him, stopping when the toes of their shoes tapped together, sending a jolt of adrenaline straight into his blood stream. He looked down at her leaning his shoulders away. *The fuck?* The closeness was jarring. Did she recognize him?

Her face tipped up, presenting him with her tear-stained beauty once more. Aiden pulled out a hanky from his jacket and offered it, needing to comfort her somehow.

"Thank y—" A sniffle and a gasp cut off her words. "…ou."

"Sorry for your loss." The rumble of his voice sounded deep as the inane words tumbled out of his mouth. He cringed inwardly. What could he say that didn't sound trite? *Hank would know what to say.*

Aiden's brown eyes drilled into her vivid green ones. She was an ethereal beauty. It was heartbreaking to witness the sadness pouring out of such perfection. Her head bobbed as she curled an unsteady hand around her throat, and burst into sobs.

"Oh sh—" He grimaced, raising a cautious hand to pat her on the shoulder. In response, she stepped into his side, grabbing onto the lapel of his jacket. Her jerky movements sent shock waves racing through his veins, the weight of her grip seeping into his bones. His mind blanked for a minute as his body took over. He shook his head to set his synapses scrambling, trying to make sense of this bizarre interaction.

When he arrived this morning, it sure didn't equate to a feeling of homecoming. He shouldn't have been surprised at the feeling of displacement and disconnection. That shit was pretty standard. But, this was Alabama. Where he grew up. The only place that had ever felt like home. Now? Sweet home Alabama? Not so much.

Standing with his arm around this stranger… this felt more like home. Aiden's eyes almost crossed from system overload. His body hadn't really *felt* anything in so long. He was used to living the life of an international nomad, roaming between photo shoots. His only interactions with others coming from behind a camera lens.

What the hell is happening?

The woman's shudders slowly lessened to the softer, rise and fall of her chest, as she breathed deeply in acceptance of his comfort. Huh. He had been able to offer something after all. It speared his soul, connecting him to another in a way he had forgotten existed. His breathing slowed in time with hers, every inhale drawing her delicate, jasmine perfume, and the scent of salty tears. Aiden was drawing as much comfort as he was giving, the exchange probably weighing more heavily in his favor. In a moment of tortured surrender, this petite woman had made him see how lonely he was.

Loneliness was his MO.

His life sucked.

Goddamn.

It made him want to wrap himself around this woman, and never let go.

Their cocoon of comfort was shattered as she yanked her body away from his, crossing her arms, consternation written all over her face. At a loss for what to do, he shoved his hands in his pockets. Aiden dimly registered the sounds of car engines starting as the mourners lined up to leave, and the whispers of those few who remained.

"Are you coming to the wake?" Her eyes were almost pleading.

"Yes," his mouth spoke without connecting to his brain. His intention had been to pay his respects and leave, unsure if he'd even be welcome. Actually, he was certain he was unwelcome. Why was she asking him, a stranger?

Her head jerked in approval, before she again burrowed in the envelope of her friend's arms, the women then marched away. Aiden hadn't even noticed the blond move toward them. He'd been blissfully oblivious, completely absorbed by a woman for the first time in…forever.

He stood on liquid legs, elbows loose, missing the feel of her. Bewilderment doused his ability to think, as he watched her retreat. Something about the texture of her movement stirred the familiarity again. His memories rose closer to the surface, but faded again as she disappeared out of sight.

The energy in the air was noticeably different. Heaviness descended over him again as he turned to the grave to add a shovelful of dirt. Three other men remained to do the same.

"It's good to see ye again, Aiden. Sorry it couldn't have been under happier circumstances." Harry, his friend's brother, gave him a slap on the shoulder in greeting. The sentiment confused and chipped at his expectation to be treated like a stranger.

He paused to collect his wits, gathering the appropriate words from unused corners of his brain. "I'm crushed that I didn't get to see him again. He was more of a father to me than my own." The truth came rushing out, striking him straight through the heart. "I'm so sorry for your loss." He addressed all three men, again frustrated that he couldn't think of anything better to say. Harry's younger brother, Harvey, and Mr. Saunders, the neighbor from across the street, joined Harry.

Hank had been the oldest brother. A tall and sturdy Irishman with masses of black hair, and a beard to match. The younger brothers had inherited red hair from their mother, but they all had the same goliath stature.

In comical contrast, Mr. Saunders was a petite man with thin white wisps of hair. His eyebrows and eyelashes almost invisible against his pale pink skin.

All three men were in their sixties now. Patches of white had bleached the red hair at the brothers' temples, with several strays flecked about, elsewhere. It was shocking, how much they had aged. He supposed they could say the same about him. He was not yet sixteen when his parents moved him north.

"Would ye like a lift to the wake, then?" Harry asked.

"I don't suppose ye've got a car, at the minute?" Harvey threw a heavy arm around Aiden's shoulder, stretching slightly, as they were the same height.

"That'd be great, thanks."

Harry and Mr. Saunders took a more luxurious, Buick, while Harvey promptly guided Aiden to a rusty, old, Chevy pick-up. He knew that it used to be candy apple red. The painted logo of Harvey's Auto Shop had faded from the hood over time.

The slamming of their doors was loud, but the rumble of the engine was deafening. His shoes slipped and crunched on the collection of empty chip packets and coffee cups strewn on the floor of the passenger side. Harvey looked over to investigate, propping his sunglasses on his nose. "Sorry 'bout the mess. I needed sustenance to get me through the long hospital waits. Just kick it out of the way." He waved his hand as if brushing the offending items away, stirring the smell of sweat and stale coffee.

Aiden took in the scenery as the old truck bumped along; its shock absorbers not up to the task. The town had changed in his absence. Grassy fields had made way for new housing developments. The single traffic light had spawned some friends, though the center of town had mostly remained in its time capsule.

Aiden's knee jiggled against the door as his nervous energy found an outlet. He was still reeling from the weirdest moment of his life. Seeing his friend put underground, and experiencing what felt like salvation all within moments of each other. He had to put *her* out of his mind and focus on Hank.

"How long was he ill?"

"Oh, he had the first stroke about a month ago. It wasn't too bad. He could still talk, though his words were slurred. We thought he'd recover. He was starting rehab, but then he had a massive stroke. Turned him into a vegetable. No coming back from that. He was in a coma for a week before he died. Nasty business, seeing a strong, proud man brought to his knees. Even more horrible, seeing a brother suffer."

Aiden kept a steady eye on the road, using the horizon to ground him, and stop the flow of tears that threatened. He swallowed against a tight throat before attempting to speak. "I didn't know." He cursed under his breath. "I would have come." *I should have been here.*

"I just happened to look up the local paper online. I don't even know what made me do it. His name caught my eye while I was skimming." Aiden swallowed again, and turned to the window to squeeze his eyes shut.

He felt a firm grip on his shoulder. "Per'aps you wanted news of a certain young lady, as well as her pa?"

Hank's daughter, Angel. If he weren't in the habit of denying his true desires, he'd admit that he'd been searching the group of mourners for her. The girl he would never forget no matter how hard he tried. Angel. An appropriate name for the girl who weaved through his thoughts whenever he let them drift.

He sucked in a breath. Light dawned, and memories of green eyes that used to be shadowed behind glasses rose abruptly into transparency. Climbing trees and fishing, later became holding hands and kissing.

Angel.

His plans just changed.

Acknowledgements

I actually don't know how I managed to write this book. My life turned on its head while I sat my butt down and made myself keep typing. I wrote some of it at my friends' places, and sent it to my editor while sitting in a driveway. It was meant to be shared with the world, and I was determined to get it out there.

The list of names I need to give thanks to is growing with every book, but these ladies are my foundation and my unwavering support, so they get first mention. In alphabetical order: Belinda, Deb, Emma, Katja, Lachele, Paula, and Robyn. You carried me on your shoulders, even when I got really freakin' heavy, and stopped me from falling into the chasm that opened up before I knew it. Dramatic, I know, but seriously that's what you did. Thank God for you.

Ruth! Once again, you came to my rescue and volunteered to beta read for me. You are a super star, and I will always have your back whenever you need me to return the favour.

Big thanks to my editor, Eeva, who became very ill during the editing of this book, but still soldiered through. I feel personally responsible, and I hope you can forgive my impatience. I'll try to pare back the profound word play in future, but I do love it so.

Jennifer at More Than Words Promotions, thank you for helping me to get my work out there. And for being patient with my re-scheduling and the ARC delay. Love the teasers!

Nicole Andrews Moore and the team at Love Kissed Author Promotions, you are such an inspiration. Thank you all for being awesome and accommodating.

To my reader group, JM's Gems, y'all are the bomb. Thanks for listening to my bullshit and giving me feedback on the snippets I share. I'll have some goodies just for you on release day!

To my ARC readers, thank you so much for being excited to read an advanced copy, and a massive thanks to all those who reviewed the book. It's so nerve wracking to send out those first copies, so thanks for going easy on me.

Likewise, to the bloggers who work so hard to help authors spread the word, you are all so important and deserve a heck of a lot more credit.

And to you, my readers, you wonderful souls, you. Thank you for buying this book. It means the world to me that you wanted to read it. I hope you liked it.

I've left the most important people until last. My three little Jedi. You are my world. I know I spend too much time working, but I'm doing it for you. I want to give you guys the best, but I also want to show you what it takes to follow through on a promise and chase your dreams. Whatever you choose to do, you know I'll be there, backing you all the way. Love you to bits.

About the Author

Former nurse, reluctant romantic, chocolate lover and serious reading addict, J.M. Adele is the author of paranormal and contemporary romance, and romantic suspense. After years of indulging in her addiction to reading, her own characters started to tell their stories. They were relentless, forcing her to put pen to paper and release them into the world.

On most days you can find her juggling authorhood with motherhood while carrying a book in one hand. When everyone else drifts off to dreamland she escapes into the worlds conjured by the characters in her head.

Follow J. M.

Links to my newsletter and my Facebook reader group
can be found on my website.

www.jmadele.com

www.facebook.com/authorjmadele

@JMAdeleBooks

@j.m.adele